Myrtle, Means, and Opportunity

A MYRTLE HARDCASTLE MYSTERY

T0385386

Myrtle, Means, and Opportunity

A MYRTLE HARDCASTLE MYSTERY

Elizabeth C. Bunce

ALGONQUIN YOUNG READERS 2023

Published by Algonquin Young Readers
an imprint of Workman Publishing Co., Inc.
a subsidiary of Hachette Book Group, Inc.
1290 Avenue of the Americas
New York, New York 10104

Printed in the United States of America
Design by Carla Weise

The publisher is not responsible for websites (or their content) that are not owned
by the publisher.

LIBRARY OF CONGRESS CATALOGING-IN-PUBLICATION DATA
Names: Bunce, Elizabeth C., author.
Title: Myrtle, means, and opportunity / Elizabeth C. Bunce.
Description: First edition. | New York, New York : Algonquin Young
Readers, 2023. | Audience: Ages 9–12. | Audience: Grades 4–6. |
Summary: Twelve-year-old Myrtle Hardcastle's plans to bring her father
and governess together are jeopardized when she investigates a murder and
cursed treasure on a Scottish island, and finds herself being hunted by
another who will stop at nothing to find the treasure for themselves.
Identifiers: LCCN 2023006318 | ISBN 9781643753140 (hardcover) |
ISBN 9781523524280 (trade paperback) | ISBN 9781523526246 (e-book)
Subjects: CYAC: Mystery and detective stories. | Murder—Fiction. | Scotland—
History—Victoria, 1837–1901—Fiction. | LCGFT: Detective and mystery fiction. |
Novels. Classification: LCC PZ7.B91505 My 2023 | DDC [Fic]—dc23
LC record available at https://lccn.loc.gov/2023006318

ISBN 978-1-64375-314-0 (hardcover)
ISBN 978-1-5235-2428-0 (paperback)
ISBN 978-1-5235-2624-6 (e-book)

10 9 8 7 6 5 4 3 2 1
First Edition

For my MacEwens, my McKuens,
and my Manros (including Monroe)
But most of all
for my McNells

Myrtle, Means, and Opportunity

A MYRTLE HARDCASTLE MYSTERY

1

A Woman's Home Is Her Castle

Philosophers and artists have long glorified the ownership of property, but they have given much less attention to the practical aspects of maintaining it.

–A Guide to Modern Estate Management,
Comprising Advice on Financial and Legal Matters;
Livestock and Domestic Animals; Agriculture and
Timber Holdings; Mineral Resources; Fishery
and Game; Staff and Tenants; Along with Notes
on Basic Domestic Maintenance, Including
Carpentry, Landscaping, and Plumbing (with a
Particular Focus on the Importance of Drains),
by a Country Gentlewoman, 1894

"I've never even heard of Augustus Horatio MacJudd." Miss Judson, my governess, regarded the telegram on the dining table, its edges curling like the legs of a prematurely dispatched insect. Her lip curled in a matching expression of distaste. "How can he have left me his estate?"

Father studied the letter, which had arrived moments after the telegram. It had come from a solicitor in Argyll, far away in Scotland. "It seems that your uncle—make that *great-uncle*, rather, on your father's side—having reached the age of seventy-seven without producing offspring, specified that his relation Ada Eugenia Judson, of Swinburne, England, was the most worthy of his possible descendants to inherit Rockfforde Hall—with two small *f*s—on the island of Dunfyne, Loch Fyne—one *f*—Argyllshire. The aforementioned great-uncle having passed away on 12 April, the lands and holdings have fallen to you." Father looked up. "Mr. Macewan, Esquire, sends his condolences. And this." *This* appeared to be a picture in a frame, wrapped in brown paper to protect it from the travails of cross-country post.

"It must be a hoax," said Miss Judson. "See—he hasn't even got my name right. It's Eugénie, not Eugenia."

I clutched my fork, doing my best not to spear the telegram with it so I could look for myself.

"Aren't you excited?" I said. "It's a whole estate! In Scotland! You had an uncle," I added, somewhat belatedly. I gave up trying to resist and snatched up the telegram after all. Although it had come from her parents in French Guiana, it was in English (having been written by her father).

ADA: UNCLE AUGUSTUS DEAD. GO SCOTL'D
EARLIEST CONVENIENCE TO SETTLE
ESTATE. SOLICITOR TO CONTACT YOU
WITH DETAILS. -J. JUDSON.

Telegrams are expensive—you pay by the word—and international cables pricier still, but this seemed terribly curt to me, and Miss Judson was certainly not receiving it with a great deal of warmth. Anyone would think she'd just been diagnosed with the mumps, not inherited A Whole Estate. In Scotland.

"I'm with Myrtle," Father put in unexpectedly. "This is terribly exciting."

"It's terribly inconvenient," she corrected. "We are in the middle of the Reign of Terror." She'd been teaching me the French Revolution with particular fervor, taking especial interest in its effects on her maternal homeland.

"Mlle. Guillotine can wait," said Father. "I'll telephone the station and arrange your tickets."

My heart thumped in surprise, but I let Miss Judson answer. She quirked a dangerous eyebrow. "Tickets? Plural?"

"You'd hardly deny Myrtle the educational opportunities of seeing the great kingdom to the north! And there's no telling what the state of the kitchens in the Dear Auld Hame might be, so you'll have to accompany them, Cook—"

Cook, lurking unsubtly in the doorway, nodded briskly. "Quite so. And Herself? There'll be herring, no doubt."

She meant our cat, Peony, lurking with her. "*No,*" Herself replied, meaning yes.

"No doubt," agreed Father. "And I'll join you when my current case wraps up."

Miss Judson looked faint. "Anyone else?" she said. "Aunt Helena, perhaps? Magistrate Fox? What about the Colliery Band?"

"You're the heiress," he said cheerfully. "You can buy their tickets."

Miss Judson put her head down on the table in defeat.

❧

I followed Father out of the dining room, up the stairs to his study. He was whistling merrily. He'd been in uncommonly high spirits the past few weeks. His newest client, Viscountess Snowcroft, was the source of more work than he could handle on hwwis own, so he'd taken on our good friend Mr. Blakeney as his clerk in charge of estate law. Father's regular job as Swinburne's Prosecuting Solicitor had likewise kept him busy. He was on a murder trial—as a witness this time, not the prosecutor—which was expected to conclude shortly. But that wasn't the reason for his good cheer.

I slipped into the room behind him and closed the door. "Is it here yet?" I demanded. There was almost too much excitement at the moment, and I couldn't decide which foot to stand on. (Dear Reader, you will perhaps be thinking *both* would be a sensible choice—but I challenge you to stand still on two feet with such anticipation . . . well, afoot!)

Eyes twinkling, Father beckoned me to the desk. I perched on the edge of the chair but could hardly stay put. My stockings and petticoats prickled. With solemn ceremony, Father opened his desk drawer and withdrew a small leatherbound box shaped like a miniature book, complete with a tiny gold clasp.

"It's splendid," I breathed. "She'll love it."

Father sat back without handing me the box. I bit my lip, bracing myself for whatever he meant to say next. "Well," he said carefully.

"No *well*!" I cried. "Just do it, already. Before she—" Father's unspoken objection finally sank in. I sank into my seat. "Oh."

"Oh, indeed," he agreed. "This changes things."

"It doesn't have to," I argued.

Father smiled sadly. "Our Miss Judson is about to become independently wealthy," he said. "A woman of means. And a good deal more means than I, from what I can tell. I can't offer her an estate in Scotland."

"She already has one of those! Why would she want another one?" But I knew what he meant. "She won't need us anymore."

Father clicked open the tiny latch on the tiny box to

regard its contents—which I *still* could not see, however I craned my neck. "Never mind. You're off on a Grand Adventure, and we shan't spoil it with idle conjecture of things that may never come to pass."

He snapped the box closed and tossed it back into the drawer, and I kicked my chair legs. The way he was dithering, they *wouldn't* come to pass. Father tugged his waistcoat smooth and said, with false brightness, "Who knows? The charms of Argyllshire, with its lochs and legends, will surely pale in comparison to dear old Swinburne. This Rockfforde Hall can't be a patch on Number 14 Gravesend Close."

He leaned in conspiratorially. "I'm counting on you, Myrtle," he added.

I sat up straighter. "Sir?"

"This won't just be a holiday," he warned. "I have a Very Important Job for you."

"I'm ready." Miss Judson's uncle already had a solicitor, so I doubted Father would entrust the estate law to my hands, but I'd been giving a thorough study to Scottish criminal law. I'd followed every bit of the Ardlamont murder trial this winter—a supposed hunting accident that left a young nobleman dead. "Do you think Dunfyne Island is near Ardlamont?"*

"What?" Father scowled. "Don't get distracted, now.

---

* I checked the map, Dear Reader: it *is*. I therefore immediately began scheming a visit to the crime scene.

I need you to do everything in your considerable power to keep Miss Judson's mind on coming back home."

"You mean, don't let her fall in love with Scotland?"

Father stared heavily at his desk drawer and the tantalizing treasure within. "Exactly."

﹏

That evening I hoped Miss Judson and I might discuss this radical change in her fortunes, but when I approached her room, I had second thoughts. She sat at her small neat desk, regarding the parcel the solicitor had sent. It *was* a photograph, of two gentlemen—young and old—standing before a grand house. I could make out nothing else, but Miss Judson picked up a card and read it aloud: *"Rockfforde Hall in happier times."* She touched the glass, and my heart gave a guilty squeeze, sure I was Observing something private.

As if she'd heard the Guilty Squeeze, Miss Judson glanced up from the picture, and I darted away, suddenly uncertain. Miss Judson's Scottish heritage had caught us all off guard. Reverend Judson was English—I'd thought—though he'd immigrated to the tropics of French Guiana as a young man, where he'd married Mlle. Marie-Barbe Dupin, a Guianese nurse. After settling near her home, they'd sent their daughter far away to school in England. Miss Judson didn't talk about it, of course, but I supposed she had always felt somewhat adrift from her family, her blood relations.

Father was correct. Her inheritance could indeed change everything.

This was her home, though. Miss Judson would never abandon us.

But the look on her face when she beheld the picture of Rockfforde Hall had said something very different.

⁂

Travel from Swinburne to Scotland was not swift. Or efficient. We took a crowded, smoky express train (don't let the name fool you) to Glasgow—where there was some confusion with the luggage, and Miss Judson's portmanteau was nearly lost—followed by several crowded, smoky ferries; then a crowded, horsey coach; and now yet *another* ferry bound for the village on Loch Fyne where we planned to meet the solicitor . . . before we could finally sail to Dunfyne Island itself.

Miss Judson had been aloof during the journey, the cramped accommodations not conducive to conversation, and Cook and Peony were occupied elsewhere. I'd therefore spent the entire trip fretting. From Swinburne to Glasgow, squeezed into a third-class compartment with cross strangers on either side of me and a cross cat beneath my feet, I wondered what the magnificent Rockfforde Hall would be like, or the mysterious, mist-shrouded isle of Dunfyne. I'd read all about Argyll, of course—in fact, I'd longed to visit— but I hadn't inherited A Whole Estate. In Scotland.

Miss Judson had, and she was being alarmingly closemouthed about it.

We were consequently a considerably cross and road-weary (and loch-weary) party by the time we boarded what we thought would be our penultimate vessel. Miss Judson and I stayed on deck while Cook took Peony below to inspect the ferry's boilers. After the past few days, they were practically experts.

Loch is Scots for "lake," but Loch Fyne is no mere lake. It is a deep slice in the landscape into which the sea has seeped in bottomless blue magnificence, sprinkled with so many islands, large and small, that most local travel is accomplished by boat.

The motor-ferry putted us across the vast, glistening surface of the long and narrow loch, drawing us closer and closer to the uncertain future. We sat beneath the passenger shelter and Observed the scenery in mutual silence. Miss Judson held the solicitor's letter in one hand, face unreadable beneath the brim of her crisp straw hat. I swung my feet, feeling smaller and smaller as the lumpy green mountains swarmed up from the blue water, swallowing us whole.

I had a sudden disorienting image of a similar journey years and years ago, when a much smaller Ada Eugénie Judson had boarded a vessel at a port in French Guiana all by herself, bound for parts unknown in Britain. I slipped up beside her and took her gloved hand. "It's not like Kourou, is it?" I said.

To my surprise, she laughed aloud.

"Are you going to stay at Rockfforde Hall?" I asked, voice tight with anxiety.

"Let's not be premature," she said. "We must get to the bottom of things before we make any decisions." She withdrew the solicitor's letter from its envelope and scowled at it. "This is all highly irregular, and I mean to have Mr. Macewan's explanation."

"But—" I squirmed in my seat. What did I want to say? "Why didn't you simply wire this solicitor before we set off? Or telephone him?" Much had been made of the region's modern conveniences in the newspaper accounts of the Ardlamont mystery.

"This sort of matter is best handled in person." I sensed another thought lurking below the deceptively placid surface of Miss Judson's face. "Besides . . ."

"Besides *what*?"

"Well," she said frankly, "your father was so anxious to be rid of me, I hardly had a chance to object."

Rid of her! Panic clutched my chest. That was the very *opposite* of what Father wanted! "But—" Why wouldn't the words spring out of my mouth? "He's going to join us," I said in a small, useless voice.

"Yes, he is," she said ominously—and I was afraid to ask what she meant. Did she want Father to join us? Or not?

2

ESTATE LAW

In addition to the management of a land's natural resources, do not neglect the financial side of matters. An estate will fail just as easily from economic malfeasance as from natural calamity.

*–A Country Gentlewoman's Guide to Estate
Management*

We disembarked at a modest ferry terminal in a picturesque village called Tighnabruaich. This marvelous Gaelic word is in fact three words: *Tigh na bruaich*, pronounced (roughly) "*tie na brew egg*," and means "house on the hill," an apt description for the settlement perched on the rocky shore overlooking Loch Fyne.

Passengers packed the whitewashed pier, coming and going from the ferries crowding the harbor. At the ticket office, Miss Judson asked directions to Mr. Macewan's office. By the time she succeeded in making the agent understand her—using a combination of English, French, and charades—everyone in Tighnabruaich probably knew our destination. (Tourists to these parts generally come seeking fishing tours, not solicitors.)

Men waited with horse-drawn carts, but Miss Judson and Cook eschewed any assistance and we carried our luggage ourselves. Tighnabruaich proved a lively holiday destination, tidy buildings nestled together on one side of a rambling high street, chimney pots puffing smoke into the blue sky. Cook, toting Peony in her hatbox, gave the town a critical eye.

"I'll find us a spot of tea," she decided. She was attired for the journey in a most unCooklike manner—a gaily striped cotton frock with flounces and ruffles and a tiny beribboned hat that barely perched upon her thick grey hair. Odd as it was to see Cook dressed so, I had to admit she fit in with all the other holidaymakers flooding into Tighnabruaich on the steam ferries. "And I'd best find the shops. If we're to be trapped on a deserted island for who knows how long, we'll be wanting provisions."

"Cook! I'm sure they have food at Rockfforde Hall." But the alarm in Miss Judson's voice gave her away. Unconvinced, Cook hoisted Peony off to the village. If Peony offered any opinion on the mission—perhaps a tiny, hopeful burble—we did not hear.

Miss Judson watched them leave, looking somewhat bereft. "Very well," she called after them. "We'll meet back here in an hour!"

She turned and forced her way into the crowd surging the opposite direction, clearing a path with her umbrella, like a machete in the jungle. "The solicitor's office is—" she began, but was abruptly cut off when a man in a short tweed coat and a scruffy cap burst from an alley and grabbed her portmanteau.

"*Salopard!*" she cried—a French word I am definitely not supposed to know—clapping him in the head with her umbrella. His cap went flying as he let out a cry and released his grip on her bag, which tumbled to the pavement, spilling open.

Miss Judson, still shouting creative invectives in French, charged after her assailant. Startled witnesses milled about, blocking my view. Heart thudding, I was relieved to see a flash of red cutting through the crowd: the bold uniform of an English soldier.

"Stop right there!" the soldier bellowed—not as effective, perhaps, as a nice police whistle, but good in a pinch. Confident that the combined forces of the British Infantry and Miss Judson could handle any crisis, I scooped her things safely back into the bag. The glass in the photograph of Rockfforde Hall had cracked—only a little—and one latch on the portmanteau had broken. In an inspiration of evidence gathering, I also collected the assailant's wool cap.

"Lass! Are ye all right?" A kindly looking gentleman tugged me gently out of the traffic. He had fluffy white whiskers and a blue tartan waistcoat. "What is this village coming to? A bag-snatching herrre, in broad daylight?" He shook his head and frowned down at me. "Are ye hurt?"

"No—" I found my voice after the shock, although it was shaky and didn't quite sound like me. "I'm all right. But where's Miss Judson?"

"Your companion? Wait, did ye say Judson?"

My reply was forestalled by the triumphant return of Miss Judson and the soldier. They strolled arm in arm like they were on holiday in true, and Miss Judson's color was high.

Relieved to see her unharmed, I burst out, "Where's the man who attacked you?"

The soldier looked rueful. "Got away, I'm afraid. But your friend gave him an earful, I don't mind saying."

Miss Judson disentangled her arm from the soldier's. "Myrtle—my bag! Well done." She clucked sadly at the broken latch. "Does this sort of thing happen regularly? I'm afraid it will color my review."

The bewhiskered gentleman rushed to answer. "Nay, nae at all! I cannae believe it. Are ye carrying anything valuable, Miss—?"

Miss Judson was inspecting the contents of her bag. "I will try not to take that personally. Perhaps he assumed we were simply easy prey."

"I doubt that," said the soldier. "It looked like he targeted you specifically."

"That doesn't make sense," I put in. "Miss Judson is a stranger here. Why should anyone be after her?"

"Well, whatever the case, he miscalculated!" exclaimed the soldier. "He surely didn't count on you being . . . armed."

Brandishing her brolly, Miss Judson parried at the air. *"En garde!"*

"Touché," he laughed.

I coughed, loudly. The excitement over, the spectators dissipated. "Shouldn't we fetch the police? Miss Judson will need to give a statement."

Miss Judson's lips pursed as she considered this. "There's no harm done, and he's got away . . ."

"Exactly!" I said. "They'll need your description if they want to catch him."

"We're on a tight schedule," she reminded me. "We need to find the solicitor's office."

"I can help with that—" the older gentleman began, but the soldier broke in.

"Why don't I see if I can't lay my hands on the scoundrel? And if that fails, I'll make a full report to the constabulary."

Miss Judson was grateful. "That does seem most sensible. Thank you . . . Lieutenant?" she guessed.

The soldier snapped his heels together and saluted her. "Smoot. Fitzhollis Smoot, at your service."

Miss Judson took his hand. "I am most appreciative,"

she said—although she'd had the situation entirely under control, from what I'd seen.

"All in a day's work," Lt. Smoot said. "And if I might provide one further service, I believe this is your destination." He indicated a sign above our heads, which read:

H. S. MACEWAN, ESQUIRE
SOLICITOR

And standing directly beneath the sign, the bewhiskered gentleman in the tartan waistcoat. "As I was saying," he said modestly. "Lieutenant, thank ye again. I'll take the ladies from here."

Before the lieutenant could vanish, I handed him the robber's hat. "Here—take this to the police. It's evidence."

Lt. Smoot accepted it, twirling it on one finger, then saluted me and was off.

Mr. Macewan led us to his office. The door bore a curious brass knocker depicting a tree stump with leaves sprouting from its hewn trunk.

"Are ye *sure* you're all right?" he fussed. "I cannae imagine a more upsettin' welcome to our lovely country." I *was* still wound up from the encounter, but Miss Judson seemed her typical composed self. "Ye really cannae be too careful, ladies travelin' alone." He tut-tutted in disapproval—though of us or the thief, it was hard to be certain.

Mr. Macewan admitted us into a bright, welcoming chamber dominated by . . . plaid. Blue plaid carpeting spread to the threshold, and matching paper clad the walls, behind shield-shaped wooden coats of arms. A fine specimen of a telephone, mounted on the tartan wall, jangled an urgent appeal.

"Excuse me—I must take this." Mr. Macewan hastened to answer the device. "Macewan speaking." I was surprised to hear him say his name aloud. Contrary to appearances, it was evidently pronounced *Mac Ewan*. His telephone voice was booming and full of confidence. I approved. "Now, wait just a minute! Calm down. I told ye—"

He was cut off by a muffled, angry voice we could not make out.

"How could I predict that would happen? . . . I *was* prepairred—I did everything just as we discussed . . . nay, nay. I'll take care of it. Yes, ye'll get what ye're owed. Dinnae do anything hasty! We have an agreement, remember?"

Even before Mr. Macewan could disconnect the call, his angry caller responded with a tirade of disappointment, punctuated with a very final click.

The solicitor stood for a long moment, regarding the handset, then dabbed his face with a handkerchief.

"So sorry aboot that," he said, fumbling to replace the handset in its cradle.

"Disgruntled client?" Miss Judson asked.

"Aren't they all?" he muttered. "Now. We got off on rather an exciting foot!" He clasped his hands together, fluffy whiskers bristling in a smile. "Let's try this properly. I'm Hector Macewan. What do two English ladies want with an old Scottish solicitor?"

Miss Judson returned his handshake. "Ada Judson, and Miss Hardcastle. I'm Augustus MacJudd's great-niece. Apparently."

Mr. Macewan regarded her blankly for a moment. "But, my dear, why are ye here? In Tighnabruaich, I mean? Did ye nae get my letter?"

"Yes, and the photograph of Uncle Augustus with my father." She patted the broken portmanteau. "That was very kind of you. I had no idea they were close."

I shot a look at Miss Judson—her *father*! Why hadn't she said anything?

"Oh . . . ye brought it. That's—how nice." A thread of anxiety knotted Mr. Macewan's fluffy eyebrows together. "There was no need for ye to come all this way. Everything's been taken care of. I've arranged for the estate to be sold off, in accordance with Mr. MacJudd's wishes."

"Sold!" I exclaimed, entirely out of turn. "You can't do that, not unless you have power of attorney." Sell

Miss Judson's estate, before I—I mean *she*—even got a glimpse of it?

Miss Judson stepped in before I could frighten Mr. Macewan further. "I'm afraid a sale is out of the question," she said, to my immense relief. I mean *alarm*. "I can't allow any decisions to be made without a review of the will and a complete inventory of the property."

"My dear girl. Ye're still upset, and no wonder! First that shameless attack, and now ye've had anither shock. Why don't ye get a nice cup of tea while I prepare the papers for ye to sign? After yer long journey, ye'll appreciate the comfortable accommodations of the Royal Hotel."

Miss Judson slowly removed her gloves and laid them, side by side, atop his desk. "Mr. Macewan," she said with dangerous precision, "I am *getting* upset. I intend to find comfortable accommodation at Rockfforde Hall."

The solicitor gave a nervous cough. "My good woman—"

She stopped him. "My good man. Let me disabuse you of the notion that I am some fragile female who must be coddled. Such specimens are far rarer than you might suppose. I have endured the most intolerable travel conditions only to arrive in your village and be criminally accosted, and now I am being denied access to my own legal property." She glanced to me.

"Myrtle, I'm beginning to suspect that there *is* no such place as Rockfforde Hall."

I was enjoying their argument so much, it took a moment to catch up. "Perhaps there's something wrong with it," I suggested.

Miss Judson brightened. "That would explain things. Mr. Macewan, is there Something Wrong with my property? Perhaps you've misrepresented yourself to me, as well as to these so-called buyers to whom you intend to hand off my inheritance without permission. Myrtle, we may need to engage another solicitor."

"The executor of a will has very specific duties under the law," I added helpfully. "The local magistrate would want to know if Uncle Augustus's estate isn't being handled properly."

"Now see herrre!" Mr. Macewan burst from his seat. "I shallnae be bullied by twa—twa—*Englishwomen* in me ain office!" He made this sound like the very worst thing he could call us. "There is Naethin Wrrrong with Rockfforde Hall. See for yerselves!" He flung open a drawer and tossed a sheaf of papers onto the desk.

Miss Judson caught them neatly. "Was that so difficult? Myrtle, I'll let you know if I require your legal expertise."

That was a very polite dismissal, and I squelched my disappointment. Of course Miss Judson would wish to protect her privacy. While she read, I looked about Mr. Macewan's Exceptionally Plaid office. A prominent shield displayed an unusual crest: the tree stump again, encircled by a sort of strap fastened with a buckle, all rendered in silvery metal.

"Are ye interested in heraldry, lass?" Visibly calming himself, Mr. Macewan rose and unhooked the plaque from the wall. "This is the crest of Sween MacEwen, last chief of Clan Ewen of Otter." His words spun out dramatically, his Scottish accent giving them extra flourish.

"Otter?" Above the stump arched the Latin word *Reviresco*. "I . . . become green again?" I puzzled aloud.

Mr. Macewan beamed. "Chief Sween's own motto, usually translated, 'I grow strong again.' And truer words ne'er were spoken—the clan *will* have its chief again, mark my words!"

"What happened to Sween?" The notion of a chief-tainless clan was intriguing. How did they get on?

"Died in 1493. His lands passed to the Campbells, the clan broken, his people scattered tae all corners." He took the plaque back, polished away my finger-marks, and returned it lovingly to its place on the wall.

"Why don't you capitalize your E?" I indicated the plaques, with the clan name spelled differently.

"Tradition, lass! And it confuses the English," he added with a chuckle.

He was right—I'd already fallen prey. "No true Scotsman would say it wrong," I posited.

"Well, nay, cannae say as that's true." He laughed

again. "I've been working on a clan history. According to my research, the MacJudds are a sept of Clan Ewen—under the chief's protection. That's how Augustus and I became friends."

The connection between MacJudd and Judson was less perplexing: both names meant Son of Judd. "Then . . . you and Miss Judson are relatives?"

This idea did not seem to have occurred to him. "Well—er. I suppose, in a way. The bond between oor twa clans goes back centuries, cemented through the ages with the exchange of the MacJudd clan brooch."

I was getting into this tale. "The same brooch, over and over?"

"Aye, passed from one clan to t'other and back until 1745, when it was lost—on Dunfyne Island, no less. But our connection endures." Mr. Macewan brought us back to the present. "Miss Ada, the lands are yers by birthright. But being the Laird is a big responsibility. It'd be easier just to sell."

"Uncle Augustus was the Laird?" I said. "You mean the Chief of Clan MacJudd? The whole clan?"

"It's quite a wee clan."

Miss Judson looked up from her papers. "Mr. Macewan, are you attempting to say what I think you are? I've inherited not just my great-uncle's property, but his title and legacy as well?"

"Well, aye. But—"

"She's not first in line," I pointed out. "She has parents."

"Excellent Observation," Miss Judson said. "Have you an explanation for this, as well?" Her voice was brittle.

Mr. Macewan looked distinctly scared. "The chief can name whatever heir he likes. He—evidently—liked ye."

"He never met me!" Brittle evolved to shrill.

"Don't mind her," I said. "This all came rather unexpectedly."

"Myrtle!"

"Well, it did," I retorted. "You weren't expecting to inherit A Whole Estate. In Scotland."

"Indeed, I was not," she admitted. "Mr. Macewan, we seem to be on the same side—wishing the best possible disposition of my great-uncle's wishes. If he did intend to sell the island, I suppose I am bound to consider the matter. But I must inspect the property first."

"That can be arranged. But Fyne Fisheries has made a substantial offer—"

"Fyne Fisheries?"

"The buyers, of course. A consortium of commercial fishing enterprises means to convert the island to a processing facility. Progress, you know."

Dear Reader, in general I am a great supporter of Progress—scientific, technological, social, medical, judicial—but a fish-processing factory did not sound entirely desirable.

Miss Judson frowned. "I'm not certain I like the sound of that."

"These were yer uncle's wishes," he said reproachfully.

"And as I said, I shall consider the matter. *After* my associates and I have made a thorough inspection." She rose perfunctorily. "Now, shall you take us there, or do we need to arrange our own transportation?"

It was Mr. Macewan's turn to look triumphant. "I'm afraid that's quite impossible. To reach Dunfyne, ye'll sail from Otter Ferry, on t'other side of Cowal. And it's too late in the day for the boats tae run. Ye maun stay in Tighnabruaich overnight. As I was saying, we've a lovely hotel."

"Very well." Miss Judson rose and neatened her traveling costume. "Before we depart, Myrtle has a question for you."

Mr. Macewan and I regarded my governess with matching expressions. "She has?"

"I do?"

"I should be very much surprised—and disappointed—if you had not."

I realized what she meant. I stood straighter. "Mr. Macewan, if you would please tell us, what was Mr. MacJudd's cause of death?"

"Odd little lassie," he said. "I wat it's only natural, ye

wanting to know if he died peacefully. Auld Augustus went for a stroll roond his property one afternoon, as was his habit, and never returned hame. They found him aside a rrrock overlooking the loch, loyal dog by his side, like he'd settled in for a wee nap and simply fallen asleep. Never felt a thing, passed in his own lands on a fine spring day." He smiled wistfully. "May we aw be sae lucky."

I followed the report of this idyllic scene with, "Was there an inquest?"

"An inquest! Whatever for?"

"To rule out murder."

Miss Judson beheld this exchange with satisfaction. Mr. Macewan drew himself up and tugged again on his waistcoat (it was clearly too small for him, to need such constant adjustment). "There most certainly was not. There's naethin wrong wi' either the man's death, *or* his hoose. You've my word as a solicitor—and a MacEwen!"

Miss Judson appeared unconvinced, but said, "Good. Now, if you please, I'll take the will and the death certificate, and I shall expect to meet you at the ferry landing tomorrow for the first departure for Otter Ferry."

"Meet *me*?"

"You would hardly expect us to inspect the property without proper guidance, would you?"

That comment may have fooled Mr. Macewan, but it was clear she hadn't decided to trust him yet, and wished to keep him—and the valuable legal documents—under close supervision.

As we left, Mr. Macewan handed me a paperbound booklet with a tree stump on its cover. "My history of Clan MacEwen," he said proudly. "Along with some auld clan legends—tales o' lost treasure an' the fair folk."

I suppressed my disdain. What did he take me for? But I thanked him politely and tucked it into my satchel, wondering if there would be a quiz.

∾

At the hotel that night, Miss Judson drew me aside. "Tell me what you make of this."

She'd drawn a chair up beside the dresser, and spread the will atop it. The fresh loch air had sent Cook straight to sleep, and she and Peony curled together in the large bed, both snoring softly. They had been properly disappointed to miss the excitement outside the solicitor's office, Cook vowing that *she'd* not have let the assailant escape. And we'd never heard back from Lt. Smoot about whether the police had apprehended him.

I twisted my hands uncertainly. "You want me to read your uncle's will?"

"You would hardly expect me to move forward without reliable legal counsel. I'm not sure I trust that man."

That was enough for me. Eagerly, I sat down to study the document. The will was very short, only two and a half brief pages, typewritten, signed at the last by

Mr. Augustus Horatio MacJudd and witnessed by an Alan Balfour and Dr. Paul McGann. But what caught my eye was the date. "This was signed last month!" I lifted my eyes to hers. "Your uncle made a new will just before he died?"

"Mmm," she agreed. "Curious timing."

"Well, it's strange, if he was intending to sell Dunfyne Island to these herring people."

"Quite. What does that tell you?"

"Well . . ." There hadn't been an inquest, so they couldn't be certain Uncle Augustus had died of natural causes—although the scene Mr. Macewan had painted for us sounded about as natural as you could get. "Seeing as how *you* stood most to benefit from his death, you would be my chief suspect."

She let out a laugh. "I believe I have an alibi."

Shadows from the oil lamp pooled at the edges of the room, casting Miss Judson's face in a haunting glow. Her fingers tapped the paper, as if she could receive ghostly messages from the beyond via Morse code—but she did not give away her thoughts.

"We ought to look into this," I volunteered.

"Oh, there's no *question* we're looking into this. No, it's just, it all did seem too good to be true."

I searched her face, trying to make out the source of her disquiet. "Do you think your uncle was murdered?"

3

SPEED, BONNIE BOAT

As an estate may include any manner of geographic formations—from forest to farm field to
fishing waters—it is essential to familiarize yourself with the proper care of all of them.

–*A Country Gentlewoman's Guide to Estate
Management*

Now that we were on another Investigation—until we
determined whether Uncle Augustus's death was natural or not—everyone we encountered in Argyll was
potentially a murder suspect. That was nothing new
for me, of course, but Miss Judson was about to meet
all the people who had known and loved her long-
lost uncle, and that was a dreadful beginning to an
acquaintance with her extended family. What ought
to have been an exciting homecoming was now tinged
with sinister overtones.

Oddly, however, it seemed to brighten Miss Judson's
spirits. She rose early, singing softly in French, and

threw open the curtains to our little hotel room upon a scene of improbable storybook beauty. Colorful fishing boats dotted a strip of dark water, and behind them rose hillsides of deep misty green, cottages nestled among the trees. Above it all spread a blue, blue sky— so huge and bright it was hard to believe it was the same ordinary atmosphere I regarded every day from Swinburne.

Cook sat up, eyeing Miss Judson dubiously. "What's got her in such a good temper?"

I slid my bare feet to the bare floor, mindful of stalking cats ready to attack my bare ankles. "She thinks her uncle might have been murdered." There was no reason Cook couldn't be in our confidence, after all. Three heads were better than one, and Cook was already skeptical of everything Scottish. She was starting the Investigation with an advantage.

Cook gave a huff of satisfaction. "Sure enough, then. Shall we wire Himself?"

Miss Judson's sunny mood clouded over. "Hardly. I'm certain we are more than capable of handling this ourselves."

Although that was undeniably true, her ready dismissal of Father's involvement concerned me. Of course, she knew he was working and couldn't get away. But there seemed something more in her reluctance, something I was reluctant to examine too closely. Thank goodness there was a murder—potential murder—to look into instead. Not to mention the crime we'd witnessed ourselves.

"What about the police report from yesterday?" I looked up from tying my boots. "Shouldn't we make sure the local constables are on the lookout for your pickpocket?"

"We don't want to miss our ferry," she said. "I'm eager to finally see my new island for myself."

I yanked hard on my laces. Anyone might think a purse-snatching (well, attempted portmanteau-snatching) would give Someone pause about settling in such a place—but a certain Someone seemed to think it only added to the region's charms.

By the time we queued up, the ferry landing was already thronged with smartly dressed tourists with their parasols and carpetbags and cameras, admiring the sights along the loch. All manner of boats crammed the water: sailing vessels, steamships large and small, fishing fleets bringing in the day's catch of herring, touring yachts with wealthy passengers enjoying the bright clear weather and dazzling views. All along the shore, tall wooden stakes were jammed into the seabed—evidently part of some local industry whose purpose was not immediately apparent.

Cook had her nose buried in a guidebook she'd picked up on her supply-gathering mission yesterday. "It says here that it's impossible to go more than four miles in Argyll without being in sight of either a loch or the sea," she informed us. "Unnatural, that. Are we seals?"

The bustling pier attracted all sorts of traffic. "Look, there's Lt. Smoot!" I cried, immediately regretting it. Although he could not possibly have heard me, he turned, recognized Miss Judson, and waved.

Mr. Macewan failed to materialize, which piqued Miss Judson considerably. She scanned the crowds, tapped her fingers against her elbow, and finally herded the rest of us onto the boat. Dodging the handful of wagons and horses that were also making the journey, we threaded our way past the fat smokestack to the low, whitewashed observation rail at the bow. Otter Ferry was a small port on this grand vessel's route, and most of the passengers were bound for parts more glamorous. Miss Judson straightened her hat and rewarded me with a brief smile.

"Well," she said, "off we go!"

We had been going off for several days now, but I understood what she meant. This was the next-to-last leg of the journey to claim her Scottish inheritance, and even she couldn't help being excited—inconvenience or not, murder or not. I turned my face toward the loch, and tried to regard our encroaching destination with happy expectation.

Dear Reader, I have never found myself in such an alien and enchanting land. Much has been written, of course, about Scotland's magnificent lochs and the dramatic rocky land rising from amid them—but what's been neglected is how *green* everything is. Ireland is called the Emerald Isle, but it could not possibly have a thing on the myriad verdant shades of Argyll. Miss Judson had her pastels out, capturing the view: slate-colored water lapping grey and tan rocks with white froth; dazzlingly bright lawns spreading to the pine-shadowed hills. And all around, wildflowers bursting forth in every shade of springtime. It began to hurt my eyes.

I turned away to Observe the view of Tighnabruaich disappearing into the distance, and saw that Lt. Smoot had followed us aboard. He was watching Miss Judson intently. Frowning, I fixed his features in my memory, which I had failed to do in the excitement yesterday (some eyewitness I made!). He was tallish and fit, handsome in an oily sort of way, with dark hair fluttering in the wind, a matching dark moustache, and his helmet tucked beneath his arm. Our eyes met briefly before he slipped back into the crowd on deck.

"That was odd," I said to Peony, who was huddled against my chest (boats not being her particular favorite). She made no reply, pretending she had seen nothing.

The soldier's appearance made me realize that I had thus far given little attention to my singular mission of preventing Miss Judson from falling in love with Scotland. Until now there had seemed little risk of it, with the inconveniences of travel, the attempted robbery, the condescending solicitor. But standing upon the bow of the *Flora MacDonald*, sketchbook in hand, she seemed entirely at home. Simply admiring the view couldn't do much harm. Could it?

"There's Dunfyne," said a voice at my shoulder. Lt. Smoot pointed across the water to a lump of green indistinguishable amongst the other green lumps of the lumpy green shore. "Some of the finest herring to be found hereabouts."

"What are you doing here?" I demanded.

"Why, I'm your neighbor," he said. "I've a wee isle of my own the other side of Dunfyne—not an estate like Rockfforde, mind you. Just a nice little croft with a view o' the loch. I knew your uncle well."

"Her uncle," I corrected, indicating Miss Judson, still intent on her sketching. A curl of hair had escaped its pins, and I had the most curious urge to tuck it back into place before Lt. Smoot noticed. But, of course, it was already too late.

Miss Judson turned and nodded briskly to Lt. Smoot. "Good morning again," she said. "You were saying you know Dunfyne?"

He smiled broadly. "I'd be glad to show you around—the Falls, the ruins—"

"Ruins?" I said, against my better judgment.

"The ruins of Castle Dunfyne! There are medieval ruins everywhere in Argyll, but these are your very own. Augustus was quite keen on them."

I glanced to Miss Judson. I should like to see a ruined castle myself.

"We don't want to put you to any trouble," she said.

"No trouble," he assured us. "In fact, you're about to impose on me again."

Now she frowned. "Explain."

"Did old Macewan fail to mention that commercial ferries don't serve Dunfyne?"

The look on Miss Judson's face was growing deadlier by the moment. "He did indeed."

The lieutenant hastened to explain. "The island has supplies delivered every fortnight by a local puffer"—he gestured toward a sturdy-looking vessel with a thick smokestack—"but that was yesterday."

The stormy expression on Miss Judson's face showed no signs of blowing over. Her fingers tightened on the sketchbook. "I see."

"Dunfyne likes its solitude." He sounded apologetic.

"There must be other boats for hire," I said.

"It'll be hard to find one just now. It's the beginning of tourist season, and vessels go quickly."

"What will we do?" I asked—foolishly, since Lt. Smoot had an answer to this, as well.

"I'll take you, of course. I keep my yacht in Otter Ferry. She's not as grand as that, but she makes the trip."

Miss Judson made an inaudible sound of annoyance,

and I felt Peony's tail flick. "We couldn't possibly incon-venience you."

"I'm afraid you'll have to. There's but one boarding-house at Otter Ferry, and it'll be booked solid."

"Lieutenant," Miss Judson said, "why do I get the feeling we've been conned?"

The friendly soldier tossed his head back and laughed.

Ordinarily Miss Judson—not to mention every other reliable source—makes it a point to stress the inadvis-ability of accepting rides from strangers, particularly charming strangers who appear out of nowhere with offers too good to be trusted. Unfortunately, Lt. Smoot's predictions came to pass: the ferry did not run to Dunfyne, and none of Miss Judson's pleas moved the harbormaster to make an exception on our behalf. Nor was he susceptible to pounds sterling. Two other vessels docked nearby were likewise unavailable, their skippers shaking their heads at Miss Judson's entreaties.

While Lt. Smoot waited for Miss Judson's Investigations to prove fruitless, I questioned him about yesterday's events.

"Were you able to give a description of the thief to the constables?"

His attention was on Miss Judson, and I had to repeat myself. "What's that? Oh, of course." He gave me an indulgent smile.

"And you turned over his hat, for identification?"

Before he could reply, Miss Judson returned in defeat.

"You must let us pay you," she said, but he waved this off.

"I wouldn't hear of it! We're *neighbors*. We do for each other in Argyll."

Lt. Smoot was beginning to wear me down as well. Peony recognized the superior accommodations aboard the *Lass o' Loch Fyne*, which included a sun-warmed spot on the spick-and-span deck—although nowhere to sit, and no railing to keep us aboard in case of rough seas. Rough lochs. I hesitated before boarding; my singular (vicarious) experience of such a small vessel had been ill-fated, and I was none too eager to repeat the misadventures of her sorry crew,* which had included shipwreck, starvation, and murder. The only seating seemed to be within a square cavity sunk into the deck, where the helm—a well-polished wheel—waited at the ready.

"On you go." One by one, Lt. Smoot led us aboard, where an older man in a yachting cap greeted us warmly. "Ladies, allow me to introduce our skipper, Sandy Macfarlane."

The captain shook Miss Judson's hand. "Ah knew yer uncle. Ahm sorry for yer loss, lassie."

---

* See previous Investigations, Dear Reader.

"I'm afraid it's your loss," she said with a kind smile. "I never met the man."

This seemed to melt the seaman's* heart. "Nae anither like him in all Argyll," he said. "A real character, oor Augustus. Aye off on his gran' Quest, diggin' up Castle Dunfyne for buried treasure, or else wi' his hooonds." This last word seemed to go on several more syllables than necessary, accompanied by a fond chuckle. "Aye, they'll be missin' him, though, won't they, Fitz?"

"Who will?" I asked. In among the musical burrs and vowels of Captain Macfarlane's splendid accent, I'd lost track of what we were talking about.

Lt. Smoot saluted the captain. "Ladies, I'm needed at the bow, but you'll be safe with Macfarlane." He decamped to the mysterious business of the vessel's rigging, while the captain helped us descend into the cockpit.

Cook settled on the deck beside Peony, like she'd been raised aboard loch-sailing yachts and was home at long last. Miss Judson perched atop a slim cask, and I settled on a wooden crate, feeling something lumpy beneath my backside. I fished under my skirts and freed a battered wool cap that looked entirely too familiar.

"Miss," I hissed, but Captain Macfarlane had her attention.

* lochman?

"Keep an eye oot for the Falls," he called from the helm. "We sail right past, and you'll nae git a bitter view."

As we crossed the narrow strip of loch, Captain Macfarlane kept up a lively narration of the sights we passed. "Look there, lassies!" He pointed to a wide, flat-bottomed boat, almost a raft, moving gracefully across the water with the most astonishing cargo. Passengers. Some humans, two horses, and a positive army of dogs—a full set of matching white-and-brown hounds clustered eagerly at the rail, watching us watch them.

"Tha'll be yer neighbor, Kirkpatrick, headin' hame for the summer." Captain Macfarlane greeted the passing boatmen with a wave. One of the men—tall and imperious—gazed back haughtily, but at last deigned to nod, before turning back to his hounds. "Lives ootbye Inveraray full time, but keeps a lodge on Dunfyne for the hunting season. Ach, here be the Falls."

We glanced away from horses and dogs on a boat, to say nothing of the men, to see a tumult of white flash against the blackish green of the forested hillsides. A cleft in the island opened up, brisk white water tumbling down the rocks from on high. They were gone too fast for Miss Judson to capture them, but I could see she was impressed.

"Rockfforde Falls," Lt. Smoot announced. "One of the finest of the many cascades in these parts. It's why so many people were interested in your uncle's island, you know."

Miss Judson caught on immediately. "That water could power a factory."

"So it could," Lt. Smoot confirmed. "And there've been all sorts up here nosing about. Your uncle wouldn't have anything to do with them."

"He wasn't interested in developing the island?" Miss Judson's interrogation tactics were subtle and refined. "I've been told it would be a good spot for herring processing."

Lt. Smoot hauled hard on his ropes, causing a sail to swing wildly. "You've been talking to Macewan," he said, voice full of accusation. "What sort of nonsense has he been filling your head with?"

Miss Judson cocked that head to the side. (To let the nonsense run out? Not that there was any: Miss Judson was thoroughly Immune to Nonsense! Or at least she had been before we came to Scotland.) "Aren't you in favor of Progress, Lieutenant?"

"Look here," he said heatedly. "Rockfforde Hall has stood two centuries. Castle Dunfyne was here even earlier. Folk've called these islands home for thousands of years. We've done just fine without Fyne Fisheries' fingers stirring the pot." His voice rose and his cheeks flushed with more than the exertion of sailing or the wind from the loch. "Dunfyne's perfect as she is."

Miss Judson said, "Hmm," but gave me a significant Look.

"What do you know about Uncle Augustus's death?" I Inquired.

The lieutenant didn't answer directly. "This part of Scotland's been the site of quarrels and infighting, clan wars, and shifting allegiances for centuries." He gazed into the misty distance. "It's in our blood, I suppose."

"But you're English," I said, and he grinned.

"Don't let the uniform—or the accent—fool you. Loch Fyne born and bred, I am. I know change is inevitable. Your uncle knew it too. But like the good Argyll men we are, we're determined to hang on to our scrap o' heaven just a wee bit longer." To my utter surprise, he hauled me from the cockpit and positioned me at a sort of crank. "Mind this," he said. "I need to check something below."

Miss Judson stepped in to relieve me of my duties. I didn't know she could sail, but it shouldn't have surprised me. Perhaps it was her Argyll blood coming out, as well.

It was a small vessel, with hardly any opportunity for private conversation, but with Captain Macfarlane and Lt. Smoot both occupied, I made a quiet Observation. "He doesn't want to talk about how Mr. MacJudd died."

"No, he does not," she agreed. "But I get the feeling he knows more than he's saying."

"We'll get to the bottom of it," I assured her. Then

I paused. "Of course, there might not be any mystery here." And we could turn around and head right back home to Swinburne and Father and The Item waiting in his desk drawer.

Miss Judson looked out across the water at the oncoming pines and hills of Dunfyne Island. "Oh, there are mysteries here aplenty," she said. "One: why did Augustus MacJudd leave his property to someone he'd never met? Two: was he or was he not planning to sell to Fyne Fisheries? Two-A: why would his will reflect different wishes than those he supposedly expressed to his solicitor?"

"Two-B," I interjected, "why didn't the solicitor know he'd left his property to you?"

She nodded. "Three: why has the solicitor failed to accompany us to inspect the property?"

"Four: how did Lt. Smoot just happen to run into us?"

Miss Judson's lip twitched. "I believe that falls under the category of *Coincidence*, not *Mystery*."

I shook my head, hair flipping sharply against my cheeks. "He *followed* us onto the boat at Tighnabruaich," I insisted. "I saw him earlier, talking to the ferryman. He pointed you out specifically."

She held fast to her coincidence theory. "The ferryman no doubt informed him of our plans, and knowing the difficulties we'd face, suggested that Lt. Smoot offer his assistance."

I gave a noncommittal grunt.

"You have a very suspicious mind," she said, and I felt a flush of pride.

"Thank you."

"That wasn't—" She stopped. "He's our neighbor. Let's not make an enemy of him until we have good cause."

And the way he'd been looking at my governess wasn't good cause?

୶

Lt. Smoot's yacht pulled into a sheltered inlet shaded by pines. There was no dock, just a stone quay carved out of the rocky shore, concave and bare from centuries of the loch's caress. In Otter Ferry, gulls had circled overhead, crying raucously, but Dunfyne greeted us with eerie stillness, our own commotion breaking rudely into primæval silence. I shivered and held Peony closer, although it wasn't any colder. A lonely stone hut stood near the water, like it had wandered down to wait for visitors who'd never arrived.

"That's odd." Lt. Smoot frowned at the island.

"What?" Miss Judson's voice came out sharp.

"The—well, not to worry, I'm sure." He sounded too cheery. "But Balfour's usually here to meet the boats. Or Mac."

Miss Judson raised her eyebrows expectantly.

"Rockfforde's factor, the manager," he explained. "Or his man-of-all-work. Perhaps they didn't realize you were on your way. Off you go. Sandy, I'll be back shortly, aye?"

"Lad—" Captain Macfarlane was cut off by a sharp look from the lieutenant.

"What?" I detected a note of warning in Lt. Smoot's voice.

"Dinnae be lang. We've cargo tae deliverr, remem-brr? They're not gaun tae wait frreverr."

Lt. Smoot started to say something, but Miss Judson forestalled him. (Dear Reader, had *I* done it, it would be called *interrupting*, but Miss Judson is far too refined to interrupt anyone.) "Lieutenant, we wouldn't dream of delaying you further."

The lieutenant shot a sour glance at Captain Macfarlane, but answered lightly, "A sodger's time is ne'er his ain." He swung himself easily off the side of the yacht, alighting on the water-splashed landing, pro-tected from the wash by his tall shiny boots. "Myrtle first." He held out his arms.

I stepped back. "Myrtle first *what*?"

"No switherin'. Hop down, lass."

"Hop—" Into his *arms*? Mortified, I turned to Miss Judson for support.

She had no sympathy. "Time's a-wastin', lass. Off you go." And she gave me a none-too-gentle shove that practically tumbled me right into Lt. Smoot's embrace. I squeezed my eyes shut, horrified to be so close to a strange soldier holding me like a *baby*. But I grudgingly commended him for depositing me well free of the water. I gave a most Peony-like shake of my whole person, feeling the oddest urge to stop and nibble at my forelimb to compose myself.

Miss Judson's disembarkment was more dignified—a lively, athletic leap from the deck, caught in a graceful (and altogether too lengthy) dance-like maneuver, skirts awhirl, by Lt. Smoot. She was flushed and grinning when he finally released her with a laughing bow.

Cook and Peony and the luggage were likewise transported ashore. The noise of our arrival ought to have alerted someone to our presence, but we remained alone on the deserted landing. The abandoned hut proved to be a boathouse; a net hung long ago had decayed to tatters, and an oar propped against the wall was glued in place by at least a century of lichen. From all appearances, Dunfyne Island wasn't expecting us. They weren't expecting anybody—ever.

"Maybe everyone left when Uncle Augustus died?" I whispered to Miss Judson. A Whole Estate should have an army of servants to run it. So where were they?

"Hmm," was the only speculation Miss Judson would offer.

We hadn't brought much, but as our belongings accumulated on the stony beach, our arrival in Scotland finally felt very real, and really final. What had Miss Judson packed for this trip to her ancestral homestead? How many sketchbooks had she wrestled into that valise? How many crisp shirtwaists and neat brown skirts? And would she be fitting them into a wardrobe at Rockfforde Hall, or bringing them back home to Gravesend Close?

For her part, she merely glanced round, lips tightening at the growing pile of bags and trunks. "Is it far? Should we send for a cart?"

But Lt. Smoot had the solution for this too. He ambled to the boathouse and swung open its rickety door, withdrawing an aged wheelbarrow with a wobbly wheel. "At your service, ladies."

The wheelbarrow didn't fit everything, so I wound up carrying Peony's hatbox along with my valise. Cook bustled through and took charge of the vehicle. "This way, then?" Without waiting for an answer, she forged up a rocky path to the woods. A burble and determined scratching came from the hatbox's occupant, who would have preferred to arrive under her own recognizance.

Dear Reader, the sudden gloom and abrupt chill that descended with our first steps into Dunfyne's celebrated pine forest were initially a relief, after the blaring sunshine on the loch. Despite my hat's thoroughly respectable brim, my face hurt from squinting. Tension melted from my eyebrows.

An old path twined from the beach into the trees. It had once been well trodden, but now the cracked stones were half-consumed by the forest floor. Every crunch of the barrow's wheel on the stone rang out coarse and overloud. Even Peony's restive burble clashed against the pressing hush. A cloud of humming insects swarmed out of the brush, and we swatted them away.

"Midges," Lt. Smoot said cheerfully. "The plague of Caledonia."

Something rustled in the trees, making everyone jump. The lieutenant stretched an arm out to signal silence, and a moment later a huge creature stepped delicately out of the verge, brown ears flicking. A red deer, trailed by a shaggy yearling, it froze and stared at us with distinct menace. For a mad moment I forgot all principles of zoology and wondered if deer were carnivorous.

The pair lingered only a moment, sizing us up, before bounding gracefully into the trees on the other side of the path.

We resumed our trek. "Hope this young man knows what he's doing," Cook said, not remotely under her breath. I could envision the headlines: **MYSTERY IN ARGYLL: ENGLISHWOMEN VANISH ON DUNFYNE! SOLDIER KNOWS MORE THAN HE'S SAYING.** And at that moment, the trees split open, the sunshine returned, and we caught our first glimpse of Rockfforde Hall.

Miss Judson released her breath in a slow, controlled rush, Cook gave a grunt of approval, Peony scratched frantically for her own glimpse, and I simply stared.

Rockfforde Hall was *huge*. Not quite a castle,

perhaps, but the next thing to it. A castlette? Lt. Smoot had told us it was two hundred years old, dating it from the late 1600s, but parts seemed much older. Towers and battlements bedecked an ancient stone skeleton, with brick gables and windows and extra wings stacked upon each other wherever the architects had fancied or found room. Ivy crept over the whole affair like a rash, blocking out windows and strangling the drainpipes.

"Brrrb?" the hatbox said.

I pictured all those blood feuds, warring clans storming across this clearing and tossing up wings of Rockfforde Hall in between skirmishes with their enemies. I forgot all my reservations, all my obligations and orders. Any hope of keeping Miss Judson from falling in love with her new home evaporated. It was too late; I'd already lost my own head to the place.

"Brrrb!" Peony scratched frantically at the hatbox.

The yard was a jumble of cobbles choked with greenery, spiky bushes stretching out their green-hazed arms, and most curious, a vast felled tree stump, big around as a dining table and chopped off a good three feet from the ground. It overlooked the hollow carcass of a stone-lined pond, bone dry and crusted with mummified leaves. I set the hatbox atop the stump and unlatched it, whereupon Peony leaped free, refused to take in her new surroundings, and planted herself firmly on the dead wood for a bath. At which point we were distracted by the pounding of hoofbeats and a cacophony of barking.

It started off softly enough—a distant choppy wail, like angry geese—but rose to a roar, punctuated by sharp spikes of sound. And a moment later, pouring pell-mell toward us, came more dogs than I'd ever seen in my life*: white dogs, brown dogs, white-and-brown dogs with black spots, all tripping over one another like the sea rushing the shoreline—followed by a figure on horseback, thundering into the yard.

Childhood folktales about the Wild Hunt flew into my head—spectral hounds that harried their quarry through the night sky, their haunting bay raising the hackles of anyone unlucky enough to catch wind of them on moonless nights. But these wild dogs were . . . happy. White whippy bodies leaped with joy, all clumsy paws and flopping ears and ecstatic tails. They swarmed us like a tide, barking and yipping and bumping one another in their ecstasy.

The same could not be said of the rider. The horse skidded to a stop, turf flying under its hooves. "Wha the deil do ye think yer doin'?" cried an angry woman. "We might've killed ye!" Scarcely giving the horse time to stop, she slid from its back, dropped the reins, and marched through the churning sea of dogs, who fell in line—more or less (their tails couldn't seem to slow

* At one time *or* cumulatively

down, and pink tongues lolled foolishly)—as she passed through.

Miss Judson clutched the handle of her broken portmanteau and merely stared at the scene amid which she'd found herself. Cook looked on, unimpressed, and Peony hissed, back arched to a point like one of the rooftops of Rockffforde Hall. Lt. Smoot came up beside Miss Judson, grinning.

"Aye, then," he said. "Did naebody mention the hoonds?"

4
Upstairs, Downstairs

The successful management of a country estate
greatly depends on the quality of the staff. Hire
persons of even temperament, skill, and honesty—
and above all, pay them accordingly, or risk losing
them to your neighbors. In return, a loyal household will prove its value in innumerable ways.

—A Country Gentlewoman's Guide to Estate
Management

The angry horsewoman marched straight up to Lt.
Smoot, brandishing her riding crop. She was Miss
Judson's age or a bit older, with flyaway red-brown
hair, and she wore an ensemble akin to cycling clothes:
breeches tucked into tall boots and a tweed Norfolk
jacket.

Lt. Smoot intervened before she could tear into us.
"Miss Judson, allow me to introduce Miss Jessie Craig,
Mistress of the Hounds of Rockfforde Hall. Jess, this is

Miss Judson, the Laird's niece, and the Hardcastles. I think the cat's called Peony."

Instantly the expression on Miss Craig's face shifted from fury to skepticism, followed by a flash of alarm—no, *fear*. It was gone too quickly to make sense of, her changeable features settling on resentment.

"Come tae size us up for the butcher block, then, aye? Well, English, have a guid look." She waved the riding crop at the castle. "Therty-five rooms, the roof leaks, an' we cannae make the rates. Enjoy it." She made to march right on past us, but Miss Judson forestalled her.

"Good day, Miss Craig. We're sorry to impose."

Miss Craig made an immoderate sound that was mostly covered by the continuing Exceptional Din of Houndiness, clucked to her horse, and stalked off. I found myself overcome by dogs beside themselves to see us, and within moments my traveling costume—my best coat and gloves—was a disaster of white fur and slobber. It was magnificent.

Flashing me an unreadable Look, Miss Judson set off after Miss Craig. I scurried to catch up, Cook and Peony close behind—we could hardly do otherwise; it was either move with the hounds or be trampled underfoot. Underpaw. Paws. They flowed in the apparent direction of their kennels—save for the handful who kept getting distracted by attempting to tackle the Exciting Strangers and lick us into oblivion.

Miss Craig's flood path carried us to an enclosed courtyard, where people trickled from the castle's nooks and crannies. Miss Craig jammed the riding crop into her belt and yanked something from the saddle—a narrow span of metal with a set of jaws at one end. For a wild moment I assumed it was a weapon she meant to unleash upon us (no pun intended, Dear Reader!). She waved the iron device at the assembled company.

"Jess!" A severely dressed woman about Cook's age came running down the steps. "Nae again!"

"Aye, *again*. An' there's more where this came frae, an' aw. I'll kill that man if I get my hands on him." From the fiery look in her eyes, and the fiery flush of her face, I believed her.

I pressed closer for a better look, realizing what was wrong. "Is that a trap?"

Miss Craig brandished the wicked device at me. "Kirkpatrick—our so-called neighbor—laid them all through the covert. Found a fox in one this morning. Poor wee thing." She flicked away angry tears.

I was perplexed. "But—aren't they foxhounds?" I gestured toward the pack.

The horsewoman exploded. "Hunting is a *sport*— horse an' dog an' man workin' together in the open air. Killing the foxes is cruel. We juist follow them. This"— she shook the trap—"this is barbaric!"

I scrunched away, cowed by her fierceness. I rather agreed with her, but her philosophy did fly in the face of centuries of British sporting tradition. Not that there was anything sportsmanlike about the trap she held, its cruel jaws caked with rust—I hoped.

A ginger-bearded giant in a kilt and a wooly green jumper waded through the dogs with a practiced stride. "Ah'll tak tha', lass," he said grimly. "Ah'll poot it wi' the rest." He paused to regard Miss Judson, Cook, and me. "Ladies," he said, before carrying the trap away to a brick outbuilding.

Miss Judson stepped forward. "I don't mean to intrude, but perhaps you'll explain the situation, Miss Craig?"

It was the older woman who replied. "There's naethin' to conserrrn yersels wi'," she said. "It's oor ain effair."*

Miss Judson regarded her coolly. "I'm afraid it is my concern. I'm Ada Judson, Mr. MacJudd's great-niece."

"And his heir," I added helpfully, in case anyone had missed the significance of our sudden appearance.

"I ken who ye be." The lady spoke as if my governess was of no consequence whatsoever.

"Now, Mrs. Craig." Lt. Smoot came forward. I could see a resemblance between the elder and younger Craigs now. A grandmother, perhaps? "Miss Judson's come a very long way. Is this the Rockfforde welcome she should expect?"

---

* After several days, I was slowly getting the hang of Scots. This translated as, "It's our own affair." See Appendix, page 353.

Miss Judson added gently, "I can't help if I don't know what's going on."

Mrs. Craig made a derisive noise. "Ye cannae help at all."

"Catriona—" Worry drew Lt. Smoot's moustache downward. "Where's Alan?"

Fury filled the elder woman's stately face. "Gaun! And guid riddance too."

"Gone—has he quit?"

"Quit, sacked—it's aw the same tae us," Mrs. Craig spat. "Not that ye'd carrre."

"Ach, Gran, don't be like that. Nae with Augustus gone . . ." His sad tone melted a little of Mrs. Craig's frostiness. "But—" He turned to Miss Judson. "I'm afraid if Alan Balfour's gone, that leaves Rockfforde Hall with no factor. And I dinnae ken where ye'll find anither this time o' year." His accent was growing more Scottish by the moment.

"I'm sure *we'll* manage," Mrs. Craig said.

"Quite right." Miss Judson instantly aligned herself with Rockfforde Hall's fiercest guard dog. Mrs. Craig still seemed skeptical.

Lt. Smoot stroked his moustache, frowning deeply. "I dinnae like leaving you here, not with Balfour gone. You should come back to Otter Ferry for the night."

Miss Judson regarded him—at last—with impatience. "Lieutenant, I am most obliged to you. But I assure you, we will be Perfectly Fine at Rockfforde Hall. Now,

Mrs. Craig, if someone might direct us toward a pot of tea, we can get down to business. I'm sure there's a great deal of work to be done, and you're shorthanded. Of course," she added sunnily, "we could probably find the way ourselves."

Mrs. Craig recognized the threat to her supremacy. "This way, please." She swept her black skirts in a wide, graceful arc—I Observed that not a single white dog hair adhered to their pristine surface—and set off for the castle. "Jessie," she called. "I want a word when ye've finished up. And scrape yer boots this time, lass. I've jist dun the flairs."

Miss Judson glanced about for the members of our party. Cook had wandered off to inspect a water pump coated in several generations of paint. She gave the handle an experimental lift, and it let out a shriek like Peony at her most unhappy, releasing a flood of disturbingly red water. Everyone jumped.

Cook gave us a nod, happily ensconced in her latest mechanical Investigation.

Lt. Smoot took Miss Judson's hand—and, to my enormous horror, *kissed it*! And she did *not*, I'll note, yank it back and punch him—despite all the fierce telepathic signals I was sending. They must not work in Scotland.

"Well, if you're certain, I suppose I'll be on my way. I'll try to get back in a day or two to check on you. It's been a pleasure."

This required me to mutter, "Likewise," although I cannot vouch for the veracity of the statement.

Still, he lingered, helmet in both hands, looking worried. "Gran—if I might have a word?"

Mrs. Craig glowered at him, at us. "Wait fir me inside," she commanded, pointing out a battered green door guarded by an oversized boot scraper.

Miss Judson's efficient stride carried her across a crumbly stone threshold into the cavernous maw of Rockfforde Hall, but I cast one last look behind me at the hounds, and Cook, and Mrs. Craig arguing with Lt. Smoot, all in the simmering tension left behind by Jessie's furious exit. We could not hear what was said, but it seemed to irk Mrs. Craig. (In fairness, rainbows and butterflies and hot cocoa would all probably irk Mrs. Craig too.) Tossing up her hands in exasperation, she abandoned us to march across the courtyard, in pursuit of more interloping English heiresses.

That's when I noticed a face in an upstairs window.

In a room high above the courtyard, a casement was cracked, and a thin pale figure watched, fair hair riffling in the wind. As soon as our eyes met, however, the window clicked shut and my Observer vanished.

သာ

Dear Reader, I'm afraid my first impression of Rockfforde Hall's amenities was not an especially impressed one. My beloved governess may have inherited lands and a title and a Distinguished Legacy—but as far as the Whole Estate in Scotland went, it certainly wasn't putting its best foot forward. A musty chill descended beyond the doorway, an air of gloom hanging over the back passage. I felt an involuntary shiver.

"Wuff," said a polite voice.

Waiting in the dim, low-ceilinged corridor was a white dog with a curled tail and alert black ears, one paw lifted as if it was expecting to receive us.

And behind the dog, looking not a bit like she'd been expecting us, a young woman held a feather duster like a defensive weapon. "Wha'rrre ye?" she squeaked.

"Who are *you*?" Miss Judson returned, rather more kindly.

"Muriel. I do fir th' Laird."

"Well, Muriel, you'll be 'doing' for me now. I'm Miss Ada Judson, and I've inherited Rockfforde Hall."

"Naebody said."

Miss Judson sighed. "I know the feeling. Muriel, if Mr. MacJudd were here now, what would you be doing?"

The maid glanced uncertainly from Miss Judson to me. "Tea?"

Miss Judson's smile was radiant, lighting up the gloomy hall. "Tea sounds wonderful," she said. "You'll take some too, of course? Is it easier if we come to the kitchen?"

"The—the kitchen, Miss? Mum?"

"Of course. No sense airing out the parlor. We don't stand on ceremony."

Muriel dithered. But the dog turned and trotted down the passage, nails tapping the floor.

"Perhaps it's the butler?" I whispered, which roused Muriel from her stupor to lead us after the hound. She was fair and slight—Muriel, though the dog was too—and so pale in every particular, from her hair to her dress, she was the only thing visible in the dark corridor. She might have been the apparition in the window, although if so, she'd slipped down here from her Observation Post in a hurry.

"Duik 'ere," the housemaid said, bobbing low beneath a wooden beam I nearly hit my head on. Miss Judson was not quite so successful; I heard a rasp as her straw hat met an unfortunate fate.

I stumbled over another boot scraper, dodging a tray of Wellies waiting to catch English girls unawares. Someone had tacked a notice to the wall, but so many years ago its message was long lost, the print faded and paper yellowed. Dog leads hung on hooks, and the post had accumulated in a basket upon an old table. Miss Judson paused to leaf through this, squinting at it in the dimness—just as if we'd casually strolled in our very own front door back home on Gravesend Close.

"Hmm." She showed me an envelope. "Fyne Fisheries."

"What do ye think ye're doing?" And just like that, Mrs. Craig rematerialized and whisked the letter from

Miss Judson's hands. "Ye may think ye've inherited Rockffforde Hall, but ye've nae inherited our privacy."

Miss Judson, trying to keep the peace, surrendered. "We're not here to intrude," she said—which raised the question of why, exactly, we *were* here. "You must have worked for my great-uncle a long while. I'm sure it was a great shock when he died."

Her polite condolences left an opening for Mrs. Craig to fill with gruff thanks, perhaps even an Incriminating Statement or two. (I had only just met the woman, but it is never too early to be on the lookout for murder suspects!) But Mrs. Craig wasn't interested in reminiscing *or* confessing. "I'll show ye to yer rooms noo."

Abandoning Muriel and hope of tea, we followed Mrs. Craig up to a cavernous great hall, enclosed on all sides with dark wood. Shadows pooled in the corners, and a dusty silence suffused the space. A vast iron candle ring swung overhead, its stumpy candles neglected. There was hardly any furniture to speak of, just a scratched sideboard, upon which sat an indescribable brass-and-bone . . . sculpture . . . or perhaps a candelabrum . . . a clock? . . . depicting a hunting scene, the birth of Venus, and possibly the Battle of Culloden. Beside the door, a hat rack overflowed with more dog leads, a sloppy china water bowl beside it.

Mrs. Craig bustled us through, in an almighty

hurry to get us to our destination. But she paused to produce a handkerchief and dust an invisible speck from the curiosity. She did it with such loving care that I ventured to find my voice.

"What is that?"

She stiffened. Perhaps she was the sort that believed children should be neither seen nor heard. But a moment later she answered, "The Laird's Baird Stoomp."

"His what?"

"Bairrrd stoomp." She gave the monstrosity another fond polish.

"What's a bird . . . stump?"

But that was the extent of Mrs. Craig's Artistic Lecture. Miss Judson had broken ranks and was Investigating a shadowy corridor branching off the main hall. "Where does this lead?"

"Dinnae gae therrre!" Mrs. Craig's voice made her jump, and she whirled round, flushing guiltily. Mrs. Craig seemed to have startled herself, and swept fingers down her crisp apron. "It's in a dangerrous state o' disrepairr—nae been used since the roof blew in in th' storrrm of '76."

Miss Judson recovered first, but her face betrayed the faintest hint of dismay as she mentally calculated the damage. "Of course." Her smile was soothing. "I'm naturally curious about my family home. You understand."

I understood—and it gave me an uncomfortable itch. But whether or not the stern housekeeper did was fated to remain a mystery. She silently resumed the tour, mounting the elaborate stairs like the leader of an expedition afraid of avalanche, scarcely pausing to let us breathe or take in the scenery.

And that scenery was perilous indeed. Swords, bows, pikes, and shields adorned every surface, and a full suit of armor stood guard on the landing, a sunburst of swords overhead. But instead of gleaming with polish, the weapons were pockmarked with rust and frosted with centuries of dust.

A large painted crest, evidently the MacJudd coat of arms, displayed a sprig of some plant crowned with the word *Audere*, Latin for "Be Bold," and *MDCXC* below—1690, perhaps when Rockfforde Hall was built? Or parts of it, anyway.

Mrs. Craig swept past the suit of armor, which seemed to tremble in the breeze from her skirts.

"Was Uncle Augustus preparing for a siege?" My voice clanged out in the echoey space, and Mrs. Craig gave me another frozen look.

"These are Valuable Arrrtifacts." One sharp finger flew to the axes. "The weapons of Stur Judson, who was given the rrrule of Dunfyne Island by Somerled himself." She pointed to the armor. "This was worrn by Sir Ranald MacJudd in the Nine Years' War."

Mrs. Craig's lecture on Scottish history went straight over my head (and a little down my spine), but I daren't ask for further clarification.

A step behind the housekeeper, my governess looked roadworn and slightly shabby, in her rumpled traveling suit on its third day. Mrs. Craig sailed through the hallways with all the grandeur of longtime ownership. As housekeeper of a stately home, she had Duties and Responsibilities, and was the head of a whole household of staff. I supposed it might make you feel like you owned the place.

She certainly didn't seem to make Miss Judson feel as though she owned the place. "Mind where ye step," she commanded. "I've jist had the floors varnished."

"How good of you to go to such trouble," Miss Judson said.

"I didnae do it for ye!" Mrs. Craig's eyes blazed. "I did it fir the Hall. Generations of MacJudds have been born, bred, and died here." She shined the meager lamplight upon a portrait looking down from the corridor wall with disdain. "Ross, Seventeenth MacJudd," she announced, scarcely giving us time to admire his stern visage—Exceptionally Bewigged as befitted a Baroque Gentleman of Quality, an ostentatious brooch holding his fly plaid in place—before moving to the next portrait, like a gallery—"His son, Alistair, Eighteenth MacJudd"—and the next: "Angus, Nineteenth MacJudd." And so on, down the row of

Distinguished Gentlemen in their best Scottish dress of draped tartan, cockades, and furry pouches at their waists. And always, alongside every MacJudd in his finest apparel, a hound. Their names were inscribed alongside their masters': Ladygirl, Contessa, Rustin.

We came to one unprepossessing fellow who looked as overawed by the parade of his ancestry as we were meant to feel. He wore a modern dark suit with a draped tartan pinned over one shoulder, and looked more like a scholar than a grand lord. On his knee rested the head of a hound with loyal eyes and a gold saddle, tail held high and alert. The nameplate read, AUGUSTUS HORATIO, XXV MACJUDD & CLEVELAND.

"The Laird," declared Mrs. Craig, with a touch of loyalty and fondness. "Painted by none otherr than Robert Ross. Your . . . uncle."

"Great-uncle," Miss Judson murmured, taking in her ancestor's portrait. I couldn't begin to know what she was feeling, gazing into the face of a man she'd never met, but who'd spent his last days thinking of her.

"He looks like you," I said with surprise. "You have his nose."

"I most certainly have not!" she said, so severely it even startled Mrs. Craig. She touched her face. "I have my mother's nose."

Taken aback, I wasn't certain how to respond. But Miss Judson recovered swiftly. "It's unfortunate he didn't marry and leave any direct heirs to carry on the line."

Mrs. Craig straightened the frame. "The Laird understood his duties," she said stiffly.

"Then why was he going to sell the island?" I put in.

Mrs. Craig's hand tightened on her lamp at this outrageous accusation against her precious Laird. "I dinnae ken what ye've been told," she said, "but as ye're here, *that* was clearly nivver gaun tae happen. Come aloong. I've put ye in the Thistle Room."

That didn't sound welcoming—a hard bed stuffed with spiny flowers sprang to mind—but the grueling trek eventually brought us to a pretty suite decorated in tones of soft purple: flocked damask wallpaper, frosty velvet hangings, and a thick hooked rug with a pattern of wildflowers. Despite their finery, the furnishings were worn, the plaster ceiling had a disconcerting stain, and the closed shutters were splintered. Miss Judson looked around, expression unreadable.

Mrs. Craig went straight to the casement and started to open the louvers—but clicked them shut hastily, knuckles clenched on the wooden latch. When she turned back, she was impassive, but her voice was tight. "Therre's a draft."

"What was that—" I started to say, but Miss Judson wilted onto the bed.

"Thank you, Mrs. Craig. This is lovely."

The housekeeper gave us yet another of her "I

didnae do it for ye" Looks, but all she said was, "Will ye be needing aethin' else . . . Mistress?"

I could see Miss Judson trying to decide if asking to have a bath drawn up was worth offending Mrs. Craig's wounded sensibilities still further. I raised a tentative hand. "Where's the WC?"

Mrs. Craig merely regarded me stonily.

"The water closet?" Perhaps they used another term in Scotland. "The bathroom?"

Wordlessly, Mrs. Craig glided over to a curvy, gilded cabinet with a chipped marble top. She swung open the door to pass me a large china vessel—painted with thistles—and I nearly perished from mortification.

"There's no plumbing?"

Mrs. Craig did not deign to answer, but simply floated to the door, happy to dispose of her scruffy interlopers, at least briefly.

At that moment, a great alarming thunk sounded through the floorboards, as if a locomotive had slammed to a stop, complete with the squealing of brakes. "Good heavens," exclaimed Miss Judson. "What was that?"

Mrs. Craig barely blinked. "Auld hooses mak noise. Will that be all?" I was almost surprised she didn't lock us in the room when she left. "I dinnae rrecommend wandering aboot efter derrrk. We wouldnae want ye tae get lossit."

Dear Reader, I am fairly certain she wasn't joking.

Miss Judson sighed and unpinned her hat. "It's obvious I'm not her favorite person." A small laugh escaped her.

"We can probably rule her out as a suspect in your uncle's death," I said reluctantly. "She was devoted to the man."

"Unless she killed him to prevent the sale to Fyne Fisheries. I think it's Rockfforde Hall she's devoted to. I can see her wagging that finger at Uncle Augustus, saying, 'I dinnae doo it for ye! I ded it foor the Hawll!'"

Miss Judson's Scots accent was *dreadful*, but I knew better than to say anything. I was still holding the chamber pot—which I'm embarrassed to note that I really did need—and stuck it hastily back inside its cabinet. "What now? We have time to start Investigating before dinner."

But Miss Judson didn't answer. She'd lain back on the thistle coverlet, tossed her dusty hat aside, and fallen fast asleep.

5

THE FINAL PROBLEM?

The first duty upon acquiring an estate is to make
a complete survey of the property.

*–A Country Gentlewoman's Guide to Estate
Management*

The temporary indisposition of my associate was no
impediment to Investigating on my own, Dear Reader.
No sense losing time—I could begin the Inquiry into
Uncle Augustus's Mysterious Death even without Miss
Judson's cooperation. This could very well be our final
case together, after all, if I failed in my mission and did
not convince her to return forthwith to Swinburne and
home and Father.

Notebook in hand, I sat by the creaky window (it
was the only light) and tallied up what we knew so far.
There'd been no Investigation into Uncle Augustus's
death—no police inquiry, no coroner's inquest, no
attempt to trace the movements of his enemies or

ascertain a motive. The murder—if murder it was—must have been committed very carefully to leave no clues behind.

Or the people who had found Uncle Augustus were completely incompetent.

A scratching at the door suggested Peony's presence, but turned out to be the dog with the gold saddle: Cleveland, Uncle Augustus's particular favorite. He gave me a friendly sniff, tail swinging, then trotted within.

"Oh, is this your room?" He didn't exactly seem the thistly sort, but he headed purposefully to the tall bed, sprang aloft as neatly as Peony, and curled up beside Miss Judson with a contented sigh. He thumped his tail against the coverlet with a look that plainly said, *"You go ahead. I'll keep an eye on her."*

"Thank you," I told him. "Erm, any suggestions?"

The tail thumped again. "Wuff."

"Very helpful." With that, I went on my way.

Peony was nowhere to be seen. There were an awful lot of nooks and crannies and dogs about this ancient labyrinth, and there was no telling what mayhem she might cause while unsupervised. And yes, Dear Reader, I know perfectly well you are thinking the same about me.

Even with a murderer at large, there was a delicious thrill to being turned loose upon a castle, even a modest one. A castlette. I crept along the corridor (watching for feline-induced mayhem), and tried to imagine *living* here, surrounded by swords and armor and Bird Stumps and whistling stone windows over-looking the land of one's ancestors. Naturally, I tested every door I passed, but Mrs. Craig's keys hadn't been for show. When one actually opened, springing inward with a sour, unhappy creak, I nearly shut it again just as quickly.

It was a sort of Trophy Room, and I don't mean prize cups. Mounted heads of stags overlooked stuffed birds and foxes, and at least one monstrous fish—the spoils of a hunting lodge—and still more weapons: shot-guns, bows, and a display case of knives. I recognize the scientific value of zoological specimens, but these creatures looked wrathful, *staring* at me with their glassy glass eyes, as if plotting their moment to pounce down and wreak vengeance on the humans who'd dis-patched them. Or innocent bystanding English girls.

Before I could duck away again, I was distracted by the gleam of brass. Some sort of scientific instrument sat upon a library table guarded by a weasel posed in the act of striking. Was this also a laboratory?

Avoiding the gaze of dead animals judging me, I tiptoed in. Large tables stood near the windows, clut-tered with batteries, coils of copper wiring, rubber insulators ... Someone—Uncle Augustus, perhaps—had been experimenting with electrical devices. A smallish box, which jingled when I lifted the lid, held a little bell attached to two paper-wrapped batteries. I wondered what he'd been working on.

I shifted aside a chunk of rock studded with green crystals to flip open a leather journal. The handwriting was scratchy and hard to read.

> 21 March: Disturbances persist. CC and MM disclaim all knowledge.
>
> 25 March: Observations re: Disturbances Occur btwn hours of 4 pm + midnight. Aural manifestations + odd lights with no obvious source. Concentrated around Portrait Gallery, Lady's bedroom, old garderobe, + library, though witnessed elsewhere (see Notes). Duration varies.

Dear Reader, I quite approved of Uncle Augustus's Investigative Methods.

> 27 March: MM frightened from bed by "strange lights" + noises from ceiling. Could make very little sense of her account. Search of quarters revealed nothing. MM terrified; refused to return to room. Have moved her to quarters upstairs.
>
> 29 March: D—n that Balfour for a traitor! Turning my own against me, trying to steal Dunsyne's treasure.
>
> 30 March: Work continues on detector. Have sent for more powerful batteries from Glasg. but delivery will take time. Still convinced of rational explanation.

And the final entry:

10 April: Buzzards circling Rockfforde Hall.

A shiver went down my neck. Uncle Augustus had died only a few days later. What mystery had plagued him? What Disturbances was he trying to explain? I hefted one of the glass tubes, slid a weight on the scale's beam over and back, gave a shake to a sealed brass canister. Perhaps whatever he'd been Investigating had led to his death. I reached for one of the curious books—and heard a distinct *click* from the opposite side of the room.

I looked up sharply. "Peony?" My voice sounded querulous and small in the cavernous space. "Who's there?" *Old houses make noise*—but suddenly I no longer wanted to be in that room with its horrible occupants, however fascinating the equipment and journals.

What had really happened to Uncle Augustus?

Back in the corridor, I smoothed down my skirts, pausing to study his portrait once more. I searched the Laird's kindly face for echoes of my governess's countenance. Her father had spent time here as a youth; if those really were Happier Times for Uncle Augustus, why not leave the estate to Nephew James instead of a great-niece he'd never met?

A noise in the floorboards rattled through my boots

and ankles, and I hopped away, trying to shake off the strange sensation.

"'Tis the ghaist," said a mournful voice exactly in my ear.

With a hiss, I nearly jumped out of those rattling boots. The housemaid, Muriel, lurked at my elbow, still clutching her duster.

"The ghaist," she said again. "The Grrrey Laidy of Rockfforde Hall. It's hanted herrre, ye ken."

I was instantly skeptical, despite Uncle Augustus's books, instruments, and meticulous Observations. "There's no such thing as ghosts." There was no scientific proof validating the existence—or, rather, the supposed supernatural nature—of apparitions, specters, or hauntings, despite having some rather eminent minds on the case.[*]

And why, for that matter, were ghosts always Women in White, Grey Ladies, and the sort? What about a nice Ruddy Lad, with a hale complexion and sturdy form? Why should ghosts persist in making nuisances of themselves, rather than helpfully cleaning the eavestroughs or watering the houseplants? I pictured Mrs. Craig as a restless spirit, gliding down the corridors and making sure the floors were waxed. The image made me giggle.

[*] Sherlock Holmes author Arthur Conan Doyle, for one, having abandoned both literary career *and* the pursuit of medicine for the study of the paranormal with the Society for Psychical Research

"It's nae funny!" Muriel was aghast.* "She's real—you juist haird her. I'd nae sleep in the Thistle Room, nae fir aw the treasure on Dunfyne." She pronounced *treasure* with several more syllables than I'd heard before.

Mrs. Craig put Miss Judson in a haunted room? That just figured. "Wait—did you say *treasure*?"

Muriel brightened. "Ach, aye! The missing Brooch o' Clan MacJudd, lossit durin' the ooprisin."

"The oop—? Oh, uprising. You mean the Jacobite Rebellion, in 1745?"

"Slow doon, lass, I cannae understand ye."

That made two of us.

"Durin' the Risin', Argyll was fir the Ainglish, mostly. But Angus MacJudd refuised tae renounce his suppoort o' Bonnie Prince Chairlie." Her voice rang with pride. "There were a big battle, ootbye Castle Dunfyne. Angus were a-wearin' the brooch, but it were pulled frae his plaid by an Ainglish soldier an' lossit!" The word echoed from the stone walls: *Lost lost lost . . .*

This history was more familiar. Scotland and England had come to violent conflict many times over the ages, but the battles Muriel meant were in the last century, when supporters of the Scottish Stuart dynasty had attempted to overthrow His Majesty George II. Backing James Stuart's claim to the British throne,

---

* An on-point word indeed, Dear Reader: it comes from the Old English word for "ghost."

they called themselves Jacobites, after *Jacobus*, Latin for James. The wars went on for decades, but ultimately the Jacobites were no match for the English forces. The final disastrous attempt came in 1745, under the leadership of James's son, "Bonnie Prince" Charles, and the aftermath was as bloody and violent as the battles themselves. Supporters of the rising—or rebellion, depending on what side you were on—were stripped of their lands and titles, transported to the American colonies as convicts, or simply executed.

Muriel seemed to relish Rockfforde Hall's role in the storied events. "E'er since, Rockfforde Hall's been aneath a currrse! Until the MacJudd Brooch is returned to its rrrightful place, none shall prosperrr on Dunfyne Island. The ghaist o' Ross MacJudd maks sure o' it." She made a curious gesture with her left hand—akin to crossing herself—and it gave me that eerie, shivery feeling again. "The brooch maun be foond, or the fortunes of the MacJudds will perish!"

It appeared they *had* perished, as the line had died out and their house was falling down.

Muriel's mournful expression deepened. "The Laird were oot sairchin' fir't when he passed."

"Uncle Augustus was looking for this brooch when he died?"

"Aye, wi' that queer graith o' his—he said it wuid find metal in t'earth. But it kelled him, instayd."

It took a moment to sort out what she'd said. *Graith*

meant "equipment." "Uncle Augustus was killed by—some kind of—" And then it hit me, and I sucked in my breath. "A *metal detector*?" Was that possible?

"I cannae say. I onie ken he went oot wi' the whig-maleerie* an' ne'er came hame." This seemed Scientific Proof enough for the housemaid.

"What became of the device?"

Muriel looked horrified that I'd ask such a morbid question. "Mr. Balfour destrrroyed et. An' guid riddance, too!"

I tried not to betray my disappointment. Tapping my fingers against my elbow, I said, "Would this brooch be worth killing for?"

"Och, aye. Angus MacJudd was kelled by a rival becaws of it!" She added, with authority, "He hants the Auld Gallery, a-lookin' fir his sgian dubh."

The Gaelic words went right past me. "His what?"

She repeated it more slowly for the ignorant English girl. "His *skeen doo*." She led me to the portrait of the man in the kilt with the black-and-tan hound. ANGUS, XIVV MACJUDD, said the nameplate. Muriel pointed to where the dashing be-tartan'd fellow had the hilt of a knife neatly protruding from one argyle stocking. "And he can nivver find et, becaws et's a stickin' oot his ain back!"

Wonderful. Rockfforde Hall was haunted by spirits

---

* This eluded me, Dear Reader, but upon further clarification turns out to be roughly equivalent to *thingamajig*.

searching fruitlessly for murder weapons. I hope that luck didn't extend to the living—*we* couldn't take all eternity to crack the case. We only had until Father came.

I frowned at the nameplate, something nagging at me. Abruptly, Muriel gripped my shoulder with icy fingers, staring at something behind me. "That's her," she whispered, then dropped her duster and fled in the opposite direction.

Dear Reader, perhaps it was the fatigue of the journey, or the atmosphere conjured up by Muriel's far-fetched tales, but for a ridiculous, heart-pounding moment, I could not bring myself to turn around. But it was (more or less) broad daylight, I was English, and I certainly (sairtenly!) Did Not Believe in Ghosts. With some effort, I wheeled about to peer down the passage, and I'd have dropped my duster too.

A streak of greenish light fluttered in the shadows at the far end of the hall and vanished.

Heart banging, I crept forward to ascertain what, exactly, I'd seen. The instant I took a step, that eerie underfoot rattle began anew. I skittered over a crack in the floorboards, the sound rising around me. I wouldn't have thought anything non-corporeal could possibly put up such a racket—it sounded more like Cook tinkering with the plumbing. Except there *wasn't* any plumbing, not at Rockfforde Hall.

I half wished Muriel was still here. Right now I'd accept any explanation she had, even the supernatural ones. Unfortunately, there was nothing for it but to give this a proper Investigation.

"It's not a ghost," I said aloud. Miss Judson wouldn't give in to superstition. We were made of sterner stuff than that! I plucked up all my English courage and marched straight to the end of the corridor.

It terminated abruptly in a short staircase that led nowhere, just stopped dead against a paneled wall hung with a tapestry depicting—what else?—a hunting scene. A shaft of sunlight poured from arched windows, pooling gold on the parquet floor. But there was no mirror, no vast silvery shield, no shining surface whatsoever that might have caught the reflection of the departing Muriel and made me imagine a specter. Of Angus MacJudd, with the knife in his back.

A distant clanging hammered up through the walls and floor. Warily, I nudged aside the corner of the tapestry. As I touched the fringe, another sound came, lifting the hair on my neck: a thin, reedy cry, rising to an eerie wail—definitely not a foxhound. At least not one of *this* world.

And that's when I decided that I'd had enough, thank you very much, and took myself off with some haste in the direction Muriel had gone.

I did not slow down until I found the kitchen.

ꙮ

Dear Reader, let me assure you that I was by no means *scared.* I was merely exercising due caution in the face of unknown phenomena. The fact that I had never before shown such sense should be taken merely as evidence of the continued refinement of my Investigative Skills. I certainly did not subscribe to Muriel's explanation of events.

I found my way readily enough, by following the very natural sounds of an argument. I hastened onward: an Investigator can learn a lot from quarrelsome suspects. Voices echoed in the dank and chilly corridor lit only by light from adjoining rooms' windows.

"She shouldnae be here," a woman was saying—Mrs. Craig, I deduced. "Nae now, nae wi' aw that's happening!"

"There's naethin for it," said a man's voice—perhaps the bekilted fellow we'd met earlier. "We'll mak the best of it."

"The *best* of it? I'm tae entertain her Highness, wi' the house fallin' doon aroond us an' Kirkpatrick breathin' doon our necks?" A clang sounded, like a pot slamming against a table. "I've nae enough food for the fower of us, let alone adding three more mouths tae feed! Thank goodness the lad's nae here, too."

There was a sympathetic pause. I crept as close as I dared and peered round the corner. Mrs. Craig and the big, bearded man stood just outside the kitchen threshold. "Ach, Gran, things are still gaun missin'? What noo?"

"Twa boxes of candles, an oil lamp, an' some herring frae the smokehoose." Her voice broke. "An' twa ells o' muslin I've been savin' for Jess's trousseau."

Missing property was something Miss Judson ought to know about, so I inserted myself into the conversation. "Someone is stealing from Rockfforde Hall?"

Mrs. Craig's head snapped round, eyes dangerously narrow. "That's nane o' yer conserrn."

"It's Miss Judson's concern," I pointed out. "And I'm her . . . agent."

"I dinnae ken why she even brought ye," Mrs. Craig said. "A grown lassie her age ought tae be tending her ain family, not totin' anither man's bairn aboot."

"Now, Gran," chided the man—but my mouth dropped open. I hardly knew what to be *more* offended by—the insult to me, to Miss Judson, or to Father! But the one that clanged most painfully was *tending her own family*. I stepped back, eyes stinging. I *was* Miss Judson's family.

Only I wasn't. Not really.

"Oh, dinnae fash us, lassie," the man said. He had a ruddy, bewhiskered face with a broad nose and blue eyes that crinkled at me. I had never before seen a man's bare knees, and I hastily looked away. "We've all took the Laird's death hard. But we're terrible glad tae have ye both. Terrrrible glad."

Though his voice was warm, his words gave me an ominous chill. I nodded warily.

"I'll be Mac. Yer Harriet's within," he said, nudging me toward the kitchen. "An' yer wee baudron too."

Now I was thoroughly confused. But I heard a comforting clatter from the kitchen, and I spotted a familiar figure sprawled lazily on the table, washing one white paw and Observing her surroundings. Beneath the table crouched a stout black-and-tan hound, looking rather cowed. A frilly, striped backside protruded from a giant fireplace, a ruffled parasol propped against the stone surround and a wooden tool caddy within reach.

I could see Cook and Peony had made themselves at home, inspecting the equipment. There was no hob, only a vast wood-burning fireplace with an oven compartment in the brickwork, and iron hooks and an old-fashioned spit in the firebox. One squatty window buried in several feet of rough-hewn wood let in a bit of the Argyll sun, but most of the illumination came from oil lamps hanging from the ceiling, their chimneys coated with generations of soot.

"Ach, woman, mind yersel'—ye'll be scutchin' the gangin graith." Mac had followed me in.

"Don't 'gangin graith' me," replied a muffled voice. "This chimney has a crack in it you could sail the Spanish Armada through." Cook emerged, sooty but victorious. "It's a wonder you've not burnt down the whole island. I'll start repairs straight away."

"It's always sairved us weel enew," said Mrs. Craig from the doorway.

"Gran, can ye nae see the bairn's fair tae blah awa' on a breeze?" said the giant man with the giant kilt and the giant knees I was definitely not looking at. "She needs a proper tea. An' ye cuid use a cup, too."

Surprisingly, this didn't seem to ruffle Mrs. Craig's stiff black feathers. Tea sounded unlikely, with a cold fireplace and no hob, but Mrs. Craig produced an oil burner—the clever domestic equivalent of laboratory equipment. Despite the lack of Modern Plumbing, the kitchen was equipped with a pump, which spewed brownish-red water into the kettle.

"No, thank you," I declined politely.

While she worked, I Observed my two suspects. Mac seemed friendly enough—even *too* friendly. Perhaps he meant to throw me off his scent. Mrs. Craig, on the other hand, was perhaps too hostile. Surely if she'd done something to Uncle Augustus, she'd try to hide her ill intent. I did not know enough about the residents of Dunfyne Island to speculate on potential motives, but everyone here had had the opportunity to kill Uncle Augustus.

I took out my notebook to question them properly. "Will you state your full name for the record?" I asked Mac.

"The record, is it?" He looked intrigued and leaned forward eagerly. "Dougal Alastair Manro."

Writing this down, I hesitated. "Why do they call you Mac, then?"

"An auld nickname." He laughed. "I was th' only lad at school *nae* named Mac-somethin'."

"Oh." At the rate I was going, I was never going to get the hang of Scottish names. "Did you know that Uncle Augustus planned to leave his estate to Miss Judson?"

The kettle banged—hard—onto the little burner. Another exchange of glances passed, and warning radiated from Mrs. Craig. I was growing impatient. I'd spent *days* getting here, only to be slobbered over, haunted, wailed at, stranded on a deserted island *with no plumbing,* and plopped amid hostile company. As enchanting as I found Rockfforde Hall, its inhabitants were another matter, particularly compared with the company back home. Where I was duty-bound to bring Miss Judson as soon as humanly possible. Which meant settling the estate—which meant getting to the bottom of our already bottomless stew of mysteries.

"Why would Mr. MacJudd make her his heir? He must have said something to someone."

Mrs. Craig fussed noisily with the teapot. "Nivver said word tae me."

Mac answered more gently. "Ye have tae understand, lass, the Laird were a private man. He didnae confide in many folk—sairtenly nae his staff. Whateverr his intentions might hae been, he kept them tae hissel'. Mair's the pity."

I kicked at the rungs of my chair, making the worried hound whimper (not *remotely* akin to the unearthly wail that had emerged from the tapestry in the upstairs gallery, I might add). "Mr. Macewan was surprised, too," I said. "He told us Mr. MacJudd meant to sell the island to Fyne Fisheries."

Mrs. Craig stiffened. "Tha' was *his* notion— Macewan," she said, practically spitting the words. "Breakin' up the Island, sellin' to ootlanders. That man has nae respect fir tradition."

Which seemed a strange comment, considering Mr. Macewan's office had been overflowing with tradition.

"What about Mr.—" I searched for the name. Something from Stevenson. "Balfour? Why did he leave?" The departed estate manager was the one person we knew had quarreled with Uncle Augustus.

Mac gave me a look that was entirely too familiar. "These'rrre strrrange questions frae a peerie lass."

Mrs. Craig and Mac exchanged that guarded look again, as Mrs. Craig laid out the tea things, sturdy earthenware cups and silverware that looked as old as the castle. "I'm sure *we* wouldnae ken aethin aboot it," she declared staunchly. "The Laird wouldnae share his private business wi' us."

Somehow, I didn't quite believe her.

Mac took pity on me. "Nearre as we can wat, he an' the Laird jist had a fallin' oot. Alan was heerre one day, gaun the next, and naebody ivver said word aboot it. I'll tell ye this, though, lass—he's sorely messed. Sorrrely messed, aye."

"Dougal Manro!" Mrs. Craig snapped. "Ye watch yer tongue, earin' oor private effairs tae a flook o' strengerrs."

"We're not strangers," I protested. (And I was one relatively smallish girl, which hardly constituted a flock.) But what *were* we, exactly?

Instead of pondering that mystery, I wondered if there was more to Mr. Balfour's departure than anyone was saying. I recalled the tales Lt. Smoot had spun about bad blood on the islands as I regarded my teacup.

Cook finished her diagnosis of the fireplace, emerging sooty but triumphant. "No gas laid on, so they do all the cookin' from this 'ere." She tried to sound critical, but I could tell she was impressed.

"There's no plumbing, either," I volunteered—and her flushed face took on a disconcerting grin.

"Roughin' it, then, are we? I'll get things sorted, don't you worry, Young Miss." Her holiday frock was streaked with grey. She thunked the toolbox right onto the table like she was back in her own kitchen at Gravesend Close. It gave me a warm feeling, although Mrs. Craig looked none too pleased.

"These aren't half bad, for the wilderness." Cook

sorted the toolbox's contents onto the table, setting aside whatever looked promising—not only tools, but coils of wire and blocks of wood, a discarded pocket watch, and what looked like bits of a broken telephone. She seized upon one large spanner with particular relish, hefting it in her strong grip.

Mac watched with admiration. "Ye ivver dun the caber toss?"

"I'll caber toss you," she returned cheerfully.

Peony lent a paw to the efforts, tugging out a stained envelope. An envelope that looked oddly familiar.

Now Mac frowned. "Tha's Alan's kit. Cannae believe he'd leave this ahind." The toolbox was a fine piece of workmanship, sturdily built with a lovely finish, lots of compartments, and an engraved nameplate.

I rescued the envelope. "This is from Fyne Fisheries. What's it doing in there?"

Curious to see what the consortium wanted with the former manager of Rockfforde Hall, I unfolded the creased paper to read aloud.

Dear Mr. Balfour:
Enclosed find £100 for services rendered.
It's been a pleasure doing business with you, and we look forward to our continued profitable relationship.
   R. Duncan McNeill,
   Fyne Fisheries, Inc.

6

NEITHER FORTUNE
NOR FATE

An estate's lifeblood—literally—is found in its livestock, domestic animals, and game. Ensure that
they are properly cared for: quality feed, trained
handlers, and safe and healthy accommodations.

*-A Country Gentlewoman's Guide to Estate
Management*

The letter caused an immediate uproar in the
Rockfforde Hall kitchens.

"Alan Balfour! Takin' money from *them*!" Mrs.
Craig's outrage was unmistakable.

"He wouldnae," Mac insisted, but the doleful look
on his face said otherwise. "Can I see that, lass?"

It was probably evidence—although of what, exactly,
I still wasn't clear—but I surrendered it. "It says, 'services rendered.' What does that mean?"

There was no chance to speculate, for the sound

of toenails on the flagstones brought Cleveland trotting through the low doorway, accompanied by Miss Judson. She looked refreshed after her afternoon nap—refreshed and ready to get to work.

"Mrs. Craig," she said, "is that tea I see?"

Mrs. Craig knew her business, and bustled everyone out of the way to fix a fresh pot and a modest meal of oaty cakes and cold sausage. Miss Judson—practicing an interrogation technique I was miles away from mastering—said nary a word about the mysterious letter, instead complimenting Mrs. Craig on various aspects of the Hall and inquiring about her cookery.

"Now, then," she said, once everyone was settled. "What's all this fuss I heard?"

I let Mac fill her in while I nibbled experimentally at the not-quite-sconelike thing on my plate. It was hearty and none too sweet with a satisfying graininess.

"And we've no idea what these services referred to might be?"

"Ah shouldnae like tae guess, Miss," said Mac.

Miss Judson looked evenly at her assembled staff. "If there's one thing I cannot abide, it's disloyalty." Which was news to me, Dear Reader. "I certainly don't care for the notion of a member of this household consorting with that . . . consortium. Mrs. Craig, I would appreciate it if henceforth you were to promptly turn over any correspondence that arrives from those Fyne Fisheries people." She imbued that with all the scorn and distaste of which only Miss Judson is capable. Mrs. Craig's hand dipped tentatively into her pocket and returned with a folded envelope.

"Mrs. Craig, this letter is addressed to me," Miss Judson said with mild reproach.

"We didnae ken ye were coming, did we?" came the frosty defense.

Miss Judson let that go, reading in silence. "This makes no mention of Mr. Balfour."

"What does it say?" I asked, but my question got lost in the adult conversation.

"Alan could nivver hae got involved wi' those folk," Mac insisted.

Miss Judson said sensibly, "We could simply ask the man, next time we see him."

"Nay, he's lang gaun. Muriel saw him off tae th' boat herself. We'll nae see hide nor hair o' him again."

⁊

As we unpacked that night, Miss Judson and I reviewed the Case. Outside, a wind had risen, howling against the castle walls and moaning through the sash. Inside, the wind had likewise risen, banging the loose window open. Miss Judson kept latching it shut, to no avail. Cleveland watched her from the bed, soulful brown eyes following her every move. She'd placed the cracked photograph of her father and Uncle Augustus close to the bed, and I fancied Uncle Augustus was watching us carefully, making sure we were protecting his legacy.

"A hundred pounds is a lot of money," Miss Judson reflected, carrying an armload of shirtwaists to a cupboard. "And yet it's *not*." The cupboard door opened upon a bricked-up wall. She shook her head and tried the wardrobe instead. I could not see past its door, but after a silent moment, she closed it soundly and returned the blouses to her portmanteau.

I knew what she meant. "It's certainly not enough to kill someone for. But Mr. Balfour might have already had a motive." I told her about the angry entries in her uncle's journal. "They quarreled about something before he died. But Uncle Augustus didn't say what."

"More's the pity. We'll add *Investigate Mr. Balfour* to the list." The List was her ever-growing catalogue of the dire issues facing Rockfforde Hall, from missing managers to missing property to missing money to replace the missing shingles (and the missing WC?). "As the staff here are unlikely to be forthcoming, we'll need to do some digging. Perhaps Mr. Macewan can offer some insight."

"We can probably rule out a mishap befalling Uncle Augustus as the 'services rendered,'" I said. According to Muriel, that Mishap had another possible cause. I explained about the Lost Treasure of the MacJudds.

She looked keen. "Is that the brooch Mr. Macewan mentioned?"

"It must be. *And* Muriel told me that Uncle Augustus

was out searching for it with a metal detector when he died."

Miss Judson and I had studied the technology, which worked on electricity and required batteries to make a portable unit, but she was unconvinced by Muriel's theory about Uncle Augustus's death. "I doubt there'd be enough charge in such a device to hurt someone, let alone kill him—and no, we shall *not* be conducting experiments to that end."

"Maybe it was an accident," I said, tucking my frozen toes beneath my knees. "Mr. Balfour tampered with the device, only intending to injure him, but fled when it killed him instead."

Miss Judson was still skeptical. "You wouldn't mistake electrocution for a peaceful death," she pointed out.

Not that we'd ever know, since there wasn't an inquest and Alan Balfour had destroyed the murder weapon. "Mr. Macewan didn't say anything about a metal detector," I conceded.

"He may not have known."

It seemed there'd been a number of things Uncle Augustus kept secret from his friendly solicitor, like his plans for the estate. My eyes lifted unconsciously to the photograph of Miss Judson's father here at Rockfforde Hall. Miss Judson's glance followed mine, but neither of us said anything.

Although I wanted to. I searched my governess's

face anxiously, looking for—what? Signs that she would leave me for Rockfforde Hall with its leaky ceilings and ghosts in the attic and surly staff? There were so many things I wanted to say, to ask, but I couldn't find the words. When Miss Judson had first come to us, she had encouraged me to ask her anything, and I had eagerly taken her up on that. Our whole relationship was founded on asking questions and getting answers.

But it turned out there were some questions I didn't want the answers to.

I changed the subject. "What was in your letter from Fyne Fisheries?"

"Oh, nothing of consequence. Just a vague threat of legal action if the sale papers handing Dunfyne Island over aren't signed."

I yelped at her. "Nothing of *consequence*? What are you going to do?"

She said the first hopeful thing I'd heard in days. "Well, it's a good thing we know a solicitor."

I was slow to catch on. "Mr. Macewan?"

"Hardly. I was thinking a little closer to home. Your father can look at them when he comes."

Home. My heart gave a happy sigh.

Miss Judson settled atop the bed beside Cleveland, who rolled over, inviting a scratch. "As you were saying, this clan brooch is supposed to restore the fortunes—"

She was rudely interrupted by a grating scrape resonating through the floor. "What on earth's that?"

"Muriel thinks it's a Jacobite ghost."

"Not a ghost Jacobite?" But instead of Investigating the source of the sounds, Miss Judson merely pulled up the covers and put out the lamp. "Old houses make noise. Get in bed."

As I climbed past the velvet hangings, I wondered: Which of us was she trying to convince?

～

Our slumber may have been troubled by disembodied specters, but it was shattered to pieces by the entirely corporeal Rockfforde hounds, who had even stronger opinions than Peony regarding the timing of breakfast. Stronger—and louder. Keening barks pierced walls, ceiling, and eardrums. I bundled myself deeper in my cocoon of bedding.

Miss Judson evidently found it bracing and inspirational. "Up," she sang, springing from bed. "We've a lot to do today."

"The operative word being *day*," I muttered. It was barely light out. But it was too late: Peony and Cleveland were awake and demanding to be let out. (Mrs. Craig hadn't forced *them* to use the primitive accommodations, I'll note.) I slid my feet out of bed just as Miss Judson was lighting a lamp. Or trying to.

"Hmm. There's no wick." In the dim half-light she demonstrated, turning the knob that raised and lowered the little cotton rope from the vessel of oil. Or would have, if the wick had been there. Undeterred, she tried a second lamp, but it had the same malfunction. Intrigued, I grabbed the candle from the bedside table—the one we'd blown out just hours before—but stopped, stumped. Someone had been overzealous in their trimming of the wick, snipping it right down to the wax.

Cold seeped through my nightdress, and I checked every other candle in the room—including a drawer full of spares in the chest with the chamber pot. When I held them up to show Miss Judson, she sighed and set her lamp down with a clink on the dresser.

"Very amusing, I'm sure."

Was that the right word?

"It's a prank," she said. "A mischievous inconvenience done in sport, a practical joke." In her own annoyance, she fell back on dictionary definitions.*

"Why?" I sputtered. "Not to mention, who? And *when*—we used those lamps right before bed. Somebody came in here while we were sleeping?" Now I really felt a chill.

"Just someone's idea of an entertaining Rockfforde Hall welcome, no doubt." She collected the wickless candles and dropped them in their drawer. "Amateurs."

"Miss?"

"I went to boarding school for nine years," she said darkly. "Trust me, they've seen nothing."

---

* While we're at it, Dear Reader, a *practical* joke—as opposed to any other sort of joke—involves props and physical action, and is altogether less amusing than those employing clever wordplay.

"What are you going to do?" I scurried into my clothes and followed her out of the room, into a hallway barely lit by dawn. "Apple-pie their beds?"

To my surprise, what Miss Judson did was nothing at all. She chose to let the matter rest, although she did have to beg replacement wicks and candles from Mrs. Craig. When pressed to explain how anyone could go through two lamp wicks and six candles in a single night, Miss Judson smiled placidly but offered no details. I wondered if she really meant to let it rest, or if she was merely biding her time.

The stately housekeeper presided over a room bustling with morning preparations. Muriel scrubbed veg at a dry sink, sleeves rolled up and pale hair tucked into a kerchief. Nelly, the black-and-tan hound, greeted Peony with a sloppy kiss. Peony hissed, but I could tell she secretly liked it.

Cook had installed herself within the fireplace, a white sheet spread across the uneven floor, her tools arrayed atop it, along with at least one bird's nest. Mac knelt beside her, handing her supplies like a surgeon's dresser.

"Ye maun be kin tae the MacIver clan," he marveled. "Aye tinkerin' wi' this an' that an' buildin' aw manner o' things frae matchsticks an' hairpins."

"Mrs. Craig." Miss Judson gave her adversary no time to prepare a defense. "I shall begin my survey of Rockfforde Hall this morning."

"Survey, Miss?" The housekeeper did not attempt to hide her skepticism.

"Of the property, the repairs needed, my uncle's records, and the estate office. And, of course, I'll need to arrange a tour of the land." I mentally added the rest of that sentence: *so we can get out of here as soon as possible.*

"Ah can handle that, Mistress," Mac said. "Be glad tae show ye roond."

"Excellent." Miss Judson's smile was radiant. Mrs. Craig slammed a drawer shut.

I was not wholly convinced by the soundness of my governess's plan, going off alone with one of our murder suspects, but Cook agreed to chaperone. By the time it was fully light out, we had divided and conquered: I would remain at Rockfforde Hall to Investigate, and Cook and Miss Judson would Survey the Property. Obviously, I had the winning side of that arrangement.

Mrs. Craig grudgingly gave me directions to the Estate Office adjacent to the stables, although she insisted that there was nothing useful or suspicious to be found within—which raised the question of how she knew that. Still, if Mr. Balfour had left as suddenly as everyone said, perhaps there was some clue to his involvement in the Fyne Fisheries scheme—or Uncle Augustus's murder.

Peony and I found the office small and cramped, but disappointingly tidy. Tidiness is much praised by parents and governesses, but it does put a crimp in an

Investigation. The missing manager had left nothing out of place. Above an organized desk hung a map of the island, Rockfforde Hall signified by a tower. To the north, a small region set off with a dashed line was marked KIRKPATRICK, trails linking the two properties.

Peony, inspecting the desk, gave a dissatisfied burble. Everything was neatly arranged, from the stately ledger to the empty letter trays, the pens lined up in a precise row behind the blotter, the tightly capped inkwell. Beside the door hung a deerstalker cap, and a bronze fox wearing hunting tweeds monitored the filing cabinets—containing, no doubt, centuries of Rockfforde Hall archives. Somewhere in all that, was there an incriminating document from Fyne Fisheries? And would I ever find it?

"*No,*" Peony said helpfully.

I opened the ledger, but the days before Mr. Balfour's departure seemed entirely mundane—unless that's what he *wanted* us to believe. The record covered everything from feed bills for the hounds to somebody's school fees, but nothing regarding Fyne Fisheries, or even the manager's disagreement with the Laird. Notably, however, the *Income* column was much emptier than *Expenses*, and I felt a stab of alarm on Miss Judson's behalf.

I made to close the ledger when Peony discovered a letter tucked inside, from a trade school in Glasgow.

It was a shame Miss Judson and Uncle Augustus had never met. It seemed he'd shared her humanitarian spirit and value of academics.

"Mrow." At Peony's suggestion, I opened the desk drawer, expecting pencils and pen nibs, but it held a collection of crystals on a bed of velveteen: prisms of purple and green and chalky rocks studded with glassy stones. I lifted one to the light, and sparks danced within its fragmented depths. A velvet bag with a jeweler's label was tucked neatly at the back. My heart skipped—it was so alarmingly reminiscent of The Item in Father's drawer back home. I glanced about furtively as I withdrew it and poured its contents into my hand.

It was a silver pendant on a delicate chain, two hearts intertwined beneath a crown. In the center of the hearts was one of the green stones, polished to emerald brilliance.

It seemed Alan Balfour had left more than his post and his tools behind. He'd also deserted a sweetheart.

I turned and gave the room another look. If Mr. Balfour had quarreled with his employer, and in the midst of that quarrel killed him—either accidentally or with malice aforethought—that would explain his abrupt departure without his most valuable possessions.

It didn't seem right to leave the necklace here, in an unlocked desk drawer in an office anyone could access, so I tucked it into my bag to deliver to Miss Judson's safekeeping.

Peony had moved on. Standing atop a battered leather armchair, she was rubbing her cheek against a tintype photograph pinned to the paneled wall. Fishermen lazed on the rocks at a tumbling waterfall, a blur of white in the background. Someone had scrawled *Alan & Donal, '87* in the margin. Here, then, was Mr. Balfour, but I could not identify his younger friend. The handwriting was familiar, though. Uncle Augustus had written those names, perhaps even taken the photograph. More Happier Times at Rockfforde Hall?

I sat down in the leather chair with a sigh. Peony took it as an invitation and hopped onto my lap, knocking a picture frame askew. I stood to fix it, and a slip of paper fell to the floor.

I straightened the picture first. It was a skillful pen-and-ink sketch of a pair of wide-winged birds wheeling above a lake. Buzzards circling Dunfyne Island? Peony, affronted at her ungraceful exit from my lap, retrieved the scrap of paper. After a brief tug-of-war, I held it to the light. It bore a hastily jotted address: *#14 Gravesend Close, Swinburne, England.*

My address.

Obviously it wasn't just *my* address, it was Miss Judson's, and that's why it had been tacked to the wall of Rockfforde Hall's estate office. So that someone could mail her something, pop down for an afternoon call, send her a telegram, let her know she had an uncle. I flipped it over and felt that sensible theory evaporate.

It was a business card for Fyne Fisheries.

ভর

Our Investigations that afternoon revealed nothing else—unless you count the six new ways I found to snag my stockings on antiques, or that Scotland has a surprising variety of insect fauna, and that apparently all of them are edible. Peony and I circled the perimeter of the castle, noting the drooping roof of the derelict wing, its boarded-up windows and ivy-clad walls, and agreed it would make an ideal home for ghosts. If there was such a thing as ghosts. Which there wasn't.

Had we discovered the Services Rendered by Mr.

Balfour for Fyne Fisheries? Giving them the contact information for Uncle Augustus's heir didn't seem worth £100 (however priceless *I* considered her). Perhaps they'd wanted to approach her with the offer to sell, intimidate her into turning over the island, sight unseen? But why not contact her immediately upon his death? And if they had her address, then they hardly needed to send her letters *here*, at Rockfforde Hall.

Where evidently she meant to make herself at home. I had readied my report, cataloguing the lack of funds and the neglected maintenance Observable everywhere throughout the castle. Perhaps it would be easiest to sell, after all. But when Miss Judson finally returned from her Expedition with Mac and Cook, she was beaming triumphantly and brandishing a string of fish they'd caught for supper.

This wasn't going to be so easy after all.

ᶜ⁓

Our second morning on Dunfyne Island began much the same way: with the world's rudest alarm clock barking up the castle. When I rose, I saw that Miss Judson had already left, taking Cleveland and her sketchbooks with her. This was hardly unusual, of course; she often sketched in the mornings before lessons, but knowing she was out there exploring the grounds on her own gave me a pang I couldn't quite understand.

With a sigh, I padded to close the window, which had swung open again. It looked out on the woods, and

I saw movement in the trees, a flash of tawny brown—another family of Carnivorous Deer, most likely. I strained to make them out, should they be planning an attack, but whatever I'd seen vanished into the thick greenery. In addition to lamp wicks, secure windows, and soundproof walls, the Thistle Room was sorely lacking in telescopes.

I found my own way to breakfast by following the lovely scent of fried fish. Did they have kedgeree in Scotland? In the kitchens, Cook and Mac tinkered away companionably with the fireplace while Miss Judson was negotiating with Mrs. Craig. I tiptoed in, wary of disturbing them.

"Mrs. Craig," Miss Judson was saying, "I am not accustomed to idleness. Why not suffer Myrtle and me to pitch in?" She might not be used to it, but there was no reason she couldn't *enjoy* it. "Understandably, some matters have not received timely attention. I wouldn't dream of adding additional tasks to your workload, but we could bring in outside help—"

Mrs. Craig snapped to like she'd been struck by lightning. Or a misbehaving metal detector—which I hoped to locate this morning, to confirm Muriel's account. "Ootlanders? Nay, indeed. Thare'll be nae more strangers on th' island, a-stoompin' and a-snoopin' aboot!"

Miss Judson bowed her head deferentially. "Please point the way to some supplies then, and we'll get started on . . ." Handling the prickly woman with an expert touch, she let this evolve in Mrs. Craig's imagination.

"Th' fountain." Mrs. Craig rummaged through the cupboards, shoving rags and brushes into a wooden caddy. "Th' pond's nae been cleaned yet this spring." To my eye, the pond hadn't been cleaned yet this decade, but I held my tongue. They were getting on, and I was not foolish enough to throw off this delicately achieved *détente*.

"But make sure ye scrrape yer boots efter."

Miss Judson solemnly accepted the supplies. "I'd have it no other way. Come along, Myrtle."

Thus I was unceremoniously cribbed into Maintenance & Repairs, without even a glimpse at breakfast.

"Scotland has child labor laws, you know."

"*Chut, ma râleuse.* It's a glorious morning. I already let you sleep in."

Out in the courtyard, Peony had made the acquaintance of another denizen of Rockfforde Hall. She was sharing-but-not-sharing a sunbeam with a plump tortoiseshell cat who barely flicked a whisker at our approach, and neither feline showed the slightest interest in whatever activities were planned—particularly if they involved The Dog. Cleveland trotted happily at Miss Judson's heels, having proclaimed his allegiance to the new regime.

Grudgingly, I confirmed Miss Judson's testimony: It *was* a lovely morning, the very picture of idyllic Caledonian springtime. The sun shone through a cloud-laced sky, birds chirped contentedly in the new growth of the trees, and a fragrant breeze carried the promise of summer. Cleveland sniffed lazily at the verge, tail swinging. And lying facedown in the dry pond was a man in a dark blue suit.

Dumbfounded, Miss Judson and I stood there staring. Then Miss Judson, with a long-suffering sigh, gazed skyward through the brim of her hat and said several very calm words in French.

"Miss! That's Mr. Macewan!" I recognized his tartan socks. I darted forward to see if we might render some sort of aid, but it was obvious that he was far beyond our help.

For all appearances, the solicitor appeared to have been visited by the unhappy specter of Angus MacJudd—or someone else had found the missing sgian dubh. Protruding from a tiny slit in the back of his jacket was a very small, very sharp, very deadly knife.

7

I MAKE SURE

Should disagreements arise, either among your
staff or with neighboring landowners, it is wise
to fall back first on tradition, and then on law.

*—A Country Gentlewoman's Guide to Estate
Management*

Prickles running across my skin, I turned an unnaturally slow circle to take in our surroundings. The killer
could be anywhere—hiding behind the stone wall,
lurking in the weeds, fled into the woods, or even back
inside the castle.

A clatter of footsteps sounded behind Miss Judson,
followed by a thin shriek.

Muriel stood at the foot of the pond, white hands
to her white cheeks. "Ye've kelled him!" she cried, and
sucked in a breath to scream again.

Miss Judson seized her firmly by the arm. "Of course

we haven't," she said severely. "Pull yourself together."
I'd rarely heard her speak so sharply to anyone—and for
a horrible, traitorous moment, I recalled the fact that
I hadn't seen Miss Judson for some time this morning.
She'd gone for a walk of the grounds. Could she have
encountered Mr. Macewan?

My irrational spell lasted only a moment. The
weapon was entirely out of character for Miss Judson:
a tiny Scottish knife? And stabbing a virtual stranger
in the back? If Miss Judson were going to kill someone,
she'd do it right to his face.

"Fetch Mrs. Craig," Miss Judson said. "I want every
member of the household in the kitchen courtyard in
two minutes."

Muriel, only too glad to be free of the grisly scene,
nodded and fled.

"We need the police," I said—but Miss Judson's face
was set and grim.

"How did Mr. Macewan get to the island?" Her
voice was low. "He wasn't on the boat from Otter Ferry
with us, and we've been repeatedly assured that there
is no other transportation available."

"Maybe he had his own boat. Like Lt. Smoot?"

"Then it will still be here," she said. "We need to
check the quay immediately."

It took me a moment to realize what she was saying.

"Unless the *killer* brought him here." My sluggish pulse leaped frantically to life. I grabbed her by the sleeves—then released her just as suddenly.

"Why are you looking at me like that?" Miss Judson asked.

"You didn't—did you notice anything on your walk?" I tried to sound innocent.

"Like the corpse in my lily pond? I'm not *that* distracted, thank you." When I didn't respond immediately, she adjusted her hat and stared at me. "I beg your pardon! You can't think *I* did this!"

"Well, of course not. But—"

"I simply cannot wait to hear the rest of that sentence."

"You did quarrel with him at his office," I finished weakly. "And you weren't exactly happy with his plans to sell the island . . ."

Miss Judson closed her eyes and pinched the bridge of her nose. Then she gave me a little push toward the corpse of poor Mr. Macewan. "You're the detective," she said. "Detect something helpful."

Obediently—and because I didn't like the direction of my thoughts any more than she did—I carefully approached the body. Mr. Macewan lay in a shallow grave of debris, which would all need to be sorted through for evidence: dead leaf from twig from tangle of ivy. He wore old, muddy boots that didn't match his suit. One arm was beneath him, the other by his side, palm upward on the dirty stones. It was clean and unblemished—no injuries suggested he'd fought back against his attacker—so perhaps the killer had sneaked up on him unawares. I tried to recall how tall he'd been, to estimate the height of the assailant. The knife appeared to be at a fairly straight angle, but only precise measurements would tell for sure.

The next notable thing was that his pockets were turned out, as if the killer had gone through them. This was an unlikely place for a robbery; highwaymen would grow old and perish waiting for anyone to come by so remote a spot. So it must have been done to recover—or conceal—evidence. Not of Mr. Macewan's identity, clearly. Even two newcomers to Dunfyne recognized him, and the killer hadn't bothered removing readily identifiable items like his distinctive socks and waistcoat.

Had the killer got what he—or she—was after? Crouched on my heels, I visually combed the stones at the edge of the pond while Cleveland sniffed at Mr. Macewan. He gave a snuffly whine and nudged my hand.

"You probably knew him, didn't you? I'm sorry."

He prodded me again with his wet nose, then pawed at Mr. Macewan's body—at the arm tucked beneath him. I knew better than to disturb a crime scene by tampering with evidence, but Cleveland was insistent—and I could only imagine (thanks to Peony) what damage an anxious dog might do. Swallowing my distaste, I wriggled my hand underneath the body. It was still warm. I caught hold of what I hoped was a coat sleeve and tried to shift his arm.

"What are you doing?" Miss Judson's sharp voice broke my concentration.

"Cleveland thinks there's something here."

"Oh, then by all means continue with your disturbance of the corpse."

"A little help might not go amiss," I grunted. A full-grown Scotsman—even a smallish one—is heavier than you'd expect. Miss Judson crouched down to grasp Mr. Macewan's shoulder, turning him to the side just enough for me to coax his arm free.

His bluish fingers uncurled and something rolled out of his hand—something shiny and round: a silver emblem encircled by a strap. A clan badge.

"Not MacEwen, though," I said. "Look, the pin's bent. He must have pulled it from his attacker." I held it to the light, trying to make out the symbol on the badge. It looked like a hand holding a knife—a bloody knife. "What's this say?" I sounded out the unfamiliar words for Miss Judson. "*I mak sikkar* . . . ?"

An unexpected voice replied. "*I make sure.*" I glanced up to see Jessie Craig staring down at the body, a look of numb horror on her face. "It's the motto of Clan Kirkpatrick."

I jerked upright. "Your neighbor? The man who set the fox traps?"

She nodded slowly, a trembling hand to her lips.

"Does Mr. Kirkpatrick wear such a badge?" Miss Judson put in sensibly.

"I couldnae say." Her voice was a ghost of itself.

"Would he have a reason to kill Mr. Macewan?" I said.

"I couldnae say." She sounded helpless. "Why wuid someone do this?"

Miss Judson faced her. "The more critical question at the moment is *who* did it. And where that person is now."

Instantly Jessie took in Miss Judson's meaning. "I'll check the beach."

Miss Judson forestalled her. "I want to secure the household first. Myrtle, collect that brooch. Everyone: courtyard."

I hated to leave Mr. Macewan unattended, but as we slipped away, I Observed that someone had relieved Cleveland at his post looking over the body. The plump tortoiseshell cat perched atop the stone wall, gazing over the scene with inscrutable gold eyes, Peony right beside her like a sentinel.

The household assembled in the courtyard within five minutes, not two, but Miss Judson was disinclined to chide them. Everyone milled about in panicked confusion, speculations flying.

"Who could do this?"

"What was he doing here?"

"What do we *do*?"

Jessie paced like a restless lion in a zoo, and Mrs. Craig put a protective arm around Muriel, who sat, trembling, upon the low stone wall. The situation had been explained, and alibis ascertained, but even Miss Judson's superhuman calm did not soothe the frightened staff.

"Shouldn't we search the castle?" I proposed. "What if—" But I hardly needed to say *what if*. Everyone already knew.

"I'll check the stables." Jessie couldn't seem to stand still—and once again, Miss Judson stopped her.

"Nobody leaves this courtyard. We're safer out here." Part of that safety was being able to see all our suspects at the same time, but she left that out. "The first task is to summon the authorities." This suggestion met with blank stares.

Finally, Mac spoke up. "Aye, that'd be ye, Mistress."

"What?" Miss Judson's voice was sharp with tension.

"Yer Laird now. *Ye* be the local legal authority."

"That's absurd," she said. "This is 1894, not the Dark Ages. Argyll has a police force—quite a good one, from what I've heard."

"We'd nae ken aboot that herrre, lass." All the staff nodded in agreement.

Miss Judson closed her eyes and was quiet a long

moment. "Fine. Then my first official judgment is that we summon the police."

"Verrry well," Mrs. Craig said. "How?"

"Why, the—" Miss Judson faltered, belatedly realizing that the only way to fetch a constable was to sail back to the mainland and collect one in person. She changed tactics. "Someone must know what business brought Mr. Macewan to Dunfyne Island this morning."

Jessie paused in her pacing and wheeled on Miss Judson. "Aye," she said. "*Ye.*"

Muriel looked up. "Aye. He'd surely come to see ye. And ye kelled him!" She fell to sobbing once more.

Miss Judson was agog. "Why does everyone here think *I'm* a murderer?"

Cook raised her spanner. "Not me, Miss Ada."

"Miss Judson hasn't any motive to kill Mr. Macewan." I may have said that a little more forcefully than necessary.

"How's this for motive?" Jessie tossed back. "Rockfforde Hall. Ye've swanned in from who kens where, claimin' to be a MacJudd—but what proof do we have? Maybe Macewan was ontae ye, and he came oot tae prevent ye from stealin' the Hall from the rightful heirs."

I frowned. "The fish people?" Or the dogs?

"The *family!* Augustus MacJudd wuid nivver hae left his land tae—tae naebodies. Tae foreigners." She was face to face with Miss Judson now—dangerously so. "Tae *ye!*" And to my horror, Jessie Craig shoved my governess right in the chest. I leaped to my feet.

Miss Judson was surprised, too. She rocked on her heels and nearly fell—but Mac stepped in and caught her.

"Nay, lassies, easy noo. We dinnae ken whit brought Mr. Macewan tae Dunfyne this morn. He maun hae had some business here, aye?" Mac's voice was soft, but his imposing size made up for it. "Aebody? Noo's the time tae speak up."

I looked at the assembled suspects in turn, watching for signs of guilt. But if anyone made one—the furtive flick of Mrs. Craig's grey eyes, the nervous tilt of Muriel's head, the defiant stare of Jessie—it was impossible to tell for sure.

"Is there anyone else on this island he may have come to see?" Miss Judson proposed. "Lt. Smoot, perhaps, or Mr. Kirkpatrick?"

"He didn't just come to the island," I pointed out. "He came to Rockfforde Hall. His purpose for coming to Dunfyne Island was clearly something *here.*"

"I hardly think his morning's agenda included being stabbed in the back."

Someone let out a snicker—hastily stifled before Miss Judson could fix the perpetrator in her gaze, which was growing deadlier by the minute. She might not have killed anyone yet this morning, but I had a feeling she was getting closer.

"Of course not," I put in quickly. "But was he looking for something? Meeting with someone? Delivering something? Fetching something?" I produced the handkerchief-wrapped brooch. "What about the Kirkpatrick clan badge we found?"

"Kirkpatrick!" The word burst like a curse from Mrs. Craig. "I might've kent."

"Let me see that, lass." Mac strolled forth, and I unrolled the cloth but held it out of his reach.

"Do you recognize it?"

"The badge, aye, but nae the owner." Then he said something I was afraid of. "Aebody kin get those, though. Shops on th' mainland sell 'em. Anie clan ye cuid want."

"Who'd want tae claim *that* kinship?" spat Mrs. Craig. "Nay, that man's your killer. Mark my words."

Miss Judson turned to her. "Why would this Mr. Kirkpatrick want to kill Mr. Macewan?"

"Why does that man do aethin? Pure meanspiritedness, if you ask me."

"Mrs. Craig." Miss Judson spoke calmly. "There is a world of difference between mean-spiritedness and murder."

But as she said that, a shiver went through me. I'd seen the trap Jessie had pulled out of the woods. I wasn't sure I agreed.

"It cannae be Kirkpatrick." Muriel spoke up, face stained with tears. "He's gaun awa' off th' island."

"She's right," Jessie confirmed—and I recalled we'd seen him too. "He only comes fir the season, and tha's just ended. There'll be naebody at his lodge." The fox-hunting season, she meant. I had a vague recollection that that happened over the winter.

"Then it was one of ye." Muriel stared at everyone with her ghaist-stricken gaze. "It was one of *ye!*"

The murmur of confusion rose to a burble of voices erupting in an argument, until it became impossible to keep track of who was saying what.

"Enough!" Miss Judson's voice clapped over the courtyard, silencing everyone in an instant. She stepped forward, boots clicking. "This is unproductive. Someone on this island killed Mr. Macewan. It *might* have been one of us—"

"Ye cannae think that," said Mac.

"I said *might*. It might have been Mr. Kirkpatrick. Or it might well have been a party who is no longer on the island. That information is for the police to determine. The next order of business is to fetch them. Is the estate in possession of a suitable vessel?"

Jessie, hugging her arms to her chest, nodded miserably. "There's one in the boathouse."

"That boat's for *emergencies*," Mrs. Craig protested—whereupon Miss Judson merely *Looked* at her. She surrendered an inch or so.

"But who will go?" Jessie asked. "It willnae hold aw of us. We might be letting a killer sail free!"

I bit my lip. She was right. We couldn't trust anyone at Rockfforde Hall—and they didn't trust us. It was like the old riddle with the fox and the goose and the bag of grain: we couldn't all go together and we couldn't leave anyone behind. "Draw lots," I suggested, before I'd even realized I had the idea. "Someone from our party goes with someone from Dunfyne."

"Clever lass," said Mac.

Miss Judson gazed critically at the rest of us before nodding. "Mrs. Craig, matchsticks, if you please. Cook, look after everyone here. No one goes near the body, understand? Myrtle, Jessie, Mac—with me. We'll fetch that boat."

If the trip from the beach to Rockfforde Hall had felt ominous, it was nothing compared to retracing our steps in pursuit of a nameless killer. Not to mention alongside two potential suspects, one of whom was armed. Jessie carried her shotgun, slung over one shoulder by a strap. Every whisper of the breeze felt sinister, each snap of a twig made us jump and cling together. I pressed closer to Miss Judson, as if proximity might somehow protect me from the others. Were they really leading us to transportation—or a secluded hideout where no one would ever find our bodies?

I wished for the friendly presence of Cleveland, but Mrs. Craig had seized the hound by his blue collar, holding him back. He'd whined softly, but sat, dejected, by the housekeeper's feet, watching us vanish into the woods.

At long last, we spotted the sparkle of Loch Fyne through the trees, and Jessie broke into a run.

"Careful!" Miss Judson called, to no avail. She hit the beach and dashed for the old stone boathouse where we'd collected the wheelbarrow.

"Hoold on, lass," Mac called, as we hastened to catch up. "Ye dinnae ken what's in there."

Jessie, still far ahead, paused to cock her shotgun. "Aye now, ye happy?"

"Not especially," murmured Miss Judson. She held me back, and the rest of us cowards let Jessie Craig inspect the boathouse for murderers by herself.

The beach was eerily silent, only a faint rustle of unsettled trees and the soft lap of the water against the stone quay. Faraway boats dotted the loch, and I could almost make out the habitations on the hillsides across the water, but the signs of life, just out of reach, made Dunfyne feel all the more isolated and alone.

"It's nae locked," Jessie said, rattling the boathouse latch. "Someone's been here." Cautiously, one-handed, she eased it open, but no armed (or, more to the point, *disarmed*) murderers leaped from within. "There's nae-body," she called back, and stepped inside.

It was like she vanished through a portal to another world. There was utter silence, not the barest whisper from within the structure. Frowning, Mac joined her, with Miss Judson and me at his heels.

Jessie lingered near the doorway, staring blankly at the empty shed. Sails and spare oars were stacked neatly—if dustily—on racks upon the walls, but the center of the bare floor was a blank, boat-shaped hollow.

"The boat's nae here." Jessie's voice shook. "We're trapped."

8

BY SEA AND
BY LAND

Careful inventory and maintenance can help
guard against accidental loss or damage to estate
property, but vigilance is the only security
against theft.

–A Country Gentlewoman's Guide to Estate
Management

Jessie paced the shore, hand gripping her shotgun.
"What're we gaun tae dae? There's a murderer on
Dunfyne, and we've nae way off the island!"

"First, we're not going to panic." Miss Judson's calm
had no effect on the young woman. "In all likelihood,
the boat has been taken by the perpetrator."

Jessie was no fool. "You dinnae ken that! We've nae
idea what happened tae Macewan." She waved the gun
in a frantic gesture encompassing the island's small
population. "It cuid've been aebody."

Perhaps Jessie's fears weren't as nameless as they seemed. "Like who?" I put in.

She whirled on me, eyes wide. "How should I ken?"

"You know everyone on this island, and whether you admit it or not, you must have known Uncle Augustus's business. Who might have had a motive to kill Mr. Macewan? What about Mr. Kirkpatrick?"

Miss Judson put a hand on my arm. "One thing at a time," she said. "Our boat is missing, yes, but so is the vessel that brought Mr. Macewan here. For now, we're going to consider this a positive sign: it means the perpetrator has left Dunfyne Island."

Jessie looked doubtful, but she took a shaky breath and nodded. She broke open her shotgun to eject the shells, tucking them safely into a jacket pocket. "What now, though? We cannae fetch the police."

"Aren't there other boats on the island?" I said. "What about Lt. Smoot?" I had to add my next thought: "Although it's possible *he's* the killer."

"Fitz?" Mac was dumbfounded.

"Of course he's nae a murderer!" Jessie said. "I've kent him since we were five years old. He'd nae hurt a pup, let alone kill a man in cold bluid."

I wasn't wholly convinced—I wasn't wholly convinced *Jessie* wasn't a murderer—but Miss Judson said, "Good. We'll deputize him, then. If we can find him."

And thus, with a final despairing look at the empty

boathouse, our party made its way once more to Rockfforde Hall.

As Mac and Jessie surged ahead, I hung back to consult with Miss Judson. "I'm right, you know. It was probably Lt. Smoot."

She jerked to a halt like I'd physically restrained her. "And on *what*, exactly, do you base that outrageous accusation?"

"Evidence," I said. "Circumstantial evidence—but evidence all the same." As we resumed our walk up the deserted path, I enumerated the facts. "He's a trained soldier. He would know how to use a knife to kill someone. That gives him means."

I could practically hear Miss Judson's skeptical eyebrow quirk in the dreadful Dunfyne silence, but she said nothing.

"Second, he didn't like Mr. Macewan's plans for the island. That's motive. And motive for your uncle's death, too, if it's true that Uncle Augustus planned to sell."

"You're assuming Lt. Smoot knew Uncle Augustus had such a plan. Neither of which—knowledge *or* plan— has been established."

I forged right past her objections. "Third, opportunity: he had access to the victim and to the island—which, you have to admit, describes very few other people."

She wheeled back—but slowly. I could tell I'd got her thinking. "So you're suggesting, what? Lt. Smoot returned to the mainland to fetch Mr. Macewan for the express purpose of dispatching him in my lily pond?"

My lily pond. That was the second time she'd said that. I pushed it aside. "Of course not. He probably just happened along, the friendly neighbor, remember? And Mr. Macewan wanted to bring you the sale papers—he did say he would assist you in the inventory of the property." I didn't mention that Lt. Smoot had also been more than eager to see Miss Judson again, giving *him* reason to come out to Dunfyne, too. "But when Lt. Smoot realized what he was up to, he killed him."

"But why do it in our front yard? Isn't it more probable that they would quarrel aboard the boat, and Lt. Smoot toss him overboard?"

"But that didn't happen," I pointed out. "He was killed at the pond. My theory at least fits the facts of the crime." Something else hit me, something that had felt off about the boathouse. "Lt. Smoot got that wheelbarrow from the boathouse when we arrived. He already *knew* it would be unlocked."

"Or he merely found it so when he went to check." Miss Judson's tireless march up the rocky path continued. We could now see Rockfforde's turrets peeking out from among the shivering leaves, hear the cries of the hounds barking for their mistress. "And you're forgetting the Kirkpatrick clan badge," she said. "Why would Lt. Smoot have had such a thing?"

I hadn't forgotten it, actually. I just hadn't figured out how it fit into the theory that was taking shape. "Mac said you could buy them anywhere. Maybe it was a souvenir. Maybe—" I hit on a revelation. "Lt. Smoot knew how angry Jessie was at Mr. Kirkpatrick over the traps. He probably brought the badge and planted it on the body to frame Mr. Kirkpatrick."

Now she stopped, a hand to my shoulder. "Wait, wait. That's several steps of premeditation. Your suggestion was that the lieutenant and Mr. Macewan got into an argument on the journey over. Now you want me to believe that Lt. Smoot planned the whole thing, and deliberately brought the Kirkpatrick badge to the crime?"

I kicked at a leaf in my path. "All right, so maybe everything doesn't fit. Yet."

Miss Judson's face was grim, her voice grimmer. "No, it doesn't," she said, and I knew she didn't just mean my theory about Lt. Smoot.

❧

We returned to Rockfforde Hall to find Cook standing guard over the body with Cleveland, Peony, and the tortoiseshell cat. She had found some willow stakes and set them at a perimeter about the body and the pond, linking them together with twine. "Thought you'd want to search the area," she said, "before we moved anything."

For move "anything" we would indeed have to do.

Vital as it was to preserve the crime scene for the police, it was apparent that the police were not coming—at least not right away. And we could not simply leave Mr. Macewan where he was. Even I had to agree that was morbid. But the greater fact was that the longer the body stayed outside, the more evidence would be lost or damaged.

"What do we do with him, though?" I said. "He needs a mortuary. Maybe there's a family chapel . . . ?" I glanced about for stained-glass windows or a stone cross, realizing how much about Rockfforde Hall we still did not know, how much we still hadn't seen.

Mrs. Craig had a better suggestion. "There's an ice-hoose. He'll be safe enough there, I wat."

"Officer thinking, Mrs. Craig, thank you." Miss Judson brought out her largest sketchbook to take down an accurate depiction of the crime scene and the manner in which we'd found Mr. Macewan (or, rather, *left* him, after Cleveland's and my disturbance of the body). Someone, perhaps to spare the Delicate Sensibilities of the Rockfforde inhabitants, had covered Mr. Macewan with a cheerful tartan blanket, making the chilling scene all the more incongruous. Not to mention contaminating the potential fiber evidence.

As Miss Judson sketched and Cook supervised, and Mrs. Craig and Mac went to prepare the icehouse, I examined the area around the lily pond. Magnifier in hand, crouched nearly double, I paced from stake to stake, studying every blade of grass, broken twig, dog print and cat print and hoofprint in the soft earth. But I found nothing more to tell me what—or who— had brought Mr. Macewan to this spot this morning. Although I searched for the prints of sturdy-heeled army boots, they'd have been indistinguishable amid the mosaic of feet that had crisscrossed this area in the last twenty-four hours. And there was no way to tell if they'd been made this morning, yesterday afternoon, or last week.

Finally, stiff and headachy from stooping and squinting, I admitted defeat. I'd done no worse than the local constables would have, but I was left with no better suspect than Lt. Smoot. And, it must be admitted, no further evidence to confirm that suspicion, either.

Miss Judson supervised the transportation of the body. Mac and Jessie hoisted Mr. Macewan onto a dog-cart (despite the name, this was actually a horse-drawn conveyance, hitched to a shaggy, patient pony) and wheeled him to the icehouse.

At first glance, Rockfforde's icehouse looked primitive, like the home of a hermit, but was in fact quite sophisticated, incorporating complex insulation and drainage. The round stone building was half buried in the earth, covered in moss and turf, with a little stair-case down to its recessed entrance. It put me in mind, all too keenly, of an ancient tomb. A tumbling creek stormed past behind it, rushing frigid water to keep the building cool. The roar of water in the distance told me we must be close to Rockfforde Falls.

Miss Judson paused in the subterranean threshold, taking in the preparations that had been made. "A rocking chair, Mrs. Craig?"

"Aye," the older woman said solemnly. "So we can sit at vigil."

Miss Judson nodded with satisfaction. "Quite right."

Jessie watched this exchange—as did I—from the stairwell leading down to the icehouse. She gave a snort of derision that her grandmother wasn't quite quick enough to scold. "Ye kin sit a-weepin' ower the man if ye like, but I've work tae do."

"Jessie, lass—"

"I'll see to her, Mrs. Craig. You'll take the first watch?"

"Aye, Mistress," Mrs. Craig said. "It'll be an honor."

I was still puzzling over Mrs. Craig's odd change of heart when first Jessie, then Miss Judson passed me up the stairs. "Jessie, wait." Miss Judson hastened to catch the Mistress of the Hounds.

Jessie spun back. "Ye may not care, but I've work. Those horses dinnae exercise themselves, ye know."

"I do know," Miss Judson replied. "And I also know that my uncle cared very much for his animals—and if he put you in charge of them, he cared very much for you too."

Jessie closed her mouth on whatever she meant to say next. What came out instead was, "It's strenge to hearre ye call him uncle."

"For me too," Miss Judson said. "But 'Mr. MacJudd' doesn't seem right, either. I'm not sure what I should call him, frankly."

Jessie thought a moment. "The Laird?" she proposed, and her voice was full of something I didn't recognize at first. I think it was fondness, respect . . . perhaps even love.

"I like that," Miss Judson said. "The Laird it is. Thank you, Miss Craig."

But for some reason, that made Jessie pull back even further. With a frustrated sigh, she stomped away.

Miss Judson watched her depart in bewilderment. "What did I say?"

⁍

That night Rockffforde Hall settled into a tense and suspicious sleep. Although Miss Judson had assured the staff that the missing boat clearly indicated that the murderer was safely off Dunfyne Island, I'm not sure anyone entirely believed her. And even so, there was still a murder *victim* on the premises, which I've learned many people find unsettling.

Mac insisted on sitting guard in the kitchen all night, and Cook joined him, Nelly the hound at their feet. Muriel was nearly inconsolable with fright—but whether of Mr. Macewan's murderer stalking the grounds of Dunfyne Island or Mr. Macewan's ghost haunting Rockfforde Hall, it was impossible to say for sure. Jessie kept to herself, retreating to her rooms above the kennels, or, more likely, prowling the estate with her hounds and her shotgun.

For my part, the *tappity-tap-tap-tap*ping—not to mention the wheezy wailing—of Muriel's Grey Lady or Headless Laird kept me wide awake. Miss Judson slept soundly, but my sleep was hampered not only by the restless creaks, thumps, and scrapes of ghosts, but the restless creaks and thumps of my own haunting thoughts. Finally I gave up and tossed the tangled coverlet aside.

"*No*," grumped Peony. She was curled into the hollow of Miss Judson's knees, and stretched out one white-booted paw in sleepy protest—while her ears swiveled and one eye flicked open, betraying her curiosity. "Mrow?"

"No, it's not time for breakfast."

There was no convincing her. Once bestirred, she was certain that I had risen for the express purpose of producing for her enjoyment the famed Fyne fruits of Loch Fyne—the stinky, herringy variety.

"Wuff?" Cleveland lifted his head.

"*No*," returned Peony—the single utterance conveying, *This mission is for Hardcastles and Felines ONLY. No foxhounds need apply.*

Cleveland evidently couldn't understand her

English accent. He untwined his leggy form from Miss Judson without disturbing her, dropped to the floor with a refreshing shake, and clickety-tapped to the doorway, right past Peony, tail waving amiably.

"This is *not* a fishing expedition," I warned them. "We are hunting ghosts." So-called ghosts. They gave me innocent looks that I did not for a second believe. Sighing, I fetched a candle (with a functional wick) and swung open the door upon the grave-dark passageway.

Peony immediately vanished into the shadows, but Cleveland waited for directions. "*I* don't know," I said. "You live here. Where do the ghosts normally not sleep?"

Dear Reader: evidently Scottish foxhounds can shrug.

We had scarcely stepped out of the room when the taps and thumps resumed, accompanied this time by a squeal that went straight into my bones. Cleveland gave me a disconcerted look, sandy brow furrowed, and tried to back out of the mission.

"Oh, no you don't." I swung the door shut to the Thistle Room. We were in this together. And I certainly wasn't venturing down the gloomy passages of Rockfforde Hall on my own.

The creaks and squeals grew louder, creakier, and squealier as we made our way down the corridors. A flash of white moved for the staircase—not a ghost, but the white signal flare of Peony's tail. Cleveland, relinquishing command, trotted after.

Our route led us beyond the Great Hall and deeper into the castle's living quarters, parts of Rockfforde Hall yet unexplored, past more arms and armor bedecked in military gore. My feeble candle shivered across steel blades and shields and blood-caked tassels suspended from poleaxes, and Cleveland's tail narrowly missed knocking a row of swords from the wall. Weapons of every variety were all too readily at hand in Rockfforde Hall. Mr. Macewan's killer would have had his pick of them.

My Fearless Guides finally stopped before a pair of double doors set back into an alcove filled with an air of eerie, disused importance. "Mrow," Peony said, scraping at the door. From within came the desperate, thready wheezing of a ghost in distress. *Eeeeeeeewfffff*...

I hesitated. But Cleveland did a little dance of joy, certain that the master had returned. My heart broke a little. "I'm sorry," I said. "He's not back."

They were not to be put off. Cleveland's wuff became a whine that rose to a near howl, and before Peony could join in and wake all of Rockfforde Hall, I did the only sensible thing.

I put my hand on the doorknob. It popped open, and they rushed past me, Peony a streak of black and Cleveland a slobbery white-and-gold battering ram. "Wait—"

They didn't wait.

Inside, a lamp burned on a desk.

I backed up, sucking in my breath, brain spinning wildly.

Lulled into a false sense of security by the scientific improbability of ghosts lurking behind this door, I had forgotten all about the absolute certainty of a murderer.

9

ERRANTIA LUMINA FALLUNT

A professional estate manager is your ally in all
matters, but there is no substitute for a thorough
familiarity with your own property.

–A Country Gentlewoman's Guide to Estate
Management

I stared at that little glowing lamp, Miss Judson's words
echoing in my head. *The killer has left the island.* He—
she—whoever *must* have left the island. But my lungs
squeezed tight, telling me something very different.

All Investigative instincts urged me onward, to discover who was prowling about Rockfforde Hall in the
middle of the night, pretending to be a ghost.

All primal instincts insisted that I flee—before the
ghost impostors-stroke-murderers realized they'd been
discovered.

All logical impulses were therefore drowned out, and what actually happened is that I tripped over Peony.

"*Hhhhh!*" she hissed, loud enough to wake the dead.

My candle went flying, bouncing across the threadbare rug, flame winking out. I landed on something hard and sharp and recognizable—a stack of books. "Oooph," I muttered, tangled in Cleveland and my dressing gown. I managed to regain my footing, but one slipper was hopelessly lost, and I had a permanent imprint from the spine of some obscure leatherbound tome that had been lying in wait—a trap laid by poachers, no doubt, to catch unassuming Investigators unawares.

"Hello."

Heart jolting, I jerked upright to see who had spoken. I saw no one.

"Up here."

I jerked my gaze upward to discover a shadowy landing in the peaks of the ceiling. And peering down at me from the railing was a very small boy in flannel pyjamas, holding very large bagpipes. An oddly *familiar* small boy in flannel pyjamas, with fair hair and a pale, elfin face. And he was waving at me.

"Hello," I said slowly, with a vague sense that this was probably not Mr. Macewan's killer.

"How did you find me?"

I opened my mouth to reply, but closed it again. I managed, "You're making a dreadful racket."

"Oh." His arm shifted, and the bagpipes let out a sad moan. "Did you tell anyone?"

I shook my head. "Muriel thinks you're a ghost."

"Good. Come up. I want to show you something."

"Show—me? Who *are* you?"

"Edgar, but everyone calls me Gus. You're Myrtle Hardcastle, and you've come all the way from England with Miss Ada Judson to take over Rockfforde Hall."

Faced with such a thorough explanation of my presence from someone I'd never set eyes on, the only thing I could think of to say was, "Gus—short for Angus? Or Fergus? Or—Asparagus?" I ran out of -*gus* names.

He laughed. "Just Gus."

"Do you live here?" Which was self-explanatory: he'd hardly *swum* to Dunfyne Island in his pyjamas.

He nodded happily. "Sometimes. Come *up*," he urged again. "You'll want to see this."

Dear Reader, it went against most sensible instincts at my disposal to follow strange boys into dark corners, but the expedition had gone rather sideways, and it seemed easiest just to go along with him. Gus indicated a beautiful set of portable spiral stairs wheeled into position. Wheeled *squeakily*, I Observed, at my first step. Well, one mystery solved, at least. Muriel's ghosts were nothing more otherworldly than bagpipes and library stairs (each of which, to be fair, had its eerie aspects).

At the foot of the stairs, Cleveland's tail beat like a frantic metronome, ecstatic with recognition. Peony, thoroughly Uninterested in Boys, went to see if the herring was perhaps hidden underneath the desk or inside the fireplace.

"What are you doing up here?" I inquired.

"Hiding from my sister."

I glanced back. "There—there's a girl in here?"

"Nay, silly." A pause, and then, "You cannae tell her I'm here. *Promise.* Promise or I won't let you come up." He glared at me over the bagpipes with all the force of his slight frame. There really was something naggingly familiar about him. I realized now he was the person who'd been spying on the courtyard the afternoon of our arrival, but it was more than that.

"Who's your sister, Muriel?" I guessed. He had her paleness. And her lurkishness.

"Her?" His face twisted in distaste. "Nay, of course not."

"What are you really doing up there?"

"Looking for treasure. What about you?"

"Looking for ghosts. Wait—did you say treasure? You mean the brooch?" I'd made it to a sort of miniature gallery overlooking the space. Bookcases and cabinets covered the walls, like a library. Or a museum.

"Ghosts? Oh, sorry. Just me." He gave the bag another squeeze, and it emitted its unearthly sigh. Books and papers sprawled across the landing. A lantern stood nearby—a little *too* nearby for my comfort—and I Observed, even deeper in the shadows, a nest of blankets like Peony would make.

"Are you living up here? Don't you have a room?"

"Of course I have a room." He seemed affronted by the suggestion. "The Bog Myrtle room, upstairs from you."

"Bog *Myrtle.*"

"It grows all round here—it's the symbol of Clan MacJudd, you know. It repels midges.* Anyway, it has the best view of Castle Dunfyne. But I'm not using it right now, because—"

"You're hiding from everyone. To search for treasure. Because Uncle Augustus has died and the fortunes of Rockfforde Hall will perish if the Clan Brooch isn't returned to its rightful home." For an accomplished Investigator, I really was being awfully sluggish about things. (I blame the bagpipes. They'd momentarily thrown me off. Which, I understand, is a natural reaction.)

Gus took a deep breath and a story poured out. "I ran away from school. They think I'm sick—well, I am. Sort of. Rheumatic fever. I was supposed to wire home,

* It wasn't working, Dear Reader.

but I didn't want anyone to know I was coming. They'd just send me back. But I *had* to come!" he cried. "Mr. Augustus—the Laird—" He took a shaky breath. "He needs my help. Especially now."

I didn't understand everything Gus was saying—or, rather, not telling me—but I was piecing together a partial sense of things. And I'd solved another of Rockfforde Hall's mysteries. Gus's clandestine presence explained not just Muriel's ghost, but the missing food and candles too. I took in the heap of bedding, the papers, the lamp that looked perilously close to burning down the whole castle at one wrong wag of Cleveland's tail.

"Don't you know how dangerous this is? You can see everything outside, right?" I gestured toward a window. "Did you see what happened this morning? To Mr. Macewan?"

He looked away, then shook his head. Far below us, Cleveland whined. "I was reading," Gus mumbled. "When I finally looked out, it—it was too late. You'd found him already," he added, absolving himself.

"If you saw who did it," I said, "you have to tell me. I won't tell anyone you're here." Although how I would manage both reporting the suspect and keeping Gus's secret was beyond my powers of elucidation.

"I really didn't. I wish I did. Mr. Macewan was nice. He understood about things." Gus didn't say what things, and I didn't press him. He took another shaky breath, like he might cry, so I changed the subject.

"What do you know about the Lost Brooch, then?" He had everything up here—handwritten documents going back to the probable origins of Clan MacJudd itself, an Ordnance Survey map of the property like the one in Mr. Balfour's office, books of every age and description, and piles of notes in a messy schoolboy scrawl.

"Oh, everything. Except where it is, of course. But I'm going to find it. Do you want to help?"

Well, Dear Reader, I should think that was obvious, but in his defense, Gus had only just met me. Although he'd evidently been Observing me for some time.

"Muriel said it's been missing for a hundred and fifty years," I pointed out. "How are we going to find it?"

Gus grinned, showing a missing tooth (the first premolar). Although he was small, I guessed he was only a little younger than I was. (For the record, I was likewise small, which is why I do not recommend height as a guide for estimating age.)

"This." With triumph, he produced a handwritten page of what looked like poetry. "Angus MacJudd left a riddle explaining how to find the missing brooch."

"I thought he lost it in a battle."

"That's *one* theory. I think it's hidden here in the castle, to keep it from the English. Look." He thrust the poem beneath my nose. I had to bend close to the lamp to read it.

> Atwixt stump and stane: the Means
> Atween lock and key: the Might
> Aneath W but owre X: the Way
> Seek ye the hidden path
> To restore what was lost.

Excitement shivered through me. "Where did you get this?"

"The Laird. I was helping him search. And we were getting closer, before—" He stopped to gulp, composing himself. "Mr. Macewan was helping too."

I looked up from one riddle to another. "Mr. Macewan was trying to find the missing MacJudd treasure?"

"Oh, aye! It's the key to restoring the MacEwen clan chiefship, after all. He told the Laird that he'd found out about a map that showed where the brooch was hidden." He shuffled through the papers, not speaking for a moment, and it was all I could do not to prod him. "He wanted money, to buy it."

I sat up straighter, pulse flaring to life. "And did he get the map? Do you have it?"

Gus shook his head. In fact, his whole thin frame shook a little. "The Laird wouldn't pay for it. He called it a wild goose chase. He said—" Gus faltered, shoulders fidgeting.

"You can tell me. It could be important. It might have to do with what happened to Mr. Macewan." And to the Laird.

"I've been thinking about that," Gus said. "But I can't see how. I mean, he didn't have the map, so why would someone want to hurt him for something he didn't have?"

Recalling Mr. Macewan's turned-out pockets, I wasn't so sure. "Whoever killed him was searching for something," I said. "Maybe he got the money somewhere else."

"I just ken that the Laird said he wouldnae fund any more of Mr. Macewan's harebrained schemes, and the treasure of the MacJudds was much closer to home. That's why I'm sure it's here, in the castle."

"You witnessed this? Overheard them talking, I mean?" I clarified, at Gus's odd expression.

"I'm good at hiding," was all he said.

I bit my lip, pondering all this, and how it fit into the other mysteries of Rockfforde Hall. Muriel had told me the brooch was worth killing for—it had happened before, after all. Could Mr. Macewan have dispatched Uncle Augustus, hoping that his heiress would be more amenable to the Harebrained Schemes? Perhaps this sale of the island to Fyne Fisheries was only a cover, so Mr. Macewan could get his hands on the MacJudd treasure.

But before he could make good on his own search for the brooch, someone else had killed him for the mysterious map. The theories rolled out in all directions, like dropped balls of yarn, and I wasn't sure which one to follow.

One thing didn't fit, though. "Muriel told me that Uncle—that the Laird was out hunting for the brooch with his metal detector when he died."

This piqued Gus's interest. "A metal detector? That must have been something new. He liked to build things," he added with a touch of pride.

"But he wasn't searching at the castle. He was out . . . near the ruins." I slowed down as I realized that this testimony was now in doubt. "That's what Mr. Macewan told us, anyway."

Gus frowned, pondering along with me. "I never heard what happened. I just—Gran sent a telegram, saying I was to finish out the term. I didn't even come back for the funeral." He blinked rapidly, and I didn't say anything. *Gran* . . . I looked closer at him, studying his grey eyes with their long black lashes, the determined set of his narrow jaw, with a gradual swell of recognition.

"Gus . . . Craig?" I guessed. "Jessie's your sister." No wonder he was hiding.

He glanced up anxiously, nodding. His shoulder twitched again, a sort of half shrug.

"I won't tell her," I promised. As we sat in the snug landing in our pyjamas, Gus's little nook felt covert and cozy, perfect for plotting midnight adventures. But across the estate, in the chill lonely icehouse, Mr. Macewan's body put to rest the notion of a thrilling game. This matter of the Lost Brooch had become deadly serious. As much as I wanted to focus on solving Mr. Macewan's murder—not to mention settling the estate so I could get my governess and my cook and my cat home with all due haste—I could hardly let Gus tackle something so dangerous on his own.

"Where do we start?"

10

Hoc Majorum Virtus

A family estate is not just land and buildings. It
also encompasses the history, traditions, and lore
of the people who call it home.

-A Country Gentlewoman's Guide to Estate
Management

Gus and I stayed up most of the night studying the
riddle. Gus gave me the abridged course on Clan
MacJudd, filling in the Scottish history my education
had omitted, and he found my English ignorance both
scornful and unsurprising.

"But what does the brooch have to do with Mr.
Macewan?" I asked. "Isn't it a MacJudd relic?"

"It goes back to the days when we were part of Clan
MacEwen. Dunfyne Island was originally part of the
Barony of Otir held by the MacEwens."

"Otter? Mr. Macewan mentioned that, and Lt.
Smoot brought us from Otter Ferry." I'd been rather

hoping to see an otter, but they'd evidently been scared off by all the traffic.

"*He* brought you?" Gus frowned. "It's really *Otir*. Gaelic for—um, like a sandbank.* Anyway, every generation the brooch passed from one clan chief to the other to seal the bond between families—MacEwen to MacJudd, then MacJudd back to MacEwen, and so on. When the last MacEwen chief died, his lands passed to the Campbells."

"In 1493," I put in, remembering what Mr. Macewan had said.

"Right. But Ross MacJudd had bad blood with the Campbells and refused to swear fealty to them. And with his dying breath he swore that Dunfyne Island would never return to Clan MacEwen as long as the brooch was on Dunfyne. *And we never have.*" Gus spoke with relish, but then he sobered. "There's still bad blood between the families, four hundred years later."

I shivered—bad blood. Would a MacJudd kill Mr. Macewan over the brooch, so many centuries on? But *Miss Judson* was the only MacJudd here.

"That's not Muriel's story." I explained about the brooch being lost during a battle in the Jacobite Rebellion.

* Disappointing. I'd seen plenty of those.

"Rising," he corrected me. "But you're English, so I guess it's a rebellion to you."

He grinned as he said this, but I couldn't tell if he was teasing me—and moreover, I wasn't sure exactly how I was supposed to feel about it all. Miss Judson hadn't covered that, either.

I reviewed the little verse. "*The means, the might, and the way.* What does that mean?"

Gus adjusted his feet. "The Laird thought there must be three parts to the puzzle, with one part to be found at the solution to each clue, and we'd understand once we found everything."

This was getting more thrilling by the minute. In all probability, if the brooch even existed, somebody would have found it ages ago. But Gus's eagerness was catching, and in the hazy, predawn light of Uncle Augustus's study, with all its artifacts from Clan MacJudd's long history, anything seemed possible.

Or at least it did until I took a closer look around. There were two full stories of shelves crammed with every manner of relic and oddment imaginable. It was still too dark to make most of it out, but I spotted more scientific specimens, rocks, statues, goblets, and the miniature of Mrs. Craig's Bird Stump, under an old teapot.

Sometime over the centuries, someone had hidden another tiny object somewhere in this castle or its lands. Taking it all in, I began to feel discouraged about our chances if we had to search this room *and* thirty-four others like it.

"Anything could be in here, from King John's jewels to the—" I ran out of analogies.

"The monster of Loch Ness?"* Gus proposed. "Well, the Laird *was* trying to catalogue it all. Something distracted him recently, though."

We descended to the main part of the room. Peony was skeptically examining a claymore mounted near the fireplace, and Cleveland had gone to sleep on my slipper. Neither assisted as we toured the library, examining the treasures of Rockfforde Hall that weren't lost.

There were weapons, of course, and plenty of them. A display case held an array of knives on a felt-lined bed—distinctive Scottish knives with short blades and ornate handles.

"Sgian dubhs." Gus was at my side, gazing through the wavy glass with me. A helmet mounted overhead stared down menacingly.

An ominous notion struck me. "Do you know how many were in here?"

Gus chewed on his little finger. "I never counted them. Why?"

I tugged on the lid to the case, but it was stuck fast.

---

* Improbable tales of an unclassified creature lurking in the depths of another loch have circulated for some time. See Billy Garrett No. 42: *The Highland Beastie.*

"If somebody took one out, then he had a key to this case. Or she."

"Is that how he was killed—Mr. Macewan?"

"Mmm. A sgian dubh. In the back."

"Well, it wasnae one of *us!*" Gus exclaimed. "Although . . . we all did have access to this case. And naebody much liked Mr. Macewan, except me." He sucked in his cheek, working something out. "A sgian dubh is part of full clan regalia—you know, when you wear a kilt. Everyone has one. *I* have one. Mine's just wood, though. You couldnae kill someone with it."

My next thought unspooled before I could stop it. "Mac wears a kilt." I could likewise not forget the clan badge clutched in Mr. Macewan's dead fingers. And who had told me you could buy them anywhere, *any clan ye like*?

"Mac didnae kill him! Ye take that back."

"You just told me the knife is worn with a kilt!"

"Oh! Ye dinnae ken aething!" He made a sound of frustration. "That's just a regular kilt. Lots of men wear those. I mean a *fancy* one, for formal occasions."

Something about the way he said that made it sound funny—yet I knew better than to laugh. But Gus didn't. He let out a little snicker, clapping his thin hands over his gap-toothed mouth. The laugh escaped anyway, and soon we were both hopelessly caught up in it.

When I finally caught my breath, I gasped out, "A *fancy* kilt!" And we fell to hysterics again.

It took a *wuff* from Cleveland and an expression of Utmost Scorn from Peony before we composed ourselves. "I'm sorry," I said. "I don't really think Mac did it."

Gus shifted his feet. "I know. But somebody did."

ॐ

The mood at Rockfforde Hall that day was darker and more unsettled than ever, and Dunfyne Island seemed to feel it too. A knot of low, gloomy clouds gathered over its frosty green hills, wisps of fog shrouding the castle towers. Miss Judson made a halfhearted effort to bolster morale, but even Cook was unnaturally grim, clanging disconsolately at the fireplace while Mac sat tensely by, stroking Nelly's ears. Mrs. Craig presided over her kitchen kingdom like a solemn judge, and Muriel attached herself to Miss Judson with an urgency that rivaled Cleveland's, as if proximity to the new Laird would afford some supernatural protection.

Until the police arrived from the mainland, Investigation into Mr. Macewan's death was stalled. We'd done all we could for now. That left me two other mysteries to address—assuming I could escape Miss Judson's oversight. Of course, she ought to be Investigating her uncle's death with me, and I was put out that she'd apparently set the matter aside to focus on mundane things like roof repairs. But it did mean her attention was less likely to fall on Gus, at least for a while, and I could help him solve the riddle. Today, however, my governess had abruptly decided that lessons should resume, beginning with a practicum on Medieval Architectural Maintenance. Which is to say, *chores.*

Before we could be press-ganged into that endeavor, Peony and I dodged Miss Judson and her gloomy shadow and their nefarious plans, and set off in search of lost treasure.

And almost instantly regretted it. The turrets and battlements and bloody history that had seemed so enthralling upon our arrival now harbored any number of unseen dangers. Each sharp bark from the kennels sounded like an alarm, every flash of movement just outside my vision made me whip my head round for lurking killers.

"Don't be ridiculous," I scolded myself. No sensible murderer would linger about a crime scene, waiting to be caught. Logic dictated that the culprit had fled, far away not only from Rockfforde Hall and Dunfyne Island, but surely well beyond the reach of the famous Argyll Constabulary.

"*No,*" Peony said unhelpfully.

Ignoring her, I concentrated on my search. Gus had made me memorize the riddle, and I let its beguiling rhythm soothe my nerves. *Betwixt stump and stone.*

Between lock and key. Beneath W but over X. On the surface, none of it made sense, but simply saying "I've stored the brooch in the second-story linen cupboard behind the dustpan"* would have been much less secure.

Gus remained steadfast in his belief that the brooch was concealed within the castle walls—which was just as well, since it was safer if he remained indoors. I therefore set off with an eye toward examining every stump, stone, lock, key, W, and X *outside* of Rockfforde Hall.

The felled tree stump in the courtyard was the obvious place to begin. I still didn't see how it could possibly be as old as the riddle, but perhaps generations of MacJudds had ensured that a tree always be grown on that very spot so it could be chopped down again. (Some as-yet-unrecognized scientific process that protected the wood from deterioration was probably more likely.)

Peony and I circled it slowly. I traced its gnarled bark, scraping lichen into dust (which Peony promptly ate), but it gave up no hints regarding the treasure. No one had carved a helpful arrow upon its aged surface, pointing the way to the *stane* in question. That could mean *Rock*fforde Hall, with its stony walls and stonier name. But that left rather a large expanse of courtyard

---

* It was not there. Gus had already checked.

between the stump and the stones of the castle to search—with any number of stones therein.

I scowled at the prospect from the stump to the castle archway. Before me lay one particularly notable stony landmark, where someone keen to find the brooch had stood, barely twenty-four hours earlier: the empty pond. I put myself in Mr. Macewan's place yesterday morning. What had he seen? I nudged the pond's cobbled bed with my toe. Though dirty and neglected, the stones fit together securely, undisturbed. If Mr. Macewan had come here to dig up the pond, he hadn't got very far.

I tapped thoughtful fingers against my elbow. *I* couldn't see it yet, but that didn't mean Mr. Macewan hadn't figured something out.

A thorough examination of Mr. Macewan's body had not been possible when he'd been facedown in the lily pond yesterday. But he was now in the best conditions Dunfyne Island could provide. A better opportunity was unlikely to arise. I set off for the ice-house, Peony leading the way.

It was not the ideal morning for a stroll in the woods. In the chilly mist, sinister murmurs rustled in the trees like an ominous Keep Out notice. I hunched into my coat, pulling it closer. Peony, playing Scottish Wildcat,* stalked me from the verge. The path disappeared in the

---

* *Felis silvestris silvestris*

underbrush, and I had to watch my feet to keep from tripping over hummocks, swiping branches away from my face—all the while on guard for Carnivorous Deer. Was that a flash of brown, *there*, in the trees? At last I heard the welcome burble of the stream, and found the tortoise-like icehouse crouching on the forest floor.

I hastened to the building and was just tiptoeing down the steps when a voice from nowhere said, "*Psst*, Myrtle."

I let out a strangled hiss and whirled round, heart hammering. "*Gus!* I thought you were the murderer!"

"Sorry I scared ye."

"You didn't," I said stoutly. (All evidence to the contrary, Dear Reader.) "You said you were good at hiding."

"Aye." He glanced about the clearing. "Donal taught me."

The young man from the photograph in Mr. Balfour's office? "Who's that?"

"Donal Airlie—he's the gillie at the Kirkpatrick lodge." Gus made a face. "And he and Muriel are courting."

"Gillie?" That sounded like a species of waterfowl.

"Like a hunting guide. Rich folk have them."

I filed this colloquialism away for future use. "You were supposed to stay inside," I reminded him.

"And *you* were supposed to search for the brooch." He nodded to the icehouse. "I came to, erm, pay my respects."

This left a gap to explain why *I* had come, but I demurred. Instead, we made our way inside, carefully wiping our feet ("Gran'll kill us if we dinnae"). A stone lintel bore Roman numerals, MDCCXL.

"1740," I translated aloud.

"One of the renovations," Gus said. "The Jacobite Wing's from then too."

"The part destroyed in the storm?"

"Just the roof," he said defensively. "An' the windows. An' maybe the stairs. We never use it."

The icehouse was like a tomb, silent and dark and cold, as the heat from any lighting—particularly the sun—would hasten the deterioration of its frozen contents. Not that there was any sunshine to speak of. But by propping the door open with one of Dunfyne Island's ubiquitous loose stones, we caught a serviceable amount of midmorning light filtering through the trees into the subterranean vault. A ghostly mist plumed from the ice, and our breath came in puffs.

Gus seemed shy in the presence of Mr. Macewan's body. The space wasn't exactly welcoming, freezing and foggy from the blocks of ice, colder still from the unintended contents. He pressed closer to me, shivering in his tweed jacket.

"Have you ever seen a dead person before?" he whispered. (Dear Reader, I managed not to laugh.)

"My mum." That was the closest example I had to what he was feeling.

"My parents died when I was a baby," he murmured. "I don't remember them."

I gave Gus a moment with the body. He'd missed Great-uncle Augustus's funeral, after all; it only seemed fair he get a chance to say goodbye to Mr. Macewan.

Mrs. Craig had done more than sit vigil with Mr. Macewan; she'd also prepared his body for burial, violating every principle of crime scene preservation. But adhering to the highest standards of Good Housekeeping, she'd also preserved every scrap of clothing the man had been wearing, and his belongings—including the murder weapon (which, alas, she'd wiped clean).

I didn't want to uncover the body with Gus here, so I examined Mr. Macewan's clothes first. The killer had already taken anything of value from his pockets, but I could study the garments themselves.

"What are you doing?" Gus's voice was a hoarse whisper.

"Looking for evidence. Something that might tell us what Mr. Macewan was doing on the island." I went through each neatly folded item, searching the plaid waistcoat for hidden pockets, concealed keys, or notes sewn into the lining; shaking out the tartan socks; even checking the cuffs of his trousers. The slit in the back of the jacket, and the waistcoat, and his shirt, and his underflannels gave me a dreadful chill, unrelated to the frigid building. Such small tears—but terribly efficient. There would be one final matching hole, a fatal one.

Gus crept close enough to finger one of the tears, eyes haunted. "Can ye tell aething?"

I didn't want to admit defeat, but the killer and Mrs. Craig had been too thorough.

"What was that?" Gus's head whipped round. "I heard something."

I glanced toward the icehouse door. "Probably just Peony." My feline sidekick had not accompanied us within, not being overly fond of cold.

Gus didn't seem convinced. "Is someone out there?" he called, venturing toward the doorway. "Jessie? Mac?"

"Do—do you see anyone?" My voice was not as steady as I'd have liked. "Is it the deer?"

"What?" He poked his head round the door. "I dinnae see anyone," he said doubtfully. "Peony?"

"*No*," replied my cat—from behind me. I gave a little hiss, and Gus scurried back to my side.

"We're probably imagining things."

He was imagining things; I hadn't heard a sound. "We should finish up." I took one final look at Mr. Macewan's still form beneath the blanket, but there was nothing there to identify the culprit or explain Mr. Macewan's visit to Dunfyne Island.

I paused, hugging my arms in the cold. Something *had* suggested the purpose of that visit. Something I'd already Observed. Mr. Macewan had been wearing sturdy, mud-caked workboots when we'd found him, at odds with the rest of his pin-neat solicitor's suit, as if he'd decided at the last minute to do some exploring. While Gus hovered near the doorway, I lifted up the pile of clothes, which I'd tried to refold neatly, but the boots were not there. Nor were they underneath the bench where Mr. Macewan lay. I looked all around, peering into the shadows behind the blocks of ice, but found nothing.

"Mr. Macewan's boots are gone."

Gus spun back. "What?"

"His boots. They're not here."

"Someone *took* them? Why?"

That was an excellent question.

We carefully shut the icehouse up when we left, but we didn't get far before Gus tugged me to a halt again. "Look." He pointed at the icehouse steps, where muddy footprints tracked down from the path.

Muddy footprints far too large to be our own.

11

Touch Not the Cat without a Glove

Discord among your staff is not to be tolerated.
Do your utmost to clear the ranks of malcontents
and troublemakers.

–A Country Gentlewoman's Guide to Estate
Management

We did not discuss the Footprints. Gus accompanied me back to the castle, hastening me onward through the menacing woods like it was his job to protect me. He assured me he'd make it back to hiding safely—and secretly—so I reluctantly parted ways with him at the old stump.

"*No*," Peony said mournfully, watching Gus slip back into the shadows, silent as a gillie.

I found Miss Judson in the Estate Office with Muriel, the office door standing open to the courtyard. Jessie worked nearby, as the hounds lounged or wandered about, noses pressed to interesting corners, tails waving.

Bent over paperwork on Mr. Balfour's desk, Miss Judson did not seem to notice my arrival.

"I dinnae ken, Mistress," Muriel was saying. "That were Mr. Balfour's job."

Miss Judson sighed. "And I suppose you can't tell me where Mr. Balfour might have disappeared to?"

"Nay, Mistrrress."

I burst upon them. "Mr. Macewan's boots are missing!" And someone was lurking about the icehouse—which I did *not* mention. No need to get myself confined to quarters.

Jessie, rinsing up at the pump, set her bucket down and halted the flow of bloodred water. "What's this? Somethin's missin'?"

"Mr. Macewan's shoes. I was just in the icehouse, examining the evidence, and they're gone. Someone's taken them."

"Who'd want a dead man's shoon?" said Jessie.

Miss Judson's expression suggested we'd interrupted her Vital Labors to tell her *my* shoes were missing. "I'm sure there's a reasonable explanation."

"Covering up evidence. Obviously. They were on the body when we transported him to the icehouse, and now they're *gone*. Mrs. Craig said they were there this morning."

She rubbed her temple. "Myrtle, I'm sorry. I don't

see what the shoes have to do with anything. Muriel, have you seen the schematic of the summerhouse?"

I whipped the schematic of the summerhouse from the desk. "Miss! Mr. Macewan? Murder? Remember?"

She gave the great suffering sigh she reserved for only the most tiresome of individuals—not me. *Never* me. "I'm hardly likely to have forgotten. There are other matters commanding my attention at the moment, however."

I stared at her. "What other matters?"

Before she could reply, Jessie barked out, "Muriel!" like she was summoning one of her hounds.

The maid blinked. "Aye, Miss?"

"Do ye know aething aboot these missing boots?"

"Aye, Miss."

"Aye, *and*?"

Muriel gave her a blank, wide-eyed look. "I burnt them, of courrrse."

I gave a wordless yelp.

"Ye maun burn them," she insisted, nodding her kerchiefed head. "So his soul can be rrreleased. Otherwise he'll hant the place."

"Ye silly lass," groaned Jessie.

Miss Judson said, "There you go. Everything's explained."

"They were *evidence*," I said weakly. I wanted to shake Muriel. Or Miss Judson. It was really hard to say at the moment.

"Nivver mind, Mur," Jessie said. "Gae along by and tell Gran so she disnae fret, aye? She wants tae see ye too," she added to Miss Judson. "Dinnae forget tae scrape yer boots."

Muriel bobbed to Jessie like *she* was the Mistress of Rockfforde Hall, and she and Miss Judson vanished through the heavy green door, Miss Judson looking like she was about to get her hand slapped by the headmistress.

As we watched them leave, Jessie shook her head. "Hard tae believe aebody so superstitious grew up in Glasgow, nae out in th' country. Muriel nivver used tae be sae flighty."

"How did she wind up here?" On an island in the middle of nowhere.

"Came tae us frae trade school when she was juist peerie. Gran's fair fond o' her, but she's that glaikit."

Dear Reader, I had no idea what that meant, but I agreed wholeheartedly.

I'd followed Jessie into the stables, which turned out to be the most hospitable part of Rockfforde Hall yet, warm and horsey and well lit with cozy oil lamps. The MacJudd horses enjoyed better accommodations than the humans. I might have accidentally said that aloud— but Jessie wasn't offended.

"That was the Laird's way," she said, hanging her coat on a peg. "See tae the animals first, then the tenants, and if there's aething left, then it can gae back

intae th' estate. Trouble is, there nivver *is* aething left."
She fingered a pendant at her neck, a green crystal
on a leather thong. She tucked it out of view when she
Observed my eyes upon it.

We were in a sort of tack room-stroke-office, with
a rolltop desk in a corner beneath bits of harness. A
padlocked gun cabinet stood beside shelves holding
bottles, packets, and neatly folded rags. Garnet, Jessie's
horse, snorted from her stall, and the pony stuck his
nose out, hoping we'd brought apples. The last stall
held a startlingly non-equine occupant, regarding me
with undisguised suspicion.

"Is that an eagle?" American illustrations flew to
mind. The huge, noble bird had beautiful tawny feathers, a soft white breast, and a stately black beak that
could take my whole arm off.

"Buzzard," Jessie said. "They nest here. This lassie
broke her wing somehow. The Laird an' I were nursin'
her back tae health." Jessie blinked furiously, and the
buzzard shifted uncomfortably on her perch, both
upset over the loss of their friend. "He used tae say he
cuid feel them circling roond Rockfforde, but I nivver
kent what he meant."

I looked into the buzzard's fathomless brown eye.
Uncle Augustus *had* probably seen her brethren soaring over the castle, but I couldn't help thinking there
was a different significance to that ominous comment.

All around the space, ribbons, trophies, and

photographs were on display. Handsome hounds posed with silver prize cups in most of them, but several showed Jessie with Uncle Augustus. My gaze fell on a tintype of a young boy and girl accompanying an older gentleman in hunting tweeds. Jessie cradled a rabbit in her arms, the boy brandished a slingshot. The man's attention was on Jessie, fond and proud.

I carried the picture back to Jessie. "You must have been very close."

She was silent a long moment, staring at the picture, before nodding.

"Who's the boy?" He had fair hair and light eyes, but the picture was too old for it to be Gus.

"Oh, tha's Donal—his mam worked up the Hall, and he was aye hangin' aboot when we were bairns."

"Mr. Kirkpatrick's gillie?"

"Aye." Jessie handed the photograph back. "It's aw ruined now."

"Because"—I hazarded a theory—"of Miss Judson?"

She waved a hand, encompassing Miss Judson, Rockfforde Hall, and life in general. "The Laird was the only one who kent what it takes tae keep a place like this running—that we have tae move forrit or everything will fall doon roond oor ears."

"But you understand," I posited.

"I tried," she said. "He used tae say I was the only one he trusted, the one who understood Rockfforde best. But when I tried tae show him what I cuid do, what Alan—Mr. Balfour an' I were planning—" She shook her head. "Ach, he cuid be stubborn, too."

"What really happened to Mr. Balfour?" The way people were dropping lately at Rockfforde Hall, anything might have become of him. I didn't say *that* aloud—but Jessie gave me a sharp, closed look and didn't answer.

"I know they quarreled," I pressed. "Do you know what it was about?"

For a moment Jessie looked like she could take my arm off in one bite, but she just sighed. "Everythin'. They'd got tae quarrelin' aboot *everythin'* those last weeks. Aboot the land, an' Kirkpatrick, the bills, the dogs, me—it didnae matter. Naethin' Alan cuid do was guid enew. That last morning was the worst yet. I saw them, right afore they stalked off in different directions—" She took a choking breath. "I didnae understand it—the Laird was talkin' like he might really sell tae those people, sayin' Rockfforde was doomed. It made nae sense."

I considered what she'd been telling me. "But you think Mr. Balfour had a plan to turn things around?"

Jessie sniffed. "Aye, we'd talked aboot it. Fir an estate tae thrive, it needs income. As ye can see, Rockfforde is far frae thrivin'. We've nae farming, and the pasturing is tapped oot. The timber's inaccessible. The Falls are all we have worth buyin'. MacJudds've kent as much for years, but they're all too thrawn tae let the place go. It'll be one big rrruin, but nay: we maun save the old pile of rubble until the brooch is foond. It's all blather." The more upset she got, the stronger her accent became.

"Don't you believe in the lost treasure?"

Jessie looked me square in the face before she rose and stalked off. "Rockfforde Hall *had* a treasure, and, aye, it's lossit noo. It was Augustus MacJudd."

⁊

I took that conversation back to Miss Judson. It was her uncle we were talking about, after all—and her solicitor. Jessie's obvious opposition to Miss Judson's inheritance was an excellent motive for dispatching the lawyer who'd planned to break up the estate—and maybe even Uncle Augustus. Could her desire to protect Rockfforde Hall have driven her to murder? *Twice?*

"Jessie and Mr. Balfour were the last people to see Uncle Augustus alive."

I dropped this news upon my governess as she worked amid a tangle of overgrown ivy choking the kitchen downspout. And a tangle of midges waiting to attack. She'd lost Muriel somewhere, but I still felt the maid's gloomy presence. Her talk of ghosts and specters hung over the castle, giving every creaky hinge and rattling shutter an ominous quality.

Miss Judson unearthed herself and flung aside a handful of foul black vines, swatting at a midge. "Say that again, now that I'm upright and attending to you."

I did, elaborating. "Jessie Craig had motive and opportunity."

"You're one third short of a case. We've no proof Uncle Augustus didn't die of natural causes."

"Exactly!" I was triumphant. "Who else would know how to make his death look accidental? She looks after the animals here and probably has access to all sorts of drugs, chemicals, and toxic plants. She could have used a horse sedative or something."

Miss Judson looked weary. "That's a lot of 'probablies' and 'could haves' for one theory. Have you any evidence to back this up?"

"She knew the Laird had talked about selling to Fyne Fisheries. She was awfully upset about it."

Miss Judson nodded. "From what I understand, she and Uncle Augustus were very close."

I recalled the photographs, showing their dogs and horses together. "He treated her less like a servant, and more like—" I stopped the next words with a hand over my mouth.

She waited, brows raised. "Yes?"

I fidgeted before answering, uncertain how Miss Judson might receive my next suggestion. "I was going to say, like family. Like . . . a daughter."

Miss Judson sat back, considering. "Well, now. Jessie's what, no more than twenty-five? That would have made Uncle Augustus only in his fifties when she was born."

Not an image I was particularly interested in contemplating. I moved on.

"But that leaves even *more* questions about why Uncle Augustus left the estate to you, and not to her. Jessie cares about Rockfforde more than anybody. None of it makes any sense."

"Maybe it does." Miss Judson was thoughtful. "Perhaps in some odd way he was trying to protect her from something. From debts or—" Now she stopped short, breath quickening.

"From danger?"

∽

I carried the notion of Jessie being Uncle Augustus's daughter—or something—with me the rest of that day, turning it over in my mind as I studied the pictures of MacJudds in the gallery. It would also answer another question for me. I now knew what *Gus* was short for, and it explained the interest the Laird had shown in the lad, paying his school fees, spending so much time with him.

Miss Judson hadn't said anything, but I knew she must have been thinking about this as well. Cousins! (Well, one cousin; she didn't know about Gus yet.) In Scotland! People here in Britain with whom she shared blood and heritage. *Family.*

Of course, Miss Judson had family already, but they were all far away overseas. Not practically in our very own backyard. Not people she could talk to.

Not people she might choose over me.

"No." Peony twined mournfully about my ankles. She brought up an excellent point, however. As the offspring of Augustus MacJudd, could Jessie dispute Miss Judson's inheritance? Did she *know* she might be related to the man who'd practically raised her? It cast her in a whole new light.

With a whole new motive.

12

CRAIG ELACHIE

An estate may possess sites of historical, cultural, or archæological significance. Protecting these is as important a duty as any other aspect of land management. Your ancestors—and your descendants—are relying on your care to preserve their legacy.

-A Country Gentlewoman's Guide to Estate Management

We did not have long to see Uncle Augustus's fears—whatever they might have been—pan out.*

That evening, a sweaty and riderless Garnet pounded into the courtyard. Her saddle hung skew-whiff on her back, her reins snapped. Mac caught her and tried to soothe her, but she tossed her pinkish head and pawed at the stones.

* An American expression I'd learned from Billy Garrett No. 19: *Gold Rush Glory*

"Where's Jessie?" I cried, every horrible scenario springing to mind—those where she was a victim, and those where she was a culprit.

"Wasn't anyone with her?" Miss Judson demanded.

Mac tried to soothe her, too. "It's her custom tae rride oot alane."

Miss Judson turned on him sharply. "Presumably it's *not* her custom to send her horse back without her. And where's—" She snapped her fingers, trying to recall the name of Jessie's favorite hound.

"Minna," I put in. "She'd never leave her. Something must have happened."

Mrs. Craig bustled belatedly into the yard, Muriel at her heels, tucking strands of hair into her kerchief, like she'd just come on duty. "What's all this fuss? Where's Jess?"

"Her horse has returned without her," came Miss Judson's brisk reply. "We can't rule out that she's been hurt. Where might she have gone?"

"Garnet knows," I said. Although Garnet was being less than forthcoming. "Follow her tracks."

"Guid thinkin', lass," said Mac. He huffed into the stable, taking Garnet with him, and returned with a shotgun.

"What's that fir?" Mrs. Craig cried, but Miss Judson was nodding.

"Good thinking," she echoed. "Mac and I will search for her. Everyone else, *stay here.*"

"Certainly not," came simultaneous replies from me and Mrs. Craig—who burst onto the path, heedless of danger, shouting, "Jessie! Jess!"

We all took up the anxious search, retracing Garnet's path and calling for Jessie and Minna. Mac led the charge, gun trained for unseen danger.

"Probably just took a tumble," he said gruffly, "an' she'll come walkin' back afoot aforre lang."

But she didn't. It was a long half hour of trailing down narrow deer tracks and prickly briar paths, shouting for Jessie and Minna, the woods growing thicker, too dim and dusky to make out Garnet's trail. I kept casting anxious glances to Miss Judson—could Mac be leading us astray?

"There's the rruins up aheid," Mac said.

"What wuid she be doing therrre?" Mrs. Craig's voice was sharp. No one had an answer.

Crags of grey rock loomed before us, stacks of ancient building stone, a skeletal tower, fragments of wall scattered across a clearing. In the fading light they looked like ghostly sentinels still waiting for battle.

"Stay back," advised Miss Judson, to utterly no avail. A muffled bark—a barklette—sounded from within the tumbled walls of ancient Castle Dunfyne. A moment later, we saw the white-and-black head of Minna poking nervously round a hollow doorway.

She let out a moan of pure relief and bounded for Miss Judson, then sprang away again with urgency.

"That's a lass," said Mac. "Show us where yer mistress be."

We found her, and readily enough, thanks to her bright red jacket spread on the mossy green earth.

And the bright red blood spreading beneath her head.

"Jessie!" Mrs. Craig leaped forward.

Heedless of the danger, she ran for Jessie's still form, Miss Judson quick behind her. I halted, thinking hard. Had Jessie simply fallen from her horse—or had something much more sinister occurred? What could the scene tell us about the incident?

But my pounding heart, the encroaching darkness, and the frantic onlookers made concentration all but impossible. Jessie had come into a blind spot among the ruins—an attacker might have hidden behind any number of chunks of stone or rough, broken walls. He could have struck from above, behind, or even round the next corner, and she'd have been none the wiser anyone was stalking her. I gave a shiver and hugged my arms.

A low grunt issued from the form on the ground, and Mac rocked back on his heels.

"She's awake," Miss Judson announced. "Miss Craig, can you hear me?"

"Coorse I kin hearr ye." Jessie's faint voice was welcome. Mrs. Craig let out a gasp of relief. "Oooph, me heid."

"You've had quite a fall," Miss Judson warned. "Try not to move."

"Nonsense. I'm perrfectly—*ach*." She winced. "What happened?"

"We were hoping you could tell us," Miss Judson replied. "But the first order of business is to get you back to Rockfforde—after we've made certain you've suffered no serious injuries." That was a bold statement, given the blood caked in Jessie's hair, but Miss Judson was calm in a crisis like no other soul, French, Scottish, or otherwise. "Where are you injured?"

"Foot," Jessie mumbled. "Head."

"Anywhere else?"

Jessie shook her head, wincing again.

"Please move your fingers for me."

She did more than that. She lifted a hand to her brow, which came away bloody, and blanched.

"Good," judged Miss Judson. "Mr. Manro, would you oblige?"

Before Mac could scoop Jessie from the damp and bloody earth, the thumping of footsteps made us all turn together, toward a hazy opening between craggy stones. Another flash of red emerged—followed by a pale face with a black moustache.

"Lt. Smoot!" I exclaimed.

The soldier stumbled into the clearing, sword drawn. "What's happened? I heard a scream."

We hadn't heard a scream. "Where did you come from?" I demanded. "Where have you *been*?"

He was panting. "I just put in, and—Jess!"

"Fitz," she mumbled, lifting a hand toward him. But was she greeting him? Or pointing out her assailant?

"Lieutenant, did you see anything?" Miss Judson asked. "Or anyone?"

He shook his head wildly. "Nay, the fog's come doon. It's thick as stew out therre. Had to pull in ashore—" He gestured randomly, toward a nearby beach, presumably. "And I heard—"

"What?" I said again. "What did you hear?"

He stared at me, like he couldn't fathom why he was being interrogated by a twelve-year-old (I get that a lot, Dear Reader). "I dinnae ken—a horse, maybe. Or . . ." He started to say something else, but trailed off.

Miss Judson forestalled me before I could press him on the details. Lt. Smoot fell to his knees beside Jessie, clasping her hand. "Oh, Jess."

"Gerroff me, ye great gowk," she muttered, trying to rise. At her first step, however, her injured leg buckled. Mac stepped in.

"I've got ye, lass." She made no objection when he lifted her up and carried her out of the ruins, Mrs. Craig, Cook, and Minna right on their heels.

Though dark was falling swiftly, Miss Judson and I lingered behind, taking in as much detail as we could. "What do you suppose happened?"

She looked pale and disquiet, eyes darting into the creeping shadows of the looming stanes. "Did she fall? Was she attacked?"

"And will she tell us?"

Miss Judson's grim gaze met mine.

Lt. Smoot had his weapon out again. "Jessie Craig's never fallen frae a horse in her life," he said roughly. His soldier's gaze swept the ruins for signs of The Enemy, while my Investigator's attention was focused on the ground where Jessie fell. We spotted the same suspicious stone a few feet from where we'd found her. "That looks like blood."

"Don't touch it!" I knelt to examine it. The rock was about the size of Peony, and appeared to have rolled from one of the crumbling walls.

Lt. Smoot watched grimly. "Did she *land* on that?"

"Or was she struck by it?" Miss Judson finished.

"We should take it back to Rockfforde," I proposed, but Miss Judson vetoed that.

"We haven't the equipment to analyze what occurred here. Perhaps Jessie will be able—and willing—to tell us, and perhaps not. That's the best we can do."

Lt. Smoot agreed. "Besides, it's fair dark. If there is an attacker out here, I'd rather you ladies were safely back at the castle."

And for once, Miss Judson and I did not protest.

I had questions, though. Where had Lt. Smoot been the past two days? How had he just *happened* to arrive at the moment of Jessie's accident? It was too suspicious for my liking—but I didn't voice my concerns to Miss Judson, doubting she'd be inclined to believe them. She seemed to consider the lieutenant's sudden return a miraculous stroke of good fortune.

Jessie was reasonably forthcoming, under the circumstances. When we arrived back at Rockfforde, chaos was settling into bustling order. Mrs. Craig had recovered her brusque efficiency. She moved about the kitchen, collecting first aid supplies, Muriel trailing dolefully behind. Cook joined in with boiling water and bandages, as practiced as if she'd spent some mysterious part of her past as a battlefield medic. Jessie lay atop the kitchen table, cushions heaped beneath her head and ankle. Ever close, Minna lay with her head across her mistress's belly.

Mac had taken control of the medical examination. "Look me in the eye, lass. D'ye ken the date?"

"Twenty-two April, 1894."

"An' what's my name?"

"Dougal Pain-in-the-Bahootie Manro, lang live Her Majesty Victoria Regina, an' stop *hovering*. I'm nae a hogget havin' her first lamb!"

"Yer *my* lamb, and we'll hover all we like." Carrying a basin of soapy water to Jessie's side, Mrs. Craig proceeded to clean her wounds.

Miss Judson studied the scene, arms folded. "We'll

want to speak to Jessie afterward. It's imperative we learn what happened."

"Naethin happened." Mrs. Craig held a wet towel gently against Jessie's scalp. She flinched and pushed her grandmother's hand away.

"Nay, I'll tell ye," Jessie said. "It was an ordinary ride—I was checkin' the dens tae make sure there weren't any kits missin'. They can get lossit in the fog," she explained.

"We didn't have fog," I said, surprised.

"It comes up quick on the loch." This from Lt. Smoot. Was he accepting Jessie's account because it was true, or because it corroborated his own? He didn't act like a person who'd just tried to club someone's head in with a chunk of granite castle. He looked half sick: pale and fearful, pacing the crowded kitchen. Which I suppose was possible—not all killers had to *like* what they were doing.

Especially if they'd failed.

Jessie resumed her report. "Minna heard something an' ran intae the ruins. But when we got there, the fog was sae thick I couldnae see." She winced, trying to piece the memories together. "Garnet was skittish. An'—" Her eyes lit up. "I heard a curlew."

Mac frowned. "On th' island? This time o' year? I dinnae think so, lass."

"It was fair strange. I thocht it might be hurt."

Faintly, gingerly, she shook her head. "Next thing I kent was ye lot fussin' ower me."

"Did something spook Garnet?" I asked. "Did you fall?" I registered Miss Judson's warning look but asked the next question anyway. "Were you hit?"

Jessie stared at me. "You cannae think—someone *did* this tae me? Nay, it couldnae be . . ." Her voice trailed off uncertainly, and the look Mrs. Craig gave my governess said she didn't believe her innocent account, either.

"Did you see Lt. Smoot?" There. I said it—and even Miss Judson didn't have the heart to scold me.

"Fitz? He came wi' ye." But a flicker of doubt crossed her ashen face. "Where've ye been, then, Fitz? We needed ye."

Now he looked round the kitchen—at the tense and troubled expressions. "What's happened?"

"Ach, lad." Mac put a hand on his shoulder. "There's been a murrderr."

Lt. Smoot let out a sound. "What, *really*? Who?"

"The Laird's nae-guid schemin' lawyer, that's wha'." Mrs. Craig emphasized this with a firm squeeze of her bloody rag.

Lt. Smoot put a hand to his head. "Wait—Macewan? He's been killed? Here, on Dunfyne? I'd ask if yer makin' a joke, but it's nae funny." He slid into a chair, unbuttoning his red tunic. "I *kent* I shouldnae left ye th' other day. I could tell things weren't right here." He addressed Miss Judson. "And I thought having your bag snatched was a bad start."

"What's this?" Mrs. Craig spoke up sharply. "Yer bag was stolen?"

Miss Judson smiled wanly. "An attempt only, Mrs. Craig. The lieutenant rode to my rescue. Nothing to fash yourself over." The Scots word* rolled awkwardly off her tongue, but Mrs. Craig seemed to appreciate the effort.

The next few moments settled into uneasy silence. Everyone at Rockfforde Hall had been closed and evasive since we got here, and I finally realized it was from fear. Of something—or someone? Mac looked as if he expected marauding enemies to emerge from the fireplace or behind the dry sink. Mrs. Craig was frostier than ever, and Muriel had crumbled entirely. It was impossible not to Observe that Jessie was the heart and soul of this little clan (clanlette), and her attack had made it—whatever *It* was—personal.

But who would want to hurt Jessie? And why? Did she know more than she'd admitted about the murders? I looked at the folk clustered round the table, at their grim and drawn faces, wondering yet again if one of them was a killer.

Mrs. Craig finished her bloody ministrations and headed for the kitchen door to rinse out her basin—but

* In fact, it ought to have rolled more smoothly, as its origins are French, from *fâcher* (to anger or vex).

Miss Judson forestalled her. "I'd like everyone to stay indoors tonight," she said. "Until we're sure it's safe."

"It's *nae* safe!" wailed Muriel. "There's murrderrerrs a-stalkin' the island. Wha' can ken wha's next?"

Mrs. Craig held tight to the basin. "*Nae one* will be next," she said, in a low firm voice that reverberated across the stone floor and up the ancient walls of Rockfforde Hall.

But nobody believed her.

13

GANG WARILY

Your staff must possess specialized skills. A
maid-of-all-work may be sufficient for a city
home, but a country estate requires experts in
gamekeeping, construction, real estate, farming,
accounting, tenancy laws, taxes and rates . . .

*–A Country Gentlewoman's Guide to Estate
Management*

Lt. Smoot commandeered Miss Judson for an Adults
Only discussion of the crime—crimes—never mind
that I was the one who had discovered all the evidence.
Not that I especially wanted to be stuck in that stuffy
kitchen while Lt. Smoot made eyes at my governess.
But it would have been nice if she'd preferred to go
over the case with me.

I took myself off to meet Gus instead, sneaking up
several bannocks—that was the proper name for Mrs.
Craig's oaty, sconelike cakes—which Peony naturally
decided were for her. Cleveland accompanied us, and

Gus formally introduced me to the tortoiseshell cat, who was sleeping on the portable library stairs.

"She's called Calpurrnia,* with two *r*s."

Now we sat—two small humans, two cats, and a gangly dog—in his little nook, gazing out the darkened windowpane overlooking the courtyard, where Gus had just watched us bring his injured sister home. The cozy space felt like a shrinking refuge of security in the desolate castle on its lonely island. Threats surrounded us as surely as Loch Fyne, lapping at our edges from every direction. What had really happened to Jessie? Who had struck the fatal blow against Mr. Macewan? And what about Uncle Augustus's death? Was one and the same culprit behind every incident? The long-lost Mr. Balfour? The too-convenient Lt. Smoot? Or was Muriel correct, and it was one of us?

"Do you think Jessie really fell off her horse?" I asked. When Gus still hadn't answered, I proposed my other theory. "Could Lt. Smoot have done this to her?"

Gus's whole thin body jerked with horror. "What? *Why?*"

"I don't know. But his movements are unaccounted for since he brought us here Thursday afternoon. What's he been doing all this time? He has a boat; he could have come back Saturday morning to kill Mr.

---

* Calpurnia was the wife of assassinated Roman emperor Julius Caesar, who dreamed a premonition of his death. *This* Calpurrnia's sleep seemed rather less productive, all things considered.

Macewan. And how did he just happen to show up right at the same time as Jessie's 'accident'?" My suspicions poured out, dark and thick as Mrs. Craig's honey, and I was relieved to finally have an appreciative confidant.

"Brrrb!" Affronted claws dug into my thigh.

Besides Peony, that is.

"What do you know about him?" I asked. Gus was the only person who seemed to share my skepticism of the valiant lieutenant.

He looked reluctant to answer, but I could tell he was thinking something. "Mac calls him *sleekit*—sneaky," he finally said. "He always needs money. I saw him, that day you arrived, asking Gran. The Laird helped him, sometimes—buying things from him."

"What kind of things?"

A shrug. "Old books. Liquor, sometimes. Just anything. We weren't supposed to ken."

I turned this over in my mind, unsure what to make of it. "That's not the only thing." I described the incident that had occurred in Tighnabruaich—when someone tried to steal Miss Judson's bag and Lt. Smoot came to her rescue. "And I found this on his boat." I fished in my satchel for the shabby tweed cap lost by the thief.

Gus snatched it from me. "That's Donal's hat!"

"Mr. Kirkpatrick's gillie?" My nose scrunched. "Why would he want to rob Miss Judson?" Although he had seemed awfully chummy in that photograph with

Mr. Balfour—*and* we knew that Balfour had a direct connection to Fyne Fisheries. "Lots of people have hats like this."

"I dinnae ken the first bit, but . . ." Gus turned the hat over so I could see a tear on the underside of the brim. "I did this." He looked sheepish. "Donal was teachin' me to shoot, an' he leant me his hat. I . . . might have singed it a wee bit. Now *you*. Where did you get it?"

"He dropped it at the robbery—right outside Mr. Macewan's office," I noted. "Lt. Smoot came along just in time."

Gus's expression was dark. "Aye, he does that, doesn't he?"

To keep our minds off the notion that my governess and his sister were currently in the company of a Highly Sleekit Figure who simply happened to turn up every time there was trouble—except for the one Notable Incident when a man with a boat would have been very useful to have around—Gus and I turned our attentions to the matter of the Lost Clan Brooch.

We agreed that *Atwixt stump and stane* most likely meant the span from the castle proper to the hewn stump in the yard. "But I cannae figure how aething could be between a lock and a key." Gus scratched his head. "Nae something as large as a brooch."

He wanted to show me the progress Uncle Augustus had made, so we descended the portable stairs, stepping carefully over Calpurrnia. Just as Gus set foot on solid ground, noise scraped through the ceiling—a ghastly, teeth-searing rasp. Gus jumped back onto the stairs, which skidded alarmingly. I couldn't help myself. I grabbed his shoulder, and he yelped.

"What was that?" My voice was hoarse.

"Old houses make noise?" He didn't sound convinced.

"*No*," said Peony, pressing close to my legs.

"That's the sound of Muriel's ghost," I said. "But . . . *you're* Muriel's ghost. *So what was that?*"

"Angus MacJudd, haunting the gallery?" His huge grey eyes flicked toward the shadows.

That wasn't funny—not with a real murderer lurking about. "What's above us?" I asked—but the scraping dissipated, floating into the ether. I turned to Gus with some firmness. "Ghost hunting is an activity best accomplished in daylight, with proper preparation and equipment."

He met my gaze. "I quite agree." And we shook on it.

While Gus sought a particular document that would interest me, and Peony nibbled at the claymore, I wandered through the great room, looking at Uncle Augustus's Artifacts. A rock studded with hazy green crystals caught my eye.

"Oh, that's fun!" Gus hastened to my side. "It's fluorspar. You can find them near the Falls. It glows if you rub it. Look." He took the crystal from me and gave it a swift polish with his bare hands, whereupon it let off a faint, ethereal light.

"Fluorite!" The mineral had lent its name to the word *fluorescent*. Warmth excited the molecules and made them luminesce. We spent a few minutes Amusing ourselves with the crystal. The glow was hardly visible in the lamplit room, but if we cupped our hands around the rock, we could see it.

"Jessie has one of these," I recalled.

"Mr. Balfour used to collect them from around the island. Would you like it? We have loads."

I could hardly admit that I'd already borrowed one from Mr. Balfour's own collection—as evidence—so I accepted it as a souvenir, slipping it into my satchel.

I moved to Uncle Augustus's desk, wondering how he'd got any work done at all, with his ghosts wailing all night and his dogs wailing all day. We ought to make a notation about the Disturbance we'd just witnessed, for the sake of scientific continuity. I checked the desk drawer for another diary, but it was jammed by a piece of paper. I tugged out the offending page, something torn from a technical journal, handwritten notes scrawled all over.

Hughes's Induction Balance, the caption read, a schematic for some kind of scientific novelty, like what Uncle Augustus had been tinkering with in the Trophy Room. Electrical wires coiled around tubes fastened to a wooden base. Attached at one end was—I let out a little gasp. Part of a telephone receiver. "Gus! What is this?"

He squinted, trying to make out the Old Laird's notes. "Dinnae ken. Never seen it afore."

"I have." My voice vibrated with excitement. "There were pieces of this device in Mr. Balfour's toolbox." This *whigmaleerie.* "It's Uncle Augustus's metal detector!"

∽

I could hardly contain my excitement—at last, a concrete link to Uncle Augustus's death and perhaps even a clue to his killer. But Gus remained skeptical that the schematic was significant at all. He insisted that the brooch was closer to home, within the very walls of Rockfforde.

When we parted ways that night, it was on a dark, faintly quarrelsome note. I hated to leave him in such a mood, especially when he was fraught with worry over Jessie, but it could not be helped. Someone would miss me. Eventually. I assumed.

But I wasn't quite convinced enough to put that to the test.

Back at our haunted bedchamber, I couldn't shake off my disquiet. When I pushed open the door, Cleveland let out a soft growl, and paced inside, head low. "Miss Judson?" I spoke into darkness. My candle hardly shifted the gloom, but I made myself follow. It felt like someone was inside, lurking in the shadows.

I lit a lamp while Cleveland sniffed round the perimeter, and Peony Investigated the high places, but nothing seemed amiss. Whistling, drafty window: *check*. Primitive Inconveniences: *check*. Message scrawled upon the dresser mirror—*check*.

The lamp hit the edge of the dresser with a crack, oil sloshing. I wasn't imagining things. Someone had taken one of Miss Judson's oil pastels and scrawled a rough picture and letters upon the glass.

A red sgian dubh, dripping blood, and the words

GAE HAME.

"*No!*" Peony exclaimed, bunting the mirror with her head. I fumbled in my bag for a handkerchief, dumping oddments on the dresser. I was starting to wipe away the graffiti when another light flickered behind me.

"What on earth's that?"

My hand froze, and I turned. Miss Judson strode my way, brown face illuminated by a trembling halo. I stepped aside, simmering with fear and fury.

"Another 'prank'?" I said.

Miss Judson contemplated the knife and the message for a long moment, then she tsked and collected the red pastel. "Not exactly subtle," she said—exactly as if she were marking up a disappointing essay. She held out a hand for my hankie. Somewhere I knew we ought to be preserving evidence—were there finger-marks on the pastel or the mirror? Could we match the ugly handwriting to a culprit?—but I just wanted it gone.

"What are you going to do?"

Her expression was unreadable. "Much as I'd love to *go home*, the killer has made sure we can't." She grimaced, realizing she'd inadvertently quoted the sinister Kirkpatrick clan motto. *I mak sikkar.*

"Then you admit the killer is still on Dunfyne? And is behind—this?" My voice came out sharper than I meant.

Arms folded, she frowned at the box of pastels, as if they were to blame for their misuse. Instead of answering me, she said, "Mrs. Craig was right. I'm sorry I ever brought you here."

I opened my mouth to protest—but no sound came out. What was she saying?

"This is a MacJudd problem. You shouldn't be involved."

"But—" Why couldn't I find a counterargument? Something about how her problems were *my* problems, how we were in this together. But were we? I couldn't be sure anymore.

She was muttering in French now, rubbing fiercely at the stained mirror, which was as clean as it would ever be.

She could say what she wanted, but it didn't make any difference. I squared my shoulders and took back my handkerchief. She had her duties—and I had mine.

This was my Investigation, and Miss Judson was my client, whether she wanted to be or not.

I had to solve this case.

⁓

"From now on, I don't want anyone going anywhere alone," Miss Judson announced the next morning at breakfast. We'd assembled in the kitchen round the big plank table. Jessie managed to hobble in, head bandaged, although she looked dreadful and didn't eat anything. Minna lay in a dejected, rejected heap beside the hearth, while Calpurrnia slept restlessly. I knew how they felt.

The Laird continued. "No one here is extraneous"—except, apparently, me—"and we cannot risk another . . . incident. Jessie, I would appreciate it if you'd stick to the immediate grounds of Rockfforde Hall."

Jessie struggled to her feet. "Behang this. I've work tae get back tae, an' last I heard, there wasnae any Deputy Maister of the Hunds juist loungin' aboot wi' time on his haunds."

"Jessie Craig, you sit yoursel' doon this instant. And listen to your betters for once!" (It took a moment to realize Mrs. Craig meant *elders*, although Miss Judson wasn't that much older than Jessie.) "Rockfforde Hall has lost too much already. It cannae stand tae lose ye, too."

Whether it was the anger—or the fear—in her grandmother's voice, or simply that she'd used up the last of her strength, the young woman sank into her seat. "Aye, Gran."

Miss Judson's gaze tracked round the table, taking in Mrs. Craig, Cook, Mac, Jessie, and me. "The supply boat won't be back through for several days, and Lt. Smoot has graciously volunteered to stay on, for our protection. Until we can contact the police, no one leaves Rockfforde Hall."

The news about Lt. Smoot wasn't exactly welcome—if you asked me, sailing back to Tighnabruaich to fetch the constables would do far more good. But I kept my mouth shut. No one was listening to me anyway.

When the others dissipated, leaving me alone with Cook and Nelly, I Inquired after Mr. Balfour's toolbox. "It had all those spare parts in it." I produced the schematic. "I think they make this."

Cook grunted at the drawing then huffed to the hallway to retrieve the wooden caddy, still stuffed with the batteries, wires, wooden blocks, and the pocket watch.

"What's all this for, then?" She settled beside me, and together we studied the diagram, experimentally fitting the pieces of Uncle Augustus's device together. It felt almost normal, working with Cook on something concrete and fixable, in a snug and comfortable kitchen—even one on an island miles and miles away from home.

"I think it's a metal detector."

If Cook was interested in why, exactly, we were reassembling a disassembled metal detector, she kept her questions to herself. All she said was, "You've shown this to Miss Ada, then?"

I kicked my heels against my chair rungs. "She's too busy being Mistress of Rockfforde Hall."

At first I thought Cook might scold me, but all she said was, "It's a big change, and no mistake. She'll come round in the end—you'll see."

I scowled intently at the device, crumpling the schematic in frustration.

"No, stop—Young Miss, you can't *think* it into submission. Sometimes you need a little force." Cook pulled the device closer and, leaning heavily into its fragile parts, snapped a piece into place with a satisfying click. All at once, I could see that what we had constructed very nearly matched the schematic. Nearly.

"It's missing something." I dug through the toolbox. "Where's that bit of broken telephone?"

"That earpiece thing? How could I know you'd be needing that? Hang on, then . . ." She bustled off to where she'd rigged some experimental Improvements to the oil lamps. I could not fathom what Cook had recruited the brass-and-celluloid speaker to do, but she soon had it disengaged, very little the worse for wear. I let her do the honors of hooking it up to the wires, per the diagram.

As we tinkered, I broached a second subject. Well,

a third, if you counted Miss Judson—which I didn't. "Have you ever heard Mac or Mrs. Craig mention someone called Donal Airlie? Gu—I think he might be the person who tried to rob Miss Judson."

She sat back a moment. "Not Donal, but *Airlie*—that I've seen. Hold this." She handed me the clamps, which I dutifully kept clamped in place, my fingers likewise clamping from the pressure, while Cook vanished for several minutes.

She returned with a book. "Mac thought I'd fancy this." She handed it to me, cover open to show an inscription. "Not a bad yarn, at that."

To Mrs. Bess Airlie,
for her many years of devoted
service and friendship.
With fondest memories,
~AHM

"Bess Airlie!" I nearly lost my grip on the clamps. Cook relieved me so I could use both hands for the Investigation. I flipped the book closed; it was a copy of *Guy Mannering* by Sir Walter Scott, bound in lovely green leather. "Who's she?"

"She was in service here. Died a few years back. Did a bit of everything—cook, laundress, even nanny of a sort, when Catriona's bairns were young."

I tried to piece this together. "Did she have a husband, then, or a son? This Donal?"

"That'd be a matter for Themselves," Cook said, meaning the Rockffordians. Who were about as forthcoming as Hughes's Induction Balance. I shoved the device aside with a sigh.

"This is never going to work."

"Just leave it here, and I'll see what I can do." She encircled it with her sturdy arms, giving me a stern look. "You'll get this back when you feel like explaining exactly what you want it for—and who you've been mucking about with after hours in the library."

I fidgeted in my chair, utterly failing to look innocent. "What—what do you mean?"

"Himself didn't just send me up here to fix up the kitchens, you know. I'm to look after you both."

"Father did that? It's a good thing he's not here right now."

At the possibility of all these dangers facing Father too, Cook's expression grew grim. "Well, he's safe at home, and a good thing too," she said. "You and Herself will have this sorted before he wraps up his case and joins us here."

I kicked my chair again. I wasn't sure there still *was* a "me and Herself." But another idea cheered me. "Maybe Father won't be able to get a boat."

With a sigh, I decided I needed to confide in somebody, even if it meant betraying Gus's secret. After all, there *was* a murderer on the loose—one who seemed intent on attacking the Craig family. Gus wasn't safe. Not that it eased the sting I felt at giving up Gus to an adult.

". . . And you can't tell anyone," I finished, giving Cook my sternest look.

"Now, Young Miss—"

"Please? Cook? He's really nice, and I promised I wouldn't tell on him."

"Keepin' Catriona Craig's own grandson from her don't sit right, but I suppose he's not doing any harm, a lad sleeping in his own house. But the instant things look even a mite bit dangerous . . ." She let her words trail off ominously. "And you'll tell him too. Master Craig."

I kicked the rungs of my chair, knowing she was right. "That you forced a confession out of me? All right." Absently, I fanned the pages of the book, the gilded edges spreading slightly. Something caught my eye amid the gold. "Look!"

"What's that, then?" Cook peered closer, and I set the book upon the table, carefully sliding the spine sideways, so the edges of the pages slanted, revealing a faint image imprinted there, otherwise invisible unless you held the book just so (*juist sae*). It was the MacJudd coat of arms, with the bog myrtle and the hound and the word *Audere*. Be Bold.

"Bet you that's on the whole set," Cook theorized.

"You should check Himself's library." She started to spread the pages in the other direction, in case the back side revealed another secret.

"What are ye doin' wi' tha'?"

Cook and I jerked our heads up to see Muriel lurking in the kitchen doorway.

I sprang to my feet. "Where's Miss Judson?"

But Muriel didn't answer. She marched straight up to us and seized the book. "This is Donal's mam's, God rrrest her soul!"

I wondered vaguely why she hadn't burnt it, then.

She hugged it to her chest. "It's almost the onie thing left of her, and yer rippin' it apairrt like a pack o' buzzards!"

I thought buzzards came in flocks,* not packs—but it didn't seem the moment to quibble. She was close to tears, clutching that old copy of *Guy Mannering*, and I knew what Miss Judson would do in this circumstance.

"Why—why don't you have it, then. As a memento." Muriel had seemed the most shaken by the recent events, and if this book could give her a little comfort, who was I to object?

* As it happens, they come not just in flocks, but *kettles* (while in flight) and *wakes* (while gathered to eat).

14

X Marks the Spot

Any venerable estate will possess items of great age and historical significance. A careful catalogue of these collections is essential.

–A Country Gentlewoman's Guide to Estate
Management

I was eager to share this latest discovery with Gus, even if it couldn't lead us to the treasure. I knew he'd find it as fascinating as I had. We shifted a sleepy Calpurrnia aside to reach the collected Waverley Novels by Sir Walter Scott, one of Scotland's most famous authors.

They were beautiful books, practically antiques themselves, re-bound in dark green leather with gold lettering. I pulled down *Ivanhoe*, while Gus selected *Redgauntlet*. "Mrs. Airlie must have been awfully special for him to give her one of these."

"I don't really remember her," Gus said. "The Laird was like that, though. He treated everyone at Rockfforde Hall like family. He'd think of *you* like family," he added hastily—which made my stomach give a curious twist.

I slid the gilded pages of *Ivanhoe* to the side, revealing the hidden MacJudd clan crest. Gus did the same, still chattering away. I traced my fingers along the almost invisible image, the sprig of bog myrtle, the Latin motto, the MDCXC . . . I slammed the book shut, heart thumping. "What did you just say?"

Gus was reproachful. "I was talking about *Aneath W and owre X*. I was thinking it could mean—"

"Roman numerals." The words popped out as I stared at the edge of the book.

"Well, aye," Gus said. "Except there's no Roman numeral W, so that cannae be right."

"There's no V, either."

His brow scrunched. "Aye, there is. It means five."

"I mean there's no such number as VV. Except there *is*. Come on!"

"Wait—where're we gaun?"

My heart was thumping so hard I could hardly speak. But I called out gleefully, "To look aneath W!"

I dashed out of the library and was immediately lost. "How do we get to the Gallery?" I headed for the nearest staircase, but Gus caught my arm.

"Ye cannae get there from here. The floors dinnae connect. We maun go doon to the main hall an' take the other stairs to get to that wing."

I felt like Peony. "That is not reasonable."

He grinned. "Forrget it, Myrtle, it's Rockfforde."

"But—" I peered up the narrow passage, which disappeared into darkness. "Where do *these* stairs go?"

Gus just shrugged. "Up."

Down along the twisty corridors we sped, taking care not to be spotted by the other Rockffordians: through the Great Hall past the Bird Stump and the closed-off wing, aneath all those hanging swords, trying not to give each other away by giggling. The day was overcast and drizzly—*dreich*, as Mac would say— with heavy clouds drooping the vast corridors in an eerie half-light, and I recognized the route Cleveland had taken to lead me to the library the other night. The irrational path finally brought us within reach of the proper staircase. "You ought to print maps—"

A flutter of misty green light hung in the shadows at the top of the stairs—then vanished.

Gus halted abruptly, and I nearly ran into him. "What are you doing? Go after it!" I gave him a nudge, but he didn't move.

ScrrreeeethhckTHUNK. Thunk, thunk, thunkthunk-thunk . . .

"What was that?" he whispered.

It sounded very much, Dear Reader, like someone dragging a coffin down a flight of stairs. "It's your house!"

"Well, it disnae normally do *that*."

"Maybe the ghosts don't want us to find the treasure."

"Angus MacJudd left us the riddle," Gus reminded me. "Maybe he's encouragin' us!"

"He can keep his cheers to himself," I muttered, and set off after the ghost.

But when I reached the Gallery landing, there was no sign of the specter. Again. I was starting to feel Uncle Augustus's frustration.

Gus paused midway up the steps, breath ragged.

"Hang . . . on," he panted. "I'm coming." He'd gone pink-faced from exertion.

As I waited, I examined the corridor for signs of my missing ghost—but wherever it had gone, it had done so silently and skillfully, leaving no trace.

"Aething?" Gus only joined me from the safety of the stairs when I promised the ghost was well and truly dematerialized. "Rockfforde Hall's aye been haunted." His voice was a wispy thread. "But I've nae seen the ghaists myself. I could've done athoot."

We reconvened at the portrait of Angus MacJudd, who'd been so careless with the family heirlooms and plunged his clan into a curse.

"I *knew* there was something odd, that first day. Look."

Gus stood on tiptoe for a closer look, steadying

himself against the portrait's heavy frame. It cracked loudly against the wall.

"Careful!" I said.

He was staring at the nameplate on the painting. *"Oh."*

"Exactly."

He touched the letters—numbers—that had tripped me up when I'd first seen them. *XIVV.* "That's nae how you—er, spell *nineteen.* It ought to be XIX. *W,*" he breathed, staring at the side-by-side Vs. "But what's 'neath it? Are we looking *below*—" He gestured to the paneling on the lower part of the wall. "Or *behind*?" He carefully inched the edge of the frame toward us, trying to peer behind it.

"It also says, 'over X.' Do you see any other *X*s?"

The trouble, Dear Reader, was too many *X*s—they were all over the place. Even if we confined our search to the vicinity of the Roman *W,* that left the *X*s in Angus MacJudd's nameplate, the *X*s in the portraits before his, and the *X* on the MacJudd crest that had led us here. Not to mention the diamond-shaped panes of glass in the windows or the crisscrossing parquet floorboards.

But Gus got into the spirit of the hunt. "Oh, the Laird wuid hae *loved* this!" He crouched to the floor, crawling in his short pants and long socks, cheek against the wall, trying to see the bottom of the picture frame.

I joined him, and I must say I was grateful that my skirts and petticoats offered several additional layers of protection. And people say boys' clothes are practical. I wasn't getting splinters in *my* knees, thank you very much.

Peony helpfully sought out *X*s we had missed. She hopped atop a medieval chair—the kind Miss Judson called a Savonarola chair, after the notorious Italian monk*—sharpening her claws on its venerable velvet cushion. "Mrrrrow."

"Stop that!" I pulled her down—but paused in mid-air, feline legs wheeling for purchase. A claw caught me in the cheek, but I scarcely noticed. "Gus, *look*." I dropped Peony, and she fled for safety.

"Gran willnae notice. It's aye been frayed . . . oh."

The two of us stared at the chair. Its other name rattled into my head, the one that evoked the curvy intersecting shape of its legs and arms.

An X-frame chair.

I sat back on my heels, bringing the chair with me. A segment of molding caught on the back of the chair and popped out too.

"Oh, well done!" Gus applauded my gracelessness as if it had been intentional.

Before we could Investigate our discovery, decisive

---

* Girolamo Savonarola (1452–1498), known for burning immoral books, paintings, and, evidently, chairs

footsteps echoed up the stairwell, followed by a voice. "Myrtle? Are you up there?"

Gus leaped to his feet like a hare pursued by Carnivorous Deer.

"Quick, hide!" I waved him to the recessed window, and he scrambled onto the padded seat, pulling the curtain closed just as Miss Judson tapped her way into the gallery.

She sighed when she saw me kneeling on the floor with broken pieces of Rockfforde Hall in my hands. "Didn't you hear me calling? What are you—" She abandoned that line of inquiry. "Who were you talking to?"

"Peony," I said, and the traitorous baudron looked straight at Miss Judson and impeached my testimony.

"No."

"How can you see anything up here in the dark?" She strode to the window. Her hand was upon the velvet, ready to pull it open and admit the scant daylight—and reveal her kinsman lurking within.

I blurted out the only thing I could think of to stop her. "I found *Aneath W but owre X!*"

The window emitted a muffled gasp, and Miss Judson's eyebrow twitched. A moment later and she'd find Gus for sure.

I poured out my—our—Deductions, from the faulty Roman numerals to the X-frame chair, minus Gus. I felt a twinge of guilt, but what could I do? It was either that or give *him* up. "There's a riddle," I added, rounding off my account.

"Oh, I know the riddle." At my look of surprise, she smiled faintly. "*Everyone* knows the riddle. Muriel can't stop regaling me with it. *Atwixt stump and stane? The means and the way?* I must admit I'd dismissed it. Until now." She peered at the hidden cavity. "Go ahead, see what's inside."

"Erm—it's your house." I squirmed aside.

"I'll let you have the honor of inserting an appendage into that dark hole."

I muttered my thanks and nudged Peony aside; she'd already stuck her head in, whiskers coming away festooned with cobwebs.

Trying to ignore that where there were cobwebs, there were likely cobweb *builders*, I made a fist and jammed my hand in, whereupon it struck something. "It's a . . . book?"

I pulled it out carefully—it had been in there for more than a century, after all—forgetting all about Gus. It was a sort of leather folio for storing papers in. My heart sank with disappointment. "You couldn't hide a brooch in here."

The window gave a discouraged moan.

Miss Judson was sympathetic. "Well, you could hardly expect it to be so easy."

Easy! I didn't see anybody *else* solving *Under W*, did you, Dear Reader? I teased apart the folio—the leather stuck to itself a bit—and it opened to reveal a sheet of thin, translucent paper with a scrawl of lines upon it, and a brown ring where someone had set a teacup on it. "What's this?" I turned it this way and that as if it might be more inclined to explain itself upside down. It looked like it had been torn from a larger document.

"Hmm." Miss Judson took it from me, held it to the candle like a magic-lantern slide, flipped it round to the back, and ultimately shrugged. "This clue was *the Way*, yes? Perhaps it must be pieced together with the other clues to make sense."

My triumph dissipated. I'd hoped to find the treasure itself, not *more* mysteries.

Now the window gave a clearly audible groan, and Miss Judson's eyes flicked over, narrowing. "I'll have to get a glazier out to fix that draft," she said, pulling out her list and adding it to the ever-growing tally.

༄

I managed to sneak away after dinner to leave the discovery—whatever it was—in Gus's care, but he was just as nonplussed as I was. And even more disappointed, considering how much longer he'd been on the case.

"Miss Judson thinks the other clues will turn up," I said, trying to project her confidence. "Maybe now that we've found . . . whatever that is, some of the other information you've uncovered will make more sense."

Gus just shrugged, rubbing glumly at the tea stain marring the inexplicable document.

I left him like that, studying the riddle in his dark cave of a chamber, accompanied only by Calpurrnia, and wove my way back toward the Thistle Room, mulling everything over. Miss Judson was right—we *had* managed what no one else had done in more than a century. Surely we could crack the other clues too.

Assuming Mr. Balfour didn't kill us all first.

I hoped to properly discuss the case, and all the new evidence, with Miss Judson that night—whether she wanted to or not—but I didn't get the chance. The Case rather intruded upon us instead.

When we arrived for bed, our door stood wide open. Miss Judson halted at the threshold, holding me back. A single lonely candle burned on the mantelpiece—and we definitely hadn't left it there. Its fitful flicker showed a space in disarray, all our belongings flung about, clothes and furniture and trunks scattered everywhere, as if the Wild Hunt had ridden through.

Someone had been searching our room.

Miss Judson put a finger to her lips, but Cleveland and Peony slipped inside, sniffing out the intruders. When they found no one, we humans ventured within. Every item we'd brought to Scotland was dumped onto the bed, suitcases cast aside, the chamber pot smashed (I can't say I thought that a great loss).

"They were looking for something," I said. "What could it be?"

"We don't *have* anything." She paused. "Except your new clue."

"How could they know about that, though?" And it was safe with Gus, thank goodness! But suspicions spooled out. "You didn't have anything when you were robbed in Tighnabruaich, either," I said slowly. "Or in Glasgow, when the railway lost your luggage." Could there be some connection?

Miss Judson was not in a mood to speculate. Even in the darkness, I could see color rising up her neck, and she grew far too calm. She strode about the room, gathering her belongings as if nothing worse had occurred than another practical joke. But I took in the shattered porcelain and scattered clothing, icy fingers creeping up my neck.

"Miss! This was a deliberate attack! Like what happened to Jessie. They're after *us* now, too! They've *been* after us, all along." And by *us*, I meant *her*. I took a deep breath and made my next terrible proposal. "We need Lt. Smoot to take us back to the mainland. Tonight."

She pulled me into her firmest embrace. "I am not leaving," she said into my hair, and I could not tell if she was simply being firm or trying to muffle her voice from eavesdroppers. "Is that clear? These people—"

She didn't finish. Outside, the dogs had begun to

bark—an eruption of frenzied terror. Cleveland stilled, lifted his head, and let out a high, thin howl in solidarity. The sound went straight into my bones. "Something's wrong."

Something was more than wrong.

Across the room, the door clicked shut, victim of another errant Rockfforde draft. And we caught a whiff of a faint, bitter scent.

"Did you light the fire?"

"Not me. I."

Miss Judson marched to the hearth. The grate was cold and empty, yet somewhere a thread of smoke was leaking into the room. More than a thread—a whole skein, rising like mist and circling through the chamber. Peony made a low, discontented growl deep in her throat, even eerier than Cleveland's unearthly howl or the baying dogs outside. I picked her up, and her claws dug through my bodice.

The smoke grew thicker, seeping through unseen gaps in the room's ancient construction.

I pressed the back of my hand to my nose, taking shallow breaths. "Where's it coming from?"

Miss Judson tried to keep a cool head, striding from corner to corner, searching for the source. Eyes stinging, I coughed—sucking in a huge, unfortunate breath. A moment later she reached the door and turned the knob.

It didn't open.

She jiggled it—then tugged, almost frantically. She turned back, and in a dark voice said, "This is no prank."

I hastened to the window and wrenched open the shutters. We couldn't escape that way, but the fresh air would save us.

The drafty casement, which opened of its own accord every morning, was stuck fast. I fumbled with the latch, unable to work out the problem. It was too dark, too smoky, too impossible to breathe or even think.

Miss Judson nudged me aside and gave the casement a solid strike with her elbow. The window finally obliged, cracking like a dropped egg, but somehow the wind was against us, and smoke filled the room even faster.

"Call for help," she commanded. "I'll try the door again."

But in the night below me, I saw something that took away the rest of my breath.

The castle courtyard was full of lanterns, writhing like glowworms around the kennels—and the billows of smoke pouring from the roof.

I turned to Miss Judson, voice creaking. "They're not coming."

15

Dulce Periculum

An estate must be made secure against threats
from without, but be ever watchful for betrayal
from within.

*–A Country Gentlewoman's Guide to Estate
Management*

For a terrible moment we stood at the window, watching the activity below: all the residents of Rockfforde
Hall battling a fire in the kennels. I wanted to cry, but
I couldn't find the air. My head swam.

A soft click broke the smoky silence.

"Myrtle?" An impossible voice lifted from the direction of the hearth, and through the stinging darkness
I imagined a faint wink of candlelight, a pale face. The
narrow cabinet beside the fireplace had swung inward,
revealing a concealed door.

"Gus!" I gasped—then coughed, chest splitting.

"Quick!" He beckoned. "Down here. Crawl."

We crawled—quick as any rats ever fled a burning

ship, we scrabbled on our hands and knees until Gus shuffled us, one after the other, into a tight corridor. I thunked into something soft, which scolded me.

"No!"

I nearly melted with relief, and Peony bunted me—hard—in the chin, following it up with a desperate bite.

Miss Judson squeezed in after Cleveland, Gus shifted deeper into the passageway, and the cabinet swung on its pivot behind us. Miss Judson slumped against the door, fastening it shut firmly. "Thank you," she gasped. "Master Craig, I presume?"

He lifted his free hand to shake hers. "Yes, Miss. I'm sorry for startling you."

The remark was so wildly out of proportion that Miss Judson released a rasp of laughter that turned into a fit of choking. "Quite . . . all right . . . Edgar," she wheezed. "We're much obliged. How—" She glanced about the space we'd found ourselves in. "A secret passage?"

"Nae secret," Gus insisted. "It's the servants' hall. It goes to all the bedrooms." Lifting the candle, he pointed down the narrow corridor. The faint light barely broke the darkness, but I could almost make out a doorway or two like the one that had saved us. "I heard the commotion. Oh, you're bleeding, Miss. Gran will want to look at that."

Miss Judson regarded her injured forearm without expression. "Myrtle?"

"I'm all right." I didn't know that, for a fact; I couldn't catch my breath, let alone slow the whirling of my mind long enough to give a rational inventory of my person. But we were all here—Peony, Cleveland, Miss Judson, Gus, and I—safe and breathing. It was enough for now.

❦

Gus again led the charge down the passageway. The Stygian* corridor became a flight of cramped, steep stairs that felt for all the world like a descent into an Underworld. He tried to keep our spirits up, pointing out parts of the castle as we passed behind. "Muriel uses this to spy on everyone," he said cheerfully. "And Calpurrnia's always getting stuck in the one in the Laird's bedroom."

"Well," Miss Judson found space to Observe, "this seems to explain our ghost."

Eventually we all tumbled into the dank stone corridor near the kitchen, where we could hear the shouts and barking from the courtyard.

"Outside," Miss Judson said, and I added, "The kennels are on fire," for Gus's benefit.

He turned even paler than usual, then dashed past us, through the kitchen and out into the yard.

It was a chaos of dogs and humans, barks and

---

* Dear Reader, I am running out of words to convey the layers of darkness within Rockfforde Hall. This one comes from Greek mythology, describing the River Styx in the Underworld—which is just about as dark as you can get.

shouting. Cook furiously worked the pump while Muriel passed buckets to Jessie and Mrs. Craig. Hounds scattered everywhere, skidding on the wet stones and howling piteously. Cleveland bounded up to Minna and Nelly, tails awag with relief.

Plumes of smoke rolled from the kennels. The building itself—sturdy brick with a slate roof—was probably safe from damage, but the dogs' bedding was straw. The dogs! Were they all safe? I turned to Gus, who was making a hasty tally. "Saxty-twa, saxty-three, and Cleveland makes saxty-fower. Where's Lady?" I had no idea how he could tell who was missing, with them all milling about in the dark. He started to run for the kennel door just as a bulky form squeezed out.

"Therre's naebody within, lad." Mac bore an armload of hay, from which streamed thick white plumes. Our heroes seemed to have extinguished the flames. "This'll be the culprit," he grunted, dumping it onto the cobblestones. Cook, ready with a bucket, doused it. "Burnin' green brush—nae fire tae speak of, but plenty o' smoke."

Miss Judson and I exchanged a Look.

"It's how the clans wuid signal tae each other in the auld days," he continued. "Ye burn damp brush tae make enough smoke tae carry far, but nae enough tae burn."

"It's still dangerous," Miss Judson said, voice sharp.

"Aye, Mistress."

Her lips pursed. "It doesn't seem as if the intent was to harm anyone, then."

Mac's ruddy face was creased. "Who kin say *what* the intent was heerre?"

Jessie caught sight of Miss Judson. Her face was smeared with sweat and soot, but underneath it flared with color. "Nice of ye tae join—*Gus*!" That last skirled up in a completely un-Jessie-like cry, and she flung her arms around him. "I'm gaun tae kell ye!" she said fondly, and he held on fiercely.

It seemed the crisis was over, with no casualties. Abruptly I found myself seated on the stone wall. Minna trotted over to lick my smoky face, and I followed Jessie's lead and threw my arms about her white neck.

"Is everyone accounted for?" Miss Judson asked. "Where is Lt. Smoot?"

Jessie turned slowly, color draining from her neck. "I've nae seen him. Mur?"

"Nay, Miss."

"Ye cannae think—"

Miss Judson cut that line of speculation off at its feet. "We'll know nothing until everyone's accounted for." But her cool eyes met mine, clouded with doubt.

"Gran," Gus spoke up—and I was surprised how his quiet voice carried. "Miss Judson's been injured."

All eyes turned to the new mistress. She was disinclined to allow a fuss, but was holding tight to one forearm, white sleeve blooming red around her fingers. Mrs. Craig took charge and bustled her toward the castle.

"We'll finish up oot herre," Mac assured them, and Jessie watched us trail back into the house, looking troubled.

Once inside the kitchen, Miss Judson took in her assembled staff. "Now," she said in her strictest schoolroom voice, "would someone care to tell me what *exactly* is going on here?"

"Nae until I've seen tae that arm." Mrs. Craig was firm. "Sit ye, Mistress."

Miss Judson's wound was worse than she'd let on. As she explained what had occurred in our room, Mrs. Craig removed a deadly looking spear of glass, causing the blood to flow freely once again. I have never before felt faint, Dear Reader, but watching Miss Judson sit stoically while someone else tended her injuries was enough to make even my knees a little weak. Gus clung close to me, and I was grateful for his presence. Hunkered on the table, Peony gave herself a discontented bath, complaining bitterly in a low grumble.

"Has anyone seen Lady?" Gus spoke up in a small voice.

"I'm sure she'll turn up, lad."

Nine stitches later, expertly set by Mrs. Craig, my governess's whole right forearm was bound up in white, and the others had returned. Mac frowned at Miss Judson's ashen face, her lips thin with pain.

"Perhaps a wee dram, lassie?" He offered her a flask, and Miss Judson downed a swig like a stolid old sailor, barely wincing as the Scottish whisky hit her throat.

"We've cleaned up most o' the mess," Jessie said. "The weather will do the rest." Thunder groaned overhead, and huge droplets splattered the castle.

"I repeat," Miss Judson said, "I believe I am owed an explanation."

Mrs. Craig merely went about her business, but I saw her eyes flick warningly to Jessie and Mac, daring them to speak out of turn. Finally Jessie stirred. "Gran—"

Glass plinked loudly into the basin. "Lass . . ."

"Gran, we need help! This cannae gae on!"

Mrs. Craig tossed a hand ceilingward, absolving herself of responsibility. "Fine," she said. "There've been—things happenin', hereaboots."

"Things?" Gus's brow furrowed.

"Things," Miss Judson echoed flatly.

"Bad things!" Muriel whimpered. "Terrrrible things!"

"We thocht it naethin', at first," Jessie said. "Noises in th' night, tools went missin', a lame horse, fences broken. Juist bad luck."

"But it got worse." Mac joined in but did not elaborate.

Miss Judson received this belated testimony patiently. "And what was the consensus about these . . . incidents?"

"The Laird thocht they were tryin' tae scare us off the land," Jessie said. "Intae sellin'."

"They? Fyne Fisheries?"

"Aye."

My brain finally clicked into gear. "Alan Balfour! Services rendered. Do you think they paid him to intimidate you? To do all these things?"

"Nivver!" cried Jessie.

"The Laird thocht so." Mac shifted uncomfortably.

"And he was rrright," Mrs. Craig said. "It aw stopped when Balfour left. Until—" She reined that sentence in just in time. Well, not quite.

"Until we came," Miss Judson said.

"Aye."

"But it's not Mr. Balfour now, surely. And the incidents have rather escalated, from vandalism to murder."

"Murder!" Mrs. Craig's breath came in a hiss. "Ye cannae think what happened tae Macewan's related tae aw this."

Though Mrs. Craig's protest rang through the dim kitchen, the grim faces staring back belied her assertion. Everyone clearly *did* believe that Mr. Macewan's death was part of the "bad luck" plaguing Rockfforde Hall.

"It's the currse," Muriel whispered. "Jist as Angus MacJudd swore it! It's acaws o' the lossit treasure."

"Lass," Mac chided. "Those're fairy tales."

"The Old Laird believed," she insisted.

Though the rest of the company was inclined to side with Mac, I found my gaze meeting Gus's. He gave me a very slight nod. Fairy tale or not, Uncle Augustus's search for the missing brooch had definitely stirred up trouble.

လ

The night that followed was endless. After all the confessions were made and the speculations exhausted (including Gus's explanation for his presence at Rockfforde Hall—which was not entirely well received by his kinswomen), we lingered around the old plank table, listening to the fretful Scottish weather replace the sounds of fretful Scottish dogs. And still there was no sign of the missing Lt. Smoot, or the missing hound, Lady. Even I began to worry a bit—perhaps my suspicions had been unfounded, and the soldier, too, had fallen prey to our unseen foe?

A weak banging at the old green door bestirred Nelly, who cocked her head and whined anxiously.

"Dinnae apen that!" shrilled Muriel, but Miss Judson held up a hand.

"It may be Lt. Smoot," she said. "But if it is our villain, the lot of us will subdue him. Mr. Manro, as you were."

With a grunt of resignation, the old Highlander cracked open the door, and a dazed and soaking wet Lt. Smoot tumbled in, a dazed and soaking wet white dog at his heels.

"Lady!" Gus cried.

The lieutenant had exchanged his bright red uniform for casual clothes, a tatty jumper and oversized canvas coat. Perfect for lurking about the woods.

"Wherrre've ye been?" Jessie's voice echoed from the rafters.

Lt. Smoot's story was incredible—in every sense. "I was patrolling the grounds, and I heard something in the woods. I went to investigate."

"What?" I asked, voice sharp. "What did you hear?"

"Ye won't believe me. I hardly believe it." He pushed a hand through his hair. "It was a bird, in the brush. It sounded injured."

Those cold fingers went up my neck again. That was exactly what Jessie had said too.

He slowly took in our tense expressions, the bandage on Miss Judson's arm, the spanner gripped in Cook's beefy hand. "Rough night?"

"Someone set fire to the kennels," I said. "*And* our bedroom!"

Now he stared. "What—"

"Nae a fire," Jessie said—and there was accusation in her voice. "*Smeek*, from a signal pyre. Like the Laird taught us when we were young."

"What? Jess—I'd never! Ye *know* I'd never—"

"Where were ye tonight, then? Where were ye when I was attacked in the ruins?" She marched up to him and shoved him in the chest. "Where were ye when Mr. Macewan was killed? Where were ye when the Laird died?" She pounded him with both fists. "*Where were ye?*" Her cries broke into sobs, and Lt. Smoot caught her by the wrists, pulling her closer.

"Lass," he crooned into her hair. "It wasnae me. I swear it."

But none of us believed him.

16
HOLD FAST

Keep on good terms with your neighbors. In times of strife or sorrow, they will be your best allies and first source for help.

–A Country Gentlewoman's Guide to Estate Management

Finally, somehow, that long night ended, and Miss Judson allowed us all to leave the kitchen. Her color was not back to normal yet. Of course, there was no telling her to rest (although Cook, Mrs. Craig, *and* Cleveland made a good effort). The very first thing she wanted to do was search the grounds for signs of the arsonist— is it arson if there's only smoke?—and the very second thing she wished to do was put the Thistle Room back to rights.

The first was pointless. The storm that had buffeted Rockfforde Hall all night had swept away any evidence of the culprit's identity. There was no hope of recovering footprints or of the dogs tracking him—even if the rain had not washed away the perpetrator's scent, smoke had infused every surface, fouling any possible trail.

Not that we needed a trail. We had a suspect right here, under our very roof. I hadn't yet figured out Lt. Smoot's motive for terrorizing the residents of Rockfforde Hall, but he'd never explained The Hat Incident, and his proximity to several of the crimes was too convenient to be mere coincidence.

Then again, the fires-that-weren't were the work of an expert, someone who not only possessed the skills to build a fire meant to scare, not to harm (though had Gus not come to our rescue, Miss Judson and I might indeed have met a bad end), but who knew Rockfforde Hall and its grounds inside and out. Miss Judson had dismissed Mr. Balfour as the culprit of these latest episodes, but I was not so sure.

And now I had another niggling worry. Gus's words about his secret hallway came back to me: *Muriel uses them to spy on everyone.* Could she be involved somehow? But she couldn't have locked us in our room—she had an alibi, dousing the smoke at the kennels, side by side with Cook.

Which left us with Lt. Smoot and Alan Balfour.

I wanted to confront the lieutenant about his alibi, his knowledge of the portmanteau snatching, and whatever connection he might have with Fyne Fisheries, but there wasn't a chance. He was up and off early, "patrolling" the estate. He could have fled altogether, but didn't—I'll say that much for him.

Upstairs, the Thistle Room was in a worse state than we'd left it (if that were possible). The heavy bonfire smell pushed us back, blinking away the sting. Not only was everything we'd brought with us to Scotland scattered to every corner of the suite, it had now likewise been thoroughly smoke damaged and rain-soaked. A desolate banging from the broken casement hitting the wall (*now* it opened) seemed the perfect counterpoint to the Tragic Scene.

Mrs. Craig could not quite keep her composure. She took one look at the room and a sniffly sob escaped her—but she mustered all her Scottish Mettle and marched within to fasten up the window, even though the pane was smashed.

Her defiance inspired the rest of the forces, and Miss Judson was on her heels, ticking off items we would need. "A broom—three brooms—wastebaskets, and—" She broke off. "Catriona? What is it?"

Mrs. Craig had stopped short, retrieving a fallen item from the floor. "Wherre—where did ye get this?" Her voice trembled. She held up the photograph of Uncle Augustus and the young Rev. Judson in its cracked (and now very much worse for wear) frame.

"Mr. Macewan sent it to me," Miss Judson replied. "Why?"

"This was yer uncle's favorrite picture. It disappeared

after he died. I've luikit everywhere fir it." She shook it accusingly at Miss Judson. "Why wuid Macewan hae it?"

"I assumed my uncle had him send it," Miss Judson said—but now I remembered something else.

"Mr. Macewan was upset when he found out you'd brought the picture to Argyll with you," I reminded her. "We assumed he was just upset that *you'd* come, but maybe—"

Miss Judson regarded the photograph doubtfully. "Could this be what our vandal was after?"

"Wha'd want tae steal a picture of yer uncle?" Mrs. Craig demanded. "That makes nae sense."

She was right—especially because they *hadn't* stolen it. "Somebody's been trying to find something in your belongings, this whole trip," I said. "That picture was at the station in Glasgow, at the high street in Tighnabruaich—and now here. And it *came* from here. Unlike everything else you brought."

Miss Judson's doubtful look became considering.

"Therre may be somethin' tae what the bairn's sayin'," admitted Mrs. Craig—the closest I was ever likely to get to a compliment from her.

"Well," Miss Judson said, "let's find out."

We assembled around a reasonably dry zone of the bed. Miss Judson judged my hands the steadiest, so I was given the job of carefully disassembling the frame. I took care not to damage the precious image still further as I pried up the little tabs and lifted off the velvet backing. Inside, a slip of paper covered the back of the cardboard photograph. I teased it out gently, and it popped onto the bed, looking perfectly innocent.

"What is it?" Mrs. Craig asked.

Miss Judson pinched the paper between two fingers and lifted it to the light. "I second that," she said.

But I looked at the page, with its beautiful faded ink and darkened creases, and a curiously familiar teacup ring, and knew *exactly* what it was. "It's Mr. Macewan's map to the brooch!"

It made sense now—well, part of it did. It only stood to reason that an artifact shared between two clans would share the map to the item, as well. Mr. Macewan must have recovered the MacEwen half, and once we put it together with the one we'd found inside the Gallery wall, we'd have a legible map! I couldn't wait to show Gus.

A rap at the door forestalled their reactions. Muriel poked her wraithlike head in. "Mistress? Therre's an Ainglishman at the door fir ye. Claims he's a solicitor."

At once Miss Judson and I exchanged looks of alarm, and every other thought vanished from my mind as my heart plummeted to my knees. "Father!"

I dashed for the door, nearly mowing Muriel down. I barreled down the corridors and the long twisty grand staircase through the sword-bedecked Great Hall, heart wringing. As much as I longed to see Father, the idea of him *here*, at Rockfforde Hall, *now*, in the middle of all the strange happenings and deaths and ghosts and smoke attacks, made me almost wild with panic. We'd only just got him *out* of danger on our last Investigation!

I was not quite so panic-stricken, however, that I failed to Observe that Miss Judson was *not* rushing headlong for the doorway with me. I didn't care. Muriel—in an overabundance of caution, evidently—had left our visitor outside, doors barred to intruders. It took some wrestling to shift aside the great iron bar and haul open the heavy door, and I was gasping and disheveled by the time I set eyes on our caller.

A young man with curly, fair hair wiped his feet on the boot scraper. "Not the English solicitor you were expecting?" he said affably, and I fairly flung myself into his arms.

"Mr. Blakeney!" I squealed—and yes, Dear Reader, in my anxiety, that is the best description for the sound that escaped me.

"Hullo, Stephen," he returned,* gently disentangling himself. "Miss J."

My governess had at last appeared, lurking on the staircase landing, silhouetted against the MacJudd coat of arms. At the sight of Mr. Blakeney, her features

---

* He always calls me this; frankly, I'm uncertain whether he remembers my name.

registered relief, and she came down to greet him. "You are a welcome sight indeed, Mr. Blakeney. But how—?"

"Mr. H. dispatched me to check on you when you never sent word of your arrival. Everything all right here?"

"Er," she said, stalling. "There wasn't a chance to wire home, I'm afraid. The island is somewhat . . . isolated."

"You're telling me. Did you know there's no ferry?"

"How did you get here?" I demanded, desperately hoping the answer involved a well-armed naval vessel, if not the whole fleet.

"A very large woman with a very small boat took pity on me." Mr. Blakeney was casually dressed in a white-and-blue cricket jumper with an orange ascot, and he plucked at his clothes. "I think I still have herring in my pocket."

Our visitor had attracted the attention of the rest of the Rockfforde Hall staff, who'd assembled rather suspiciously in the Hall. Jessie had her shotgun, and even Cleveland looked skeptical, a ridge of fur erect along his spine.

"I say, *is* everything all right? What's happened to your arm, Miss J?" Mr. Blakeney stepped fully inside Rockfforde Hall, swinging the door shut behind him. "And does this belong to anyone? I'm afraid the correspondent left off the signature. Found it tacked to the door, with this." He held up a sheet of paper—and something that made my blood turn cold. "If this is how folk send messages hereabouts, it explains a lot."

The other item he bore was all too familiar: a short knife with an engraved black handle. A sgian dubh.

"What is that?" Jessie marched up and yanked paper and knife from Mr. Blakeney's hands. "Who are ye?" But she forgot her own questions as she took in the note's contents. Her already pale color faded still further, and she crushed the page in her grip.

"Jessie?" Miss Judson gently wrested the paper from her trembling hand. Her face set grimly as she unfolded the message—then turned it for the rest of us to see.

LAST CHANCE

"It's *him*!" Muriel shrilled. "The ghaist o' Angus MacJudd! The Laird was rrright. We'll nae be safe till the ootsiders are gaun!"

Showing an uncharacteristic lack of restraint, Jessie slapped her. "Stop yer haverin'! There's nae ghaist!"

"Jessie Isla Craig!" her grandmother cried. "What's got intae ye?"

"Enough!" Miss Judson's voice bounced off the rafters and stones and every polished steel blade in the Hall. Everyone fell silent, looking chagrined. Muriel still trembled, white hand to her red cheek. Miss Judson put firm hands on her shoulders. "Calm yourself.

Whatever is happening, I can assure you it has a wholly corporeal cause."

Muriel didn't *look* reassured; in fact, I'm not certain she understood what Miss Judson had said (in her weariness, some French was creeping into her accent). But the maid nodded, twisting her apron in a death grip.

Mrs. Craig took pity on her. "It's been a lang nicht. Get ye tae bed, an' I'll be up wi' a brew tae help ye sleep." Muriel, still nodding tremulously, slinked off to her room. Minna watched her leave, tail twitching uncertainly.

Mr. Blakeney's presence bolstered Miss Judson. "I am half sick of Strange Occurrences," she declared. "I shall not simply stand by and do nothing while someone continues to threaten us. In fact, I quite agree. This *is* the last chance. Our culprit will show himself, or so help me—"

She didn't finish. Jessie made a muffled sound—half gasp, half sob—and all eyes went to her.

"Lass?" Mrs. Craig tilted her granddaughter's chin to meet her gaze. Jessie's face was still scratched from her recent fall. "Do ye know aething aboot this?"

"No—maybe." She flailed her hand helplessly and took a great sobbing breath. "This—everything—it's all my fault."

❧

With the additional presence of Mr. Blakeney, we were outgrowing the kitchen table, so the company now assembled in the Small Dining Room, a chamber housing a twenty-six-foot oak table and chairs and *two* fireplaces, with room to spare for an entire band of pipers, their hounds, and perhaps the Scots Dragoons. It must have been close to the Thistle Room, for the air stung with smoke, and Miss Judson opened the leaded windows to admit a leaden breeze.

Mrs. Craig had fixed "a brew" for everybody, serving it in the silver tea service that evidently went with the Small Dining Room (all two dozen place settings), and we clustered at one end of the stately table, overlooked by huge bronze stags and some disapproving portraiture. I was still suspicious of Rockfforde Hall's alarmingly red water, but this conversation definitely called for tea.

Miss Judson had introduced Mr. Blakeney to the Rockffordians, although they did not yet seem to find his presence as reassuring as we did (Jessie refused to relinquish her shotgun). Nevertheless, he adopted a calm, professional air intended to put clients at ease—orange ascot notwithstanding—and sat quietly in the corner with Peony around his neck, listening to Jessie's tale.

"Now, then. Kindly explain how everything is your fault."

I recognized Miss Judson's tone—the opening of a Socratic debate to demonstrate Jessie's faulty thinking—but Jessie flinched away from Miss Judson's efforts to be kind through logic. She looked to her gran instead. Taking a gulp of tea, she began with an earth-shattering statement no one expected.

"Roan Kirkpatrick asked me tae marry him."

Mrs. Craig leaped to her feet in indignation, dropping the sugar tongs onto the silver platter with a rattle that—all things considered—did very little to soothe the frayed nerves in the room. Jessie emitted a choked laugh.

"Well, I didnae say yes! And aye, it sounds daft—it sounded daft to me, when it happened! But he *kept* asking. He thocht—I dinnae ken why—that he could somehow get his hands on Rockfforde Hall and Dunfyne Island by marrying me."

I shot a Look at Miss Judson, who replied with a nearly imperceptible shake of her head. Clearly Jessie did not suspect that she might well be directly related to Uncle Augustus. But how could Mr. Kirkpatrick have learned that?

"I said nay," Jessie continued—as if afraid we might think otherwise. "An' I *kept* sayin' nay. But when askin' nicely didnae work . . ." She waved a hand, encompassing all the Strange Occurrences.

"I can't say I think much of the man's courtship techniques," Mr. Blakeney Observed.

Miss Judson held up a hand and spoke carefully. "Is there any reason that Mr. Kirkpatrick might have believed marrying you would—as you say—bring him

Rockfforde Hall?" Her question was addressed to Jessie, but I Observed her gaze flick to Mrs. Craig.

Jessie shook her head emphatically. "Nay. It didnae make sense. Aye, the Laird and I were close—he was always kind tae us . . ." She attempted a grin at my governess. "He oughtae've proposed tae *ye*, then, aye?"

Miss Judson smiled vaguely. "Perhaps." I glared at her—how could she even joke about that? Not when—when The Item was at home waiting for her! I retract my previous statement, Dear Reader: Father couldn't get here soon enough.

Jessie sighed into her tea. "When the first things happened—the traps, the threats—I told the Laird I wuid dae it, if it meant savin' Rockfforde. But he forbade it. Said Rockfforde wasnae worth my happiness." She sniffed at the memory. "But now he's dead, and it's aw my fault!"

What was Jessie suggesting—that Mr. Kirkpatrick had killed Uncle Augustus? Followed by Mr. Macewan, just to force her hand? I sat back, turning this theory over in my mind.

"Now, lass." Mrs. Craig was stern. "You cannae think that all this is Roan Kirkpatrick's doin'. I dinnae like the man, but he'd nae stoop tae—tae murrderr."

Jessie gave her grandmother a bleak look. "If I just give myself up—"

"Don't be absurd," Miss Judson broke in. "First of all, no one in this room would permit you to take such a foolish action—marry a man you don't love?—no matter what was at stake. Secondly, we've no proof Mr. Kirkpatrick is behind any of these incidents, let alone all of them."

Jessie's bleak gaze was on the black knife on the tabletop. "Nay, it's him. It's jist like him. Ye dinnae ken—"

"If I may," Mr. Blakeney broke in. "There's some validity to what Miss Craig is saying. Not that it's your fault," he added hastily. He hauled his overstuffed brief-bag onto the table, oblivious to Mrs. Craig's look of horror. "I stopped by Miss J.'s solicitor's office in Tig—in Tichnic—Tignag—when I got to Argyll. That's how I knew where to find you. His clerk let me take the Rockfforde files. There's more in the—er, wheelbarrow."

"Clerk?" We hadn't seen any clerk at Mr. Macewan's office. "Wait—how did *he* know?"

"Know what, Stephen?"

"That Mr. Macewan is dead. How did this clerk know that?"

"Whoa, back up. Dead?" He appealed to Miss Judson. "Don't tell me—"

She replied with a pained nod. "Murdered. Here on the island. On Saturday."

Mr. Blakeney rubbed the back of his neck. "Have the two of you ever considered simply not leaving your house?"

"More often than you could imagine. Be that as it

may, there's no way anyone in Tighnabruaich* could know that Mr. Macewan would not be needing my uncle's papers anymore, unless . . ."

"He was the killer," I said. "Or in league with him. What did this clerk look like?"

"Come to think of it, he didn't exactly have the look of the law about him. Middle-aged toff, sharply dressed—top hat, silver cane."

I made a wordless growl. That didn't sound like anyone we knew. Of course, there was nothing saying the killer couldn't have accomplices on the mainland. It sounded like a Fyne Fisherman, snooping about the office.

"What did ye mean, afore?" Jessie broke in. "When ye said I might be right aboot Kirkpatrick?"

Mr. Blakeney drew his attention from one mystery to another. "It seems this Roan Kirkpatrick's been trying to buy the MacJudd lands for years, most lately under the guise of a company called—"

"Fyne Fisheries," four voices sang out, and Mr. Blakeney put the papers down.

"No sense trying to surprise you lot."

My fingers reached into my satchel and curled around the Kirkpatrick badge, with its bloody knife and *I mak sikkar* motto. What did it all mean?

* Ever the schoolteacher, she sounded this out carefully for Mr. Blakeney's benefit: "*Tie na brrew eggh.*"

"Kirkpatrick owns Fyne Fisheries? When did tha' happen?" Jessie reached for Mr. Blakeney's papers. She cast them down after barely a glance. "Did the Laird ken?"

"Better yet," I said, "did Mr. Macewan?" Because if Mr. Macewan—the man engineering the sale to Fyne Fisheries—had known all along that his buyer wanted the hand of Jessie Craig in marriage, that brought us right back to who had the motive to kill him. And *that* became a list of just two people: Roan Kirkpatrick and Jessie Craig.

❧

As we dispersed from the dining room a short time later, Miss Judson pulled Mrs. Craig aside.

"Catriona, I have a feeling you know more about this situation than you've said."

Her reply was starchy. "I dinnae ken what ye mean. How cuid I ken aething?"

"I saw how you reacted to Jessie's story. You must know we've realized that she and Gus are related to Uncle Augustus. Is she . . . ?" Miss Judson let the question hang, evolving in Mrs. Craig's imagination.

"Nay. Nae his ain. And nae bygotten, neither—I'll nae hae ye spreadin' rumors!"

"I've no intention of it, but I deserve to know if I have other family here." Miss Judson put a hand on her arm. "I *want* to know."

Mrs. Craig looked like she still meant to deny it. But she finally sighed and led us back up to the Gallery. In the farthest depths, hidden in an alcove opposite the portrait of Uncle Augustus and Cleveland, was a portrait I hadn't noticed before. She held a lamp to it, revealing three youths in old-fashioned clothes—a young man all in tartan; a young woman with a striking resemblance to Jessie; and a boy cradling a pet squirrel.

"Stewart MacJudd's children—the *Old* Laird," she said, pointing them each out in turn. "Augustus, his brother Aubrey, and their sister Isla . . . Craig. My sister-in-law."

In the midst of this revelation, I realized we must be looking at a portrait of Miss Judson's own grandfather—the one who'd come to England and taken the name Judson. *Aubrey.* My heart squeezed, and I almost missed what Mrs. Craig said next.

"Isla fell in love with my husband's brother Neil, but the Old Laird wouldnae let them marry. They were only crofters, ye ken. Not guid enew fir the clan chief's onie daughter.

"It didnae metter tae them—they ran awa' and married in secret. Lived ootbye Aberdeen."

Caught up in the romantic tale, I breathed, "What happened to them?"

Mrs. Craig touched the canvas sadly. "Isla passed

givin' birth tae their son, Archie. It broke Neil—couldnae bear to be athoot her. He left the bairn wi' us an' ran off tae America. Aye said he'd send fir his son when he had the means . . . but I kent he wouldnae. We raised that lad as oor ain—th' only parents he ever kent. Jess and Gus are his—their ain dear mam passed when Gus was a bairn, rest her soul, and Archie died a few years later." She took a shaky breath and continued. "The Laird—your uncle Augustus—felt it was his duty tae gather up the clan. He brought us here so his sister's kin cuid be raised at hame. Onie . . ."

"Only?" Miss Judson prompted.

"I made him promise nivver tae tell them the truth—nae tae destrroy their memories of their ain family—*or* his. Why should they wat the MacJudds didnae want them?"

"Hmmm." Miss Judson regarded the painting silently for a long moment. I could tell what she was thinking, though: if Uncle Augustus had wanted Jessie and Gus to know their true heritage, why hadn't he named *them* in the will? They were as close in line to the MacJudd chiefship as Miss Judson was! Not to mention far better prepared to take on such a duty.

"You must tell them, Catriona," she finally said. "Jessie deserves to know what she's up against—and why."

"And Gus," I said softly, but I was looking at Miss

Judson, and thinking about all those relatives in the paintings, waiting for her—for us—to save their legacy. "He'd want to know his heritage, too."

Mrs. Craig sniffed. "It's jist . . . I nivver seem tae find the rrright time."

I couldn't take any more of this. "The right time is before we all get killed by crazy neighbors!"

And nobody shushed me.

17
THINK MORE

Let your home be always prepared to welcome visitors.

–A Country Gentlewoman's Guide to Estate
Management

Mrs. Craig rearranged our sleeping assignments, since the Thistle Room was no longer suitable for the New Laird and her charge. We were moved to the Butterwort,* an older bedroom that was less commodiously furnished—"Naebody's slept herre since the last o' the Stuarts—" but had a functioning window and a door that didn't quite latch, making it a step up in my estimation.

After a brief but marginally revivifying nap made somewhat less restful by an awkward profusion of canine and feline limbs poking into various human

---

* *Pinguicula vulgaris*. And here I was worried about deer, when even the plants of Argyll are carnivorous!

orifices, Miss Judson and I discovered Mr. Blakeney in Gus's Bog Myrtle room (Gus preferring his nest in the library). He was standing by the tall windows, admiring the ruins of Castle Dunfyne and the view of Rockfforde Falls.

"My window at home looks out on a Picturesque Vista of a Swinburne alleyway, complete with rubbish bins. You're moving up in the world, Miss J. Literally." He made the mistake of glancing downward at the sheer drop to the earth below (far below) and paled visibly.

Miss Judson, too, had colored slightly at his remarks. I glanced between them for clues to any telepathic messages they might be exchanging.

"Have you heard anything from Father?" I said, somewhat louder than necessary. "When he might get free?" *When we might be going home?* "Did he have any messages for us?" *Any parcels to deliver?*

Mr. Blakeney turned awkwardly from the window. "I think *I'm* the message."

I bit the edge of my thumb, though I generally try to refrain from such babyish behaviors in Mr. Blakeney's presence. Had he come to check up on us—to Observe my progress in the task Father had set for me, namely preventing Miss Judson from falling in love with Scotland? That hardly seemed fair! First, there hadn't been time to address the matter, what with the murder and all. And second, one might reasonably expect a killing spree to cool her affections. But the danger to Rockfforde Hall only seemed to cement Miss Judson's bond to her ancestral home, entrenching her ever more firmly. How was I going to get her back to Swinburne and Father? What about Cook, with an endless supply of repairs here to keep her busy? Even Peony seemed poised to forsake her second-favorite English human in favor of her new clan of dogs and cats and horses and buzzards and men with bare knees.

I cast a pleading look at Mr. Blakeney, not even realizing I was doing it.

"I'd love a look round the old place," he said. "Then I thought I'd get to work on your uncle's files—*your* files, that is, Miss J."

Miss Judson was torn. "We're trying to contain the movements of the household at present, I'm afraid. So the tour will have to wait." I saw her eyes go to the stacks of paperwork Mr. Blakeney was emptying out upon Gus's desk. "I suppose I have rather been neglecting the business side of things . . ."

Mrs. Craig, lurking in the hallway, approved. "I'll bring tea," she said.

"And bannocks?" I added hopefully. They would never replace Cook's scones, but I was getting rather fond of Mrs. Craig's oaty delicacy, particularly with the honey produced here on Dunfyne Island. And we hadn't had a proper breakfast, as Peony was keen to point out.

As soon as Mrs. Craig disappeared into the bleak corridor, Mr. Blakeney turned to us, arms crossed and expression serious, ascot askew. It wasn't a Mr. Blakeney–like gesture; in fact, he rather resembled Father, standing like that.

"Now," he said, "what's really going on?"

Miss Judson cracked a wan smile. "I believe I asked that very question not twelve hours ago. It's something of a long tale."

"Why don't I begin, then?" He sifted through a stack of file folders. "I was able to spend a bit of time with these when I got in yesterday. Miss J., I'm afraid to say, you haven't much in the way of assets."

"What do you mean? She inherited A Whole Estate! In Scotland!" I waved my arm around the room—couldn't he *see* the castle, the island, the ruins, the waterfall, the miles of shoreline teeming with herring?

"Well, there is that. But that's about *all* there is. Your bank account's empty."

"Not true," she said lightly. "I've nearly three hundred pounds saved from my wages."

"You'll need it. You've an overdue tax bill that'll take every farthing. Your uncle seems to have left you a building and an island and not much else."

"You forgot the dogs." She seemed unsurprised by this gloomy report.

"Which you can't afford, either." He held out another

paper, and I caught the letterhead: *R. D. McAllister, Veterinary Surgeon.* "I hate to say it, but I'd be thinking about selling this place."

I snatched the bill from him. "Whose side are you on?" Which was an excellent question, Dear Reader: whose side was *I* on?

"It's not just you," Mr. Blakeney assured her. "Landowners all over Britain are feeling the pinch. The agricultural recession, you know." I had no idea what he was talking about, but I certainly felt the pinch of his words.

"Hence the offer from Fyne Fisheries." Miss Judson reached into her skirt pocket and withdrew a folded letter. She handed it to Mr. Blakeney.

He read it, eyes widening. "They're getting increasingly generous," he said. "And while I grant you the water power is probably your biggest asset, this seems a bit out of proportion."

"It's not just the money," I said. "Mr. Kirkpatrick wants everything—Dunfyne Island, Rockfforde Hall, the Lairdship. Jessie. We have to find that brooch!"

Mr. Blakeney cast a quizzical gaze at Miss Judson, who filled him in. "A legendary artifact linking the fortunes of Dunfyne Island and the MacJudds to the MacEwen clan. Evidently it was one of Mr. Macewan's obsessions."

"And what got him killed," I added darkly. "There's a curse on it."

"Maybe you should sell that," Mr. Blakeney suggested.

"Oh, if only we had it. It's a legendary *lost* artifact, you see."

"You don't say? You do find your way into the most interesting cases!"

I explained what we knew. "Mr. Macewan was determined to prove that the Clan Brooch existed, and to get it back."

Mr. Blakeney brightened. "You know, you're on to something, Stephen. He had a letter from somebody mixed in with your uncle's things. Erm, a Lord Lion—" He thumbed through the files, searching.

Miss Judson spoke up. "The Lord Lyon King of Arms?"

"That's the one."

"That's the Heraldic Court of Scotland," she confirmed. "They're in charge of issuing coats of arms, titles—even recognizing clan chiefs." I was hardly surprised she knew that, given the change in her own fortunes.

"Like the chief of a clan that hasn't had one in four hundred years?" I asked. "What did the letter say?"

"It's here somewhere . . . Basically, it encouraged Mr. Macewan to back up his claim with genealogies and artifacts with known provenance to Clan MacEwen history. Could this brooch have done that?"

"That's why he was so eager to find it!" I exclaimed,

pieces finally settling into place. "Mr. Macewan was after the clan chieftainship—for himself!"

"And Hardcastle & Judson haven't cracked this mystery yet? You've been here for *days* already. What have you been up to? Come on—there's a treasure to be found!"

Miss Judson tugged him back down. "I'm afraid it's too dangerous right now, with our assailant on the loose."

"Boyhood dreams dashed," he said. "You're a spoil-sport, Miss J."

"But you can help with the riddle," I offered. "I think Gus would like that."

Miss Judson explained. "An ancestor of mine penned a mystifying puzzle for the benefit of treasure-hunting progeny. Quite the head-scratcher. I believe it's in Mr. Macewan's booklet." She retrieved the book and flipped to a page toward the middle, declaiming the verse in a dramatic voice:

> *"Atwixt stump and stane: the Means*
> *Atween lock and key: the Might*
> *Aneath W but owre X: the Way*
> *Seek ye the hidden path*
> *To restore what was lost."*

A slow grin spread over Mr. Blakeney's face. "Very mysterious indeed. I saw your Venerable Stump outside—is that the starting point, then?"

"We've figured out *Aneath W* too." I explained the discovery Gus and I had made in the Gallery, and the two parts of the secret map.

"You *are* spoilsports," he complained. "What kind of a treasure hunt has a boring old map?" He made a sulky circuit of the Bog Myrtle room, which had almost as many Curious Artifacts as Uncle Augustus's Trophy Room: birds' nests, stereograph cards, bagpipe parts. He picked up a hunk of fluorspar—the largest crystal I'd seen, tall and pointed, polished to smooth brilliance. After a moment, he opened his hand. "Well, would you look at that."

Miss Judson glanced up. "Ah, yes. One of the island's minor curiosities. I believe it's the manganese in the rock that makes it glow like that. And which gives our water its delightful shade of blood."

Though I'd witnessed fluorspar's lovely parlor trick before, something about it struck me now. "It doesn't glow that brightly for me."

"That's the hot Blakeney blood, I suspect." He held out his hand to me, and he was right: it was considerably warmer than mine or Miss Judson's.

"It glows brighter with heat," I said slowly, trying to tease my idea into the open.

"I believe we just settled that."

"I want to try something." I shoved Mr. Blakeney's papers aside.

"Myrtle! We spent an hour sorting those!"

I ignored her. I fetched a lamp from Gus's bedside table, removed the chimney, and lit it from one of the others set up around the room. I carefully placed the hunk of fluorspar right in the flame, then sat back to watch. The crystal glowed, faintly, *if* you looked at it just the right way. And used your imagination.

"Is that what you were expecting?" Mr. Blakeney asked.

I scowled at it, not yet ready to give up. I was sure I was on to something. What did I need? We ought to be in Uncle Augustus's laboratory for this, but I would work with the materials at hand. The plate holding the bannocks was clear glass; I slid the cakes onto the tabletop (to Miss Judson's vocal displeasure) and balanced the plate above the flame of the lamp, followed by the fluorspar.

"Turn down the other lamps," I said eagerly, and Mr. Blakeney obliged. At once, the fluorspar acted like a glass chimney, green light pouring out in an eerie, wavering halo.

"Crikey." Mr. Blakeney sat back, staring—and I did as well. I hadn't expected it to work quite so well. I rose to my feet, unable to stand still.

I saw the ghost of a smile lift Miss Judson's lip. "Oh, brava."

There was one more piece to the test. My pedestrian handkerchief wasn't quite like two yards of premium Glasgow bridal muslin, but it would do in a pinch. I draped the hankie over the crystal, which muted the harsh glow, making it fainter and more mysterious. Carefully I started to lift the whole precarious, incendiary arrangement—lamp heavy with oil, glass plate, crystal obelisk, and handkerchief—but Miss Judson forestalled me.

"Mr. Blakeney, if you will?"

Always amenable, he gingerly hefted the makeshift assemblage and held it aloft. In the dimness of Gus's gloomy chamber, the hankie fluttered with an unearthly green flair.

"Impressive. You've created a new light source, though I must admit the color is somewhat off-putting."

"Oh, it's better than that, Mr. Blakeney." Miss Judson was practically grinning now. "Myrtle has just created a ghost."

⁂

We discussed the Ghost Apparatus all the way back to collect our belongings from the Thistle Room. I felt a deep pang of sadness that Uncle Augustus was not here to share in the exciting discovery. And he wasn't even *my* uncle! But I'd grown rather fond of him in the last several days, reading his journal, reassembling his metal detector, following him on his quest for lost treasure.

Miss Judson was more practical. "Who is behind these 'hauntings,' then? And before you say Lt. Smoot, kindly recall that the man has an airtight alibi for the incidents—he was nowhere near Dunfyne Island when Uncle Augustus recorded his Disturbances."

Unfortunately, she was correct on that point. "It has something to do with the brooch." The two elements—ghosts and treasure—didn't seem to be connected, yet they were inextricably linked in my mind. Though I could not see the link, they kept pulling together, like magnets.

Back at the smoke-fouled chamber, an unpleasant surprise greeted us. (I was beginning to think Dunfyne Island *had* no pleasant surprises in its repertoire.) In our haste to greet Mr. Blakeney, we'd simply run from the room, carelessly leaving the door wide open. It had hardly seemed necessary to secure anything within, after all, given the destruction. But once I stepped back inside, my stinging eyes immediately went to the bed, where we'd disassembled the picture frame. I scurried over, and my heart and stomach sank with dismay.

Mr. Macewan's map was gone.

18

JAMAIS ARRIÈRE

Strife within a household must be resolved immediately. Do not allow jealousy, rivalry, or other
grievances to fester or take root.

*–A Country Gentlewoman's Guide to Estate
Management*

"Miss!" I cried. "The map's gone! Someone stole it!"

Her eyes darted round the room. "Ordinarily I
would advise against jumping to conclusions, but in
this case I'm inclined to agree."

"It must have been Muriel," I said, thinking back.
"She came to tell us of Mr. Blakeney's arrival, *and* she
has an annoying habit of tidying up evidence." And
burning it, I recalled, bitterly regretting leaving Mr.
Macewan's shoes unprotected. If she'd also burned his
treasure map . . .

"Let's go ask her, then." Miss Judson turned on
her heel and led me on a typically circuitous route
through the castle—*Ye cannae get there from here*. I could

practically see her mentally renovating the hallways to improve their efficiency as we twisted and backtracked and headed downstairs only to go back up again.

We finally arrived in a narrow corridor almost directly above the Thistle Room, housing small, cloistered, cell-like rooms. Miss Judson rapped soundly on one whitewashed door.

"Muriel? It's Miss Judson." When there was no reply, she tested the knob. It had no lock, and I had a moment of outrage on Muriel's behalf: to have no privacy at all! (Not that my own bedroom had a lock on it, but still.) Miss Judson nudged the door open, and my sympathy shriveled up.

The room was empty—not only of Muriel, but of all her possessions. The modest chamber's tiny cupboard stood open, its drawer emptied. Only a discarded grey frock and white apron on the bed remained to suggest that this room had ever been lived in. Above the washbasin, a faded lithograph of Rockfforde Hall was the latest victim of violence, slashed down the middle like someone had taken a sgian dubh to it.

Miss Judson tugged on this, and the pieces fell into her hand. "Has she been abducted?" Worry tightened her voice.

"And they let her change her clothes first?" I scoffed. "No, she's run away—with Mr. Macewan's map to the treasure!"

We ought to be chasing after Muriel right this

minute, but I sank onto her bed in dejection. It was one more moment in a string of Discouraging Incidents, and I was reaching my limit.

Miss Judson sat beside me, more perplexed than disheartened. "Where's she gone? As we all know, she can't get off the island. What is she hoping to accomplish?"

"She's going to find the treasure."

"And then what? Even assuming the map alone—and half the map, at that—is enough to determine the brooch's whereabouts—and the riddle would suggest otherwise—she can't hope to vanish with it, not without outside help."

I nodded dully. Peony and Cleveland had found us. Peony surveyed the desolation, gave one judgmental burble, and decamped. Cleveland poked his head hopefully under the bed, as if Muriel was playing a strange game of hide-and-seek.

As Miss Judson and Cleveland mulled over the maid's disappearance, Mrs. Craig peered round the door.

"Mur—oh." One hand on the knob, she took in the scene. "What's become of the lass, then?"

"It seems she's left us, Mrs. Craig." Miss Judson broke the news gently. But the expression on Mrs. Craig's face was tragic, and she slumped onto the bed beside us.

"What'rre we comin' tae, then?" she said. "First the Laird, then Balfour and Macewan, an' now wee

Muriel?" She dabbed at her eyes. "That brooch truly *is* cursit, and I hope it's nivver found!"

I pointed out that Muriel now had a map to it, but Mrs. Craig wasn't listening.

"It's that lad o' hers," she said, shaking her head sadly. "A bad sort since the day he were born, Donal—led her astray, he has, wi' his dreams an' schemes." She stooped to shoo Cleveland out from beneath the bed, but paused, coverlet lifted. "Aye, then, what's this?" She withdrew two slim books bound in the green leather of the Laird's library, *Macbeth* and *Minerals of Scotland*. She sighed. "At least she was still tryin' tae improve herself."

"Is that what she was doing?" Miss Judson said, frowning slightly.

I frowned too, ideas trying to coalesce. Something about that particular combination of volumes felt significant. I took the mineralogy text from Mrs. Craig. Employing a trick used by Billy Garrett, I set it upon its spine and let it fall open. I almost didn't expect it to work, but there on the page, one underlined passage stared up at me, the entry labeled *Fluorite*.

Belatedly, the sluggish gears in my brain clicked to life. "Mrs. Craig, when did you notice that muslin was missing?"

The housekeeper gave a start. "I cannae say—what does it metter?"

Miss Judson's expression had gone keen. "I should

say it matters very much whether it was before or after my uncle died."

"Ye wat Muriel took it? Why? For her ain weddin'?"

"Quite the opposite, I'm afraid, Catriona." Miss Judson met my eyes but explained nothing more to Mrs. Craig.

༄

Gus was understandably disappointed to learn of the new map's fate. There was no chance now to compare it to the one we'd found in the Gallery wall. "I cannae believe Muriel stole it."

Once more we'd assembled in the kitchen, which felt eerily empty without the maid's haunting presence. Mrs. Craig had gone to inform Jessie and Mac of her departure, and our remaining clanlette clustered round the cold fireplace, eager for even the illusion of warmth.

"Gus, kindly share your progress on your search for the brooch," Miss Judson said. "Perhaps as a group we'll be able to work out the next steps."

"The buzzards have a head start," I added darkly.

"But they don't have *our* half of the map," said Miss Judson.

"We've nae cracked all the clues yet, an' I still dinnae ken what this means," Gus warned her, gesturing with the MacJudd map. "But I'll try."

"That's the Rockfforde spirit," she said, squeezing his shoulder.

I watched them working, still unsettled. Mr. Macewan had known that Miss Judson had his map—he'd sent it to her, after all. *Why* had he sent it? He must have known the other buzzards were after it. He'd seemed surprised—no, upset—when she told him she'd brought the photograph to Argyll. What if he'd come to Dunfyne that morning to retrieve it, and that's why he'd been killed?

And with that, I realized something else.

Mr. Macewan and Lt. Smoot knew each other—Smoot had said so himself. But they'd pretended to be strangers that afternoon in Tighnabruaich. When Donal Airlie tried to steal Miss Judson's bag. They *all* knew each other—Macewan, Kirkpatrick, Smoot, Donal, Muriel, and Mr. Balfour! I recalled the love token in Mr. Balfour's desk—had that been for Muriel? Perhaps he, and not the gillie, was her secret sweetheart. Was *everyone* on Fyne Fisheries' payroll?

The buzzards circled, coming closer and closer. What were they up to, attacking each other, attacking us? All I knew for certain was that until we found that brooch, no one would be safe at Rockfforde Hall—not Jessie, not Gus, and most especially not Miss Judson.

There was no more time to waste.

"Mayhap this'll help." Cook bustled to the table, bearing a bulky contraption—a mad, glorious whigmaleerie—in her ruddy hands. Uncle Augustus's metal detector was fully assembled, with a few parts I didn't recognize.

"You got it working!" I exclaimed as she handed it to me.

"Naturally. Followed the Laird's notes. Added a couple Improvements of my own."

"Naturally," Miss Judson said. "What does this do, exactly?"

Cook and I answered at the same time. "It finds metal," I said—while she replied, "It finds ghosts."

I stared at her. "It—what?"

"It's in the diagram," Cook said. "Your Laird had something mighty particular in mind when he came up with this thing, and I don't think it was any old gewgaw."

"Cook, how did you read any of this?" Miss Judson held the schematic to the light. "I can't make out Uncle Augustus's scrawl."

Gus reached out for the paper, but Mr. Blakeney beat him to it. "Hand it here," he said. "I read MacJudd." But he'd Observed Gus's gesture, so he slid the paper between them to study it together. Two fair male heads bent together and conferred.

I sank into a chair under the crushing weight of the device. I'd had such high hopes for this! Even without the map, surely the riddle and the metal detector—and the keen deductive minds of Miss Judson, Gus, and me (and now Mr. Blakeney)—would reveal the brooch's location. I stared at the coils of wire, the balance beam, the batteries in their paper wrappers, the telephone receiver, not seeing any of it. I knew Uncle Augustus had been deeply troubled by his Disturbances, and I'll admit to being proud of my own deduction regarding the glowing fluorspar—but who had time for ghosts now? There were missing treasures, runaway house-maids, mad smokers . . . smokerists . . . smeekists, evil neighbors, and murderers to find!

Peony refused to be discouraged. Stretching languidly, she made her delicate way across the table and bit the power switch to the detector, activating it. I felt it kick to life in my lap, the wire coils drawing power from the batteries. It hummed and vibrated, the pocket watch ticking steadily through the speaker, tinny and far away.

Mr. Blakeney gave a whistle of appreciation.

"Does it work?" Gus leaned over the table. I handed him the probe, and he poked about at objects on the table. When he touched it to the cast iron teakettle, the ticking fell silent. He withdrew the probe then tapped it again, once more halting then reinstating the sound. I watched, impressed, but with a growing realization that Miss Judson had been correct: the device did not have enough power to injure someone. It couldn't have been Uncle Augustus's murder weapon.

"Bravo!" Miss Judson said. "But if I may . . . You've proved that it does indeed identify metal. How exactly does it detect the presence of Supernatural Visitations?"

"Maybe the kettle's haunted," Mr. Blakeney suggested. "With that water . . ." He shuddered.

"Electricity," I said eagerly, recalling what I'd found in Uncle Augustus's laboratory—everything pointed to an exploration of the intersection of ghosts and electricity. The little box, with the bell and the batteries—perhaps that was his first attempt at a Ghost Detector. "The ghosts must do something that interrupts the electrical current," I said, "just like metal."

"Perhaps it's their rattling chains," Miss Judson said mildly.

"Aye, she's right." Gus spoke to the schematic, finger tracing one of Uncle Augustus's notations. "Hark what the Laird wrote: '*Researchers theorize Spectral Disturbances produce Electro-Magnetic fields.*' And here: '*Detectable by interrupting the localized current?*'"

"Well spotted, Master Craig," Mr. Blakeney said.

Gus looked at him oddly. "Crrraiiigh," he trilled.

"Creg," Mr. Blakeney tried again. "Creygg."

Gus grinned, and the other Rockffordians laughed. "Close enew," said Mrs. Craig.

"Thank you, Catriohna," he said—and we all flinched, not just because it was terribly forward to call her by her given name.

"Ca*tree*na," she growled, but Mr. Blakeney was unfazed.

"I've heard it both ways," he said. "Stephen, grab the Ghost Detector. We have a Ghost to Detect!"

We filed out of the kitchen in a crowd guaranteed to frighten away all but the most stalwart of ghosts. I called back to Gus: "Grab the schematic!" We didn't want a reprise of this morning's fiasco* with the map, after all.

Cook, surprisingly, did not join us. "Don't you want to see the device in action?"

Cook settled comfortably in her chair. Well, Mrs. Craig's chair. "Not me," she said. "I know when to leave the dead well enough alone. Unlike Some People."

Dear Reader, I really don't know what she meant by that.

Jessie accompanied us, materializing in the Great Hall like one of Muriel's specters. "I dinnae believe in ghosts," she declared. "But I'd like tae see what that whigmaleerie does. The Laird wuid nivver tell me."

This surprised me. "Uncle Augustus was Investigating the ghosts of Rockfforde Hall. Didn't you know he thought it might be haunted?"

She scoffed. "He heard noises—we all hear *noises*. Auld—"

* A delightful word borrowed inexplicably from Italian, where it means "bottle"

"*Old houses make noise,*" I finished for her, and she smiled faintly.

"Aye. But I nivver thocht he was serious." She paused, hugging her shoulders like she'd felt a chill. "Till noo."

We decided to begin in the Gallery, where I'd first seen Muriel's ghost, and where Uncle Augustus had recorded most of his Disturbances. As I'd predicted, however, the thumping of an army of English and Scottish feet through the corridors of Rockfforde Hall had chased our subjects into hiding. We heard nothing—not a scrape, not a skitter, not the faintest wheeze or whimper or the least hint of a skirl.

"No ghosts so far," Miss Judson Observed.

"It is full o' metal, though," Jessie pointed out helpfully.

"Well, let's move the suit of armor, then," said Mr. Blakeney.

Dear Reader, it turns out that Moving a Suit of Armor is something of an epic endeavor, which was swiftly abandoned as impractical. After chasing down part of a greave that rolled down the corridor and halfway down the stairs,* Mr. Blakeney rapped the wall behind the tapestry. "What's behind here?" he asked. Mr. Blakeney had briefly studied engineering before

---

* Dear Reader, there may have been some Feline Agency involved in the rolling thereof, but you can't make me swear to it. An Alternate Theory of the Crime involves the wayward tail of a dog.

turning to the law, so he brought some structural expertise to this Investigation.

"Naethin," Jessie said. "It's the tower o' the Grreat Hall. That wall gaes tae th' outside."

"I don't think so." Mr. Blakeney rapped again. "Hear that? Hollow." He strode to the adjoining wall, full of windows, and thumped again. The sound was flatter, dead. "That's stone."

"Well, check it, then," I urged, momentarily forgetting that I held the device that did the checking. Gus and I approached the hollow, wooden wall. I handed Gus the probe—which Cook had put on an extra-long extension wire, to make it even more maneuverable—and I managed the controls. "All right, everyone be quiet."

I flipped on the detector, and its happy hum and companionable tick burst to life, rattling away as Gus passed the probe over the walls. He went slowly—slowly enough that the probe found the nails holding the paneling in place—but nothing else. Eventually, he dropped the probe in defeat. "Naethin."

Mr. Blakeney was still inspecting the space, opening doors that revealed solid brick walls, kicking experimentally at the baseboards. Something *thwicked* across the floor beneath his feet, making him jump—almost into the arms of the suit of armor.

"Therre's me brave Englishman," Jessie said with a grin, patting him on the shoulder. "Gus, weel dun. Ye lot've built a full braw mouse detector. But I'm gaun back tae work."

Miss Judson sighed. "I agree. This was a fine effort. Cook will be pleased. Shall we?"

"But . . ." Gus and I stared after them, the metal-but-not-ghost detector still humming away. Why were they giving up so soon? There was an entire castle to Investigate!

"Mr. Blakeney?" I said hopefully, but he gave a shrug.

"'Fraid I'm with Miss J., Stephen. Better luck next time, eh?"

When we didn't join the departing company, Jessie turned back. "Aren't ye comin'?"

Gus hesitated, kicking absently at the floorboards.

His sister marched back up to us. Everyone else had disappeared down the corridor. In the distance, some-where indeterminately overhead, I was still expecting the vague thumping of the ghost. Why had it chosen *now* to be silent?

"The pair o' ye are schemin' somethin'. I can tell," Jessie said. "You fess up right this minute, Edgar Augustus Craig, or I'll have Gran on yer hide faster than Minna on a fox's trrrail."

We actually weren't scheming anything—that I knew about, anyway. Jessie's dark gaze fell on the metal detector, like she wished to smash it to pieces again.

"Why didnae he tell me?" she asked, reaching out to touch its wooden base. "I'd hae luikit wi' him."

Gus snatched the device back. "You gave up on the treasure! Ye nivver believed like the Laird an' me. Did ye ken he was oot searching fir the brooch wi' this, when he died?"

For some reason, Jessie looked to me for confirmation. "I nivver heard that. Aye, he passed on a walk ootbye Castle Dunfyne, but—yer tellin' me he had *that* thing wi' him?"

"That was Muriel's version of events, anyway," I admitted.

Jessie's frown only deepened.

"But weren't you the one—er, who—found him?" I managed to *almost* wind that down before saying something too tactless.

She shook her head. "Nay. Alan—Mr. Balfour did. That's what Gran said, anyway."

Gus's eyes lit up, and I said, "The pieces of the device were with Mr. Balfour's tools." Things were starting to make a bit more sense. First he'd killed Uncle Augustus, then he dismantled the metal detector so that no one would learn what the Laird had discovered. The ugly theories just piled up and up. "Maybe he and Muriel were in it together."

Jessie looked like I'd slapped her. "Nay, he'd never—" but she stopped herself, a hand to her bruised temple.

"I dinnae ken nae more. Naethin' makes sense." She glared at the device, but her expression was far away. "But I cannae believe Alan wuid *hurt* us."

"He and Uncle Augustus quarreled about something," I said. "And there's the money from Fyne Fisheries."

Something made up Jessie's mind. "Bring the whigmaleerie," she ordered. "Gus, fetch a coat. You too, Myrtle."

"Erm, what are we doing?"

Jessie's face was set. "Searching the castle rrruins, of course."

19

D<small>ECERPTÆ</small> D<small>ABUNT</small> O<small>DOREM</small>

Be not quick to dismiss the local knowledge and
methods of your staff. There is likely an excellent reason certain things have always been done
a certain way, and woe betide the outsider who
attempts to impose "improvements" upon the
system.

–A Country Gentlewoman's Guide to Estate
Management

To my vast surprise, Miss Judson did not immediately
put a stop to this expedition. It was probably because
Jessie didn't let us notify the others of our plans. A
reluctant Minna accompanied us, hanging her head
the whole way, and I spotted two Disturbances in the
underbrush that would have borne a striking similarity
to Peony and Calpurrnia had I got a better look.

"What about the—er, killer?" Gus glanced about

anxiously, pale hair aflutter. "Miss Judson said to stay at Rockfforde . . ."

But Jessie didn't pause to answer his excellent question either.

I told myself that I had wholly exonerated Jessie from any suspicion, and that it was a good thing she'd brought her shotgun along—for *protection*—and that she *certainly* wouldn't do anything awful to me while her little brother was there to witness it. But the thick trees and eerie silence of Dunfyne's woods—not to mention the Ghost Detector toted by Gus—weren't exactly reassuring. I pressed close to him, as if he'd offer any protection against lone murderers, Carnivorous Deer, Mr. Balfour, or any of the other dangers lurking outside the dubious safety of the castle.

Soon enough, however, we heard the roar of Rockfforde Falls in the distance, and then the aged stones of Castle Dunfyne emerged from the woods. Heaps of grey stone rose from hummocks of brilliant green earth, rough edges frosted with lichen. There was no trace of the fog that had trapped Jessie here the other night. Sunlight streamed through the trees, dappling the stones with drops of gold.

Jessie was grimmer than ever, looking about the ruins with a closed, set face. I doubted she'd completely recovered from her attack, though she refused to betray any sign of injury. She reminded me of another Judson of my acquaintance, in fact. She hitched her shotgun higher on her shoulder. "Let's snap tae it, then. Does tha' thing work, or nay?"

Silently, I switched on the detector, and Gus once again took the probe. The slantwise sunlight and dramatic shadows made it hard to see well, but out here in the nail- and armor-less outdoors, we ran into fewer false leads.

We ran into no leads, in fact. We crept all through the ragged old castle grounds, but whatever Uncle Augustus had come here to find, it was either too well concealed, or it was gone.

Minna gave a restive whine, pressing against Jessie's leg. Jessie soothed her, stroking her black ears and murmuring Scots phrases I couldn't understand.

According to Muriel, there'd been a battle here, in which Angus MacJudd had lost the Clan Brooch, giving rise to the curse and the rumors and hauntings. Although naturally I didn't give any credence to such things, there was a quality in the twilight atmosphere of this remote ruin that made the *idea* of ghosts appealing. You could almost imagine the spectral defenders of Dunfyne Island still waging their ghostly battle. Were those defenders here now—and what were they defending against?

I rubbed at the edge of the detector's base, pondering the incidents and their targets. Jessie was attacked here in the ruins. Nobody would consider *her* a threat to Dunfyne Island and Rockfforde Hall. Her every waking thought was how to preserve the estate for future generations of MacJudds. It was outsiders we were worried about. Who were they? And what did they want?

Scaring everyone off Dunfyne was the obvious answer. Well, that or simply *killing* everybody—although scaring was a far less risky approach. There were two obvious camps: the people who wanted to sell the island to Fyne Fisheries, and those who wanted to clear the island so they could find the treasure.

What if those competing interests were, in fact, the *same* interest? Mr. Macewan had seemed interested in both fates for Dunfyne. Nobody wanted to prove the existence of the treasure more. But he was also the person orchestrating the sale to Fyne Fisheries. Unless Mr. Macewan hoped to scare everyone *but* Fyne Fisheries off the island, in the hopes of peace and quiet to search for the treasure by himself.

In which case, Mr. Macewan was an even bigger fool than everybody said, because there could hardly be a less peace-and-quiet scenario than building a massive fish factory on the island.

I continued this useless circle of thoughts as I followed Gus and Jessie through the ruins, holding fast to the detector. Portable it might be; convenient it was not. Its steady unrelenting ticking had grown monotonous, like the endless buzz of midges. Peony prowled aloft, trotting from stone to stone, tail curved low behind her. Calpurrnia pursued her Investigation with a more philosophical approach, locating a sunbeam striking a flat patch of wall and sprawling atop it, dappled flank soaking up the dappled sun.

Gus led us deep into the maze of the ruins, and as we came round the next corner, the sun went into hiding. As clouds passed overhead, the temperature dipped sharply, and I hunched into my coat. It was suddenly eerie and disorienting, a maze in true, and I lost track of where we were. It was all too easy to see how Jessie might have been lured to her doom.

Abruptly, the steady clicking stopped. Heavy silence pressed in around us, until Jessie cried, "Aye, what is it, then? Is it the brooch?" Her voice was high and tight.

Heart clattering with excitement, I crept closer as Gus waved the probe about, pinpointing the object. It was something in the earth.

"Here, clear off, will ye?" Jessie nudged us aside and fell to her knees, scrabbling in the grass. She let out a little gasp.

"Did you find it?" I held my breath—I couldn't bite my fingernails, gripping the detector for dear life.

But Jessie held up something far less ancient and venerable than a priceless bejeweled clan chief's brooch.

"A whistle?" I asked. It was small and shiny, like it had been dropped yesterday. Jessie put it to her lips for a test blow, and it emitted a lovely, trilling sort of note. "A birdcall!"

Gus didn't find it lovely at all. His grey eyes stood out huge in his pale face, and he shoved his hair away from his eyes.

"What's the matter?"

Jessie answered for him. "That's a curlew," she said quietly, and icy fingers gripped my chest.

I flicked the metal detector's switch off. "You were lured here by a curlew," I reminded them unnecessarily.

"An' Fitz heard one last night." Jessie just kept staring at the little silver birdcall in her hand.

"Jess?" Gus nudged her, and she finally looked up, grey eyes stricken.

"This belongs to Alan Balfour."

Now we *all* stared at the birdcall, hearts sinking. Even Peony joined in with a mournful little "*No*," and Minna looked positively miserable. (Calpurrnia gave all appearances of being asleep, but I'm sure, in her own way, she was crushed.)

"How cuid he?" Jessie said. "*Alan?* Hit me on th' heid wi' a *rock*? I willnae believe it!" Except she looked very much like she definitely believed it. I hadn't realized how much *I* didn't want it to be true.

"Wait—" I interjected. "If this was used to lure you here a few days ago, and then someone used it again last night to distract Lt. Smoot back at Rockfforde Hall"—so *he* said, anyway—"then how did it get all the way back here?"

Gus glanced up. "He came back for something!"

Now Jessie was keen, too. "Which means we can track him. Minna!" Snapping her fingers, she called the dog over—who seemed all too relieved to be given a task only she could perform.

Gus was Not Relieved. He grabbed Jessie's arm. "What're ye doin'? He nearly killed ye!"

She jerked away, dangling the birdcall for Minna. "Aye, an' he owes me an explanation fir that." In that moment, she reminded me very much indeed of her cousin, my governess. Evidently the Judd blood runs deep.

I was torn. Gus was right: this was a wildly risky endeavor. On the other hand, it was the first clue we'd uncovered so far pointing directly to whoever was behind the mysteries plaguing Rockfforde Hall, Mr. Macewan's murder, and Uncle Augustus's death. "Can she really track that?"

"Minna's the best," Jessie said with obvious pride. "But metal's nae the best material fir scent. Still, if aebody kin do it, it's this lass."

Indeed, Minna seemed confident. She snuffled greedily at the birdcall, well knowing her work. And then, with what I swear was a nod to the rest of us, she was off, nose to the soft green earth, tail like a beacon above her.

"There ought to be a whole pack," Gus whispered as we trailed behind. "She'll lose the scent after a bit and need to rest. The others would take over."

{ 269

I wondered wistfully if we might count on Peony and Calpurrnia to take over, but it hardly bore mentioning.

Jessie knew this, of course, but she seemed so single-mindedly bent on proving Alan Balfour's duplicity that she'd abandoned common sense and training. It was apparent that, shotgun or not, Gus and I would need to be the ones to protect Jessie—from herself.

Despite Gus's dire predictions, Minna did not lose the scent. Nor did she slow down. She was a practiced huntress, going no more swiftly than her human handler could follow, trotting along with her own single-minded determination, until it was hard to distinguish hound from mistress.

"Aye, lass, there ye be," Jessie murmured approvingly as we raced along over hill and over dale.

"Over ben and over glen," Gus corrected cheerfully.

In fact, Minna was so focused on her work that after a while even Jessie's skepticism returned. "There cannae be tha' much scent," she said. "Somethin's wrong. Hold up, lass." She tried to distract the hound, catching hold of her collar, but Minna pulled away, dead certain she was on the right track.

Except the track didn't make any sense. Even a novice like me could tell that. Minna led us not just over ben, glen, hill, dale, brae, and muir,* but in between bushes, crashing through brambles, backtracking,

* This geographic term isn't confusing at all; in Scots it means a moor; in Gaelic, the sea.

skewing wide, looping round our own trail. It was the landscape equivalent of finding a room in Rockfforde Hall.

Finally, when we passed the same stunted shrub with orange catkins for the third time, Jessie called a stop. A confused Minna collapsed to the earth, sides heaving, whining in distress. Jessie offered her the birdcall again, but Minna no longer seemed interested.

Jessie swore under her breath. "She's on anither scent!" Slipping the birdcall into her jacket pocket, she stomped off into the underbrush, making an unholy racket. I looked to Gus, and he shrugged.

Peony encouraged Minna, delicately washing her weary nose. Minna returned the gesture, utterly smothering Peony's "*No!*" with her sloppy pink tongue.

Minna had led us well off the beaten track. We were deep in a copse of trees and shrubs, and the light had all but left us. Even the midges had gone silent. I edged closer to Gus, wondering what was taking Jessie (and her shotgun) so long. "Where are we?" I asked—and my voice sounded frightfully loud.

He gave his jerky shrug. "Dinnae ken. Jess?" But his call was barely a murmur. I felt the same strange urge toward silence. Instinctively, we two lone small humans took another step closer to each other, until we were nearly touching back to back. After our mad route through the brush, it was too quiet. Every sound was too loud, too close. Something *huffed* in the brush, and I spun my head round, sure the Carnivorous Deer had stalked us here to our deaths. Wasn't that one of them, whickering at us now?

Finally, the unholy racket crashed toward us, and a reassuringly angry Jessie stomped into view, still swearing. "I *kent* it," she muttered, and I Observed that she was toting a dirty burlap sack. A dirty, *smelly* burlap sack.

Minna perked up her head, thumped her tail, and howled with triumph—clearly Foxhound for *"Ye've found it! Guid human."*

"Ugh, what is that?" I demanded, guarding my nose with the back of my hand.

Jessie started to open it, but I waved her to stop. I wasn't *that* curious. "Fish," she said. "Herring. It's an auld poacher's trick. Ye drag a bag o' this through the covert tae mislead th' hounds. D—ed Kirkpatrick!"

I stared at her. "Wait—that's *real*? Red herring is a real thing?"

"Aye," she said. "What d'ye ken aboot it?"

But I didn't have a chance to answer. I opened my mouth to reply, and a hand clamped over it, stifling my voice and my breath.

20
FURTH FORTUNE AND
FILL THE FETTERS

Be certain to keep track of all the keys to your property.

–A Country Gentlewoman's Guide to Estate Management

The next thing I remember, I was shaking a dirty, smelly burlap sack (not the same one from the fish, thank goodness) from my head and saw that Gus was doing the same. The ugly scent wouldn't leave my mouth. Our hands were bound, and we were indoors. We were indoors somewhere rather *nice*. A fire roared in a huge stone hearth guarded by carved Classical Nudes, and Gus and I sat upon a furry white rug. I scrambled to the side when I realized the rug had a *head*, and it was definitely angry.

"Where are we?" I squeaked, and Gus shook his

head frantically—but to tell me he didn't know, or to silence me? And then I looked past him and squeaked again. Jessie lay unconscious on the floor, a needle-point cushion beneath her cheek. Flailing in a most Unladylike way, I managed to get my knees under me and shuffled over to her. "Jessie!" I nudged her with my bound hands, and she groaned, shifting over and blinking at me.

"Where's Minna?" She slowly rolled to sitting. "Och—wherr'rre *we*? What's that smell?" Her face drained of color as she took in our surroundings, and I worried she might be sick from her second head injury this week. "Up, up, *up!*" She struggled to her feet—her hands were tied behind her back—and somehow man-aged to drag me to standing, as well.

"What is it?" Our situation was hardly ideal, but Jessie's reaction verged on panic. Then I understood. "You know where we are."

"Aye." Her grey eyes darted round the room. "Roan Kirkpatrick's lodge."

Gus let out a gasp. "He kidnapped you!"

"And *us*," I noted.

"Hush ye," Jessie said. "We maun git awa' afore he comes back." In her fear, her Scots was getting fiercer. It gave me strength, and I surged across the room, toward a door.

"Nae tha' one!" Jessie cried. "Try a window."

But the huge Kirkpatrick Lodge windows had

sashes that slid up and down, not casements that swung outward, and we could not work them with our hands tied. Outside it was full dark, cold blue night shining through the thick glass. Gus was eerily silent, and Jessie growled with frustration, kicking helplessly at the wall.

I wove back through the firelit room. The elaborately carved door was unlocked and swung freely at my touch, revealing an antechamber with a tile floor, a staircase, and two other doors leading off it. I tiptoed to each in turn, but one was locked fast and the other shifted in its frame but wouldn't open.

"Locked?" Jessie guessed.

"Blocked," I mumbled, trying to push it open with my shoulder. The foul miasma from the burlap still clung to my nose and face, and I held my breath. The door shifted a fraction of an inch before it would move no more. "There's something in the way."

Jessie and Gus joined me, and together we managed to shove the obstacle far enough aside to peer through the gap in the door and see what blocked our path.

Jessie let out a scream—a screamlette—hastily stifled, and herded us back into the room with the bearskin rug and fireplace.

"What—what was that?" Gus's voice was high and shrill.

Jessie had gone even paler, reddish hair falling all around her face as she wrestled our door shut again. "That," she said clearly and crisply, in a perfect echo of

Miss Judson, "was Roan Kirkpatrick. An' it luiks like he's been dead fir days."

Dear Reader, I was actually surprised. I blame the bump on my head I could not remember receiving for my failure to immediately recognize the telltale odor, or correctly gauge the weight on the opposite side of the door. But mostly I was genuinely dumbfounded to discover that the man we'd been certain was behind the schemes plaguing Dunfyne Island had, in all likelihood, been dead this entire time.

My first instinct was to tell Miss Judson.

Which meant we had to get back to Rockfforde Hall with all due haste—which meant freeing ourselves from our current dilemma. We clustered at the center of the room, well away from the angry rug, to confer.

"How did we get here, exactly?" I said. "I don't remember anything."

Jessie winced. "Ah do. But nae who took us."

"One person couldn't kidnap all three of us," Gus pointed out.

"Then . . . Muriel and Balfour?" I reasoned. Something about that still didn't feel right. "And what happened to Minna and Peony and Calpurrnia—and your gun?"

"An' why?" asked Jessie. "Juist so we cuid find Kirkpatrick's corpse? That maks nae sense."

"I don't know, but that herring—it was meant to lure us into the ambush."

"Aye," Jessie said. "But *why?*"

I tried to imagine what Miss Judson would do in this situation. "Instead of standing about speculating, let's work on getting out of here. Jessie, do you have a knife?"

"Like a sgian dubh?" she said bitterly. "Aye, I *did*. Kin ye find it in me pockets?"

I managed a fumbling, two-handed search that uncovered an impressive array of sensible *graith*: shotgun shells, vestas, twine, specks of dried herring—"Tha's fir th' hunds"—a stale bannock, and her fluorspar pendant. But no knife.

"There maun be something we can use here, somewhere." Gus launched a search. We spread out through the den, Jessie scouring the walls and shelves. I took the fireplace end, and Gus examined the contents of a stately desk.

My examination turned up nothing useful, just a dusting of ash on the hearth that Peony would have devoured in an instant, and a set of (pretty but disappointingly unsharpened) fireplace tools, handles shaped like pinecones. I felt a stab of regret that Mr. Kirkpatrick—a man I hadn't even known and had considered something of a scoundrel—would never use them again.

Although *somebody* had used them—and not long ago. I was unfamiliar with the precise thermodynamics of Scottish fuel, versus the coal we used back home, but I judged the fire to have been burning for some time now, as it had caught the largest logs. But had the person who'd set the fire done so and then vanished? Or done so and *stayed*? They'd not have bothered to light a fire if they intended to kill us. I hoped.

"I've got something," Gus called.

I scurried over. "Something to free us with?"

"Oh," he said. "No—papers about Rockfforde Hall. There's a map, and this is some kind of survey . . ." He looked up. "Why would Mr. Kirkpatrick have these? An' look—" Prodding papers aside, he revealed a familiar booklet, tree stump crest on the cover. Mr. Macewan's history of Clan MacEwen! This copy had been read cover to cover, dog-eared and underlined and, at some point, apparently gone for a swim in the loch.

Facts spun in my brain and *almost* came together. The metal detector. The lost brooch. Mr. Macewan's boots. The riddle and the old books and the traps in the forest.

"Buzzards," I whispered. The buzzards circling around Rockfforde Hall—Uncle Augustus had seen them, *felt* them. And they weren't ghosts. They had a very mortal explanation, but I still couldn't make the pieces fit. I gave the documents a closer look. The survey was from a firm in Glasgow, and included a list of Dunfyne Island's assets. But the map—

A small, faintly musical crack from beside us—along with a splash—drew our attention to Jessie, standing at the corner of the desk, where a moment before had been a lovely crystal decanter of amber-colored liquor. "Oh, dear," she said flatly. "How did tha' happen. Wuid one of ye neeps* mind usin' a piece o' that glass tae cut me ootae this blessed rope?"

Dear Reader, contrary to fanciful penny dreadful accounts, cutting through a rope with a shard of fractured whisky decanter takes an absolute age, particularly when the people doing the cutting are trying to be exceptionally careful, and the person being freed is twitchy with impatience. But finally we had the ropes loose enough for Jessie to wriggle out of her restraints. As she turned to release her brother, I puzzled over the latest development in the case.

We'd *seen* Mr. Kirkpatrick leave the island—yet he'd clearly returned at some point. Had he brought Mr. Macewan over, perhaps even killed him? And then been killed *himself*? But by whom?

Maybe his papers held a clue. The survey covered the grand bits of the estate someone might want to buy: the waterfall, the ruins, the natural harbor, the kennels and stables and workshops adjacent to Rockfforde Hall. But Mr. Kirkpatrick's map of the Hall was crude, hastily sketched, pointing out a strange configuration of mismatched rooms: the Thistle Room where Miss Judson and I had been staying, the tower of the Great

* Turnips. And no, I'm not certain whether this is actually a Scottish insult, or just unique to Jessie.

Hall, the closed-off wing with the damaged roof. "Why would anyone—" I halted suddenly.

"What?" Jessie hissed. "Why wuid aebody *what?*"

"I heard voices. I think somebody's here."

That statement acted like a riding crop. "Tae the window, lad." Jessie gave her brother a push, and went to collect the fireplace poker. Just before she could give the window a mighty thwack to free us, I said:

"Wait."

Two dumbfounded Craig heads turned to stare at me.

"I want to know who it is. What they're saying."

"I wat they're sayin' how they mean tae kill us," Jessie said.

"They could have done that when they found us," I pointed out—in retrospect, probably not reassuringly. I crept toward the doorway. A heartbeat later, I felt Jessie and Gus join me.

Gradually, the voices sorted themselves into two parties, male and female.

"Muriel?" I whispered, but Jessie shushed me.

"I tell ye, it's still bleedin'," groused the man. "I dinnae even ken which o' them bit me—the dog or the lass."

"Guid hund, Minna," Jessie murmured, as Gus stifled a snort.

"Stop haverin' on like me nan," the female voice said. "We've mair pressin' issues! Like the parcels ye left in the fireroom, aye?"

"What else was I gaun do? Let 'em get awa'?"

I barely recognized Muriel's voice, and the man's didn't seem familiar at all.

"They willnae be a problem once we get back to the Haugh," she said. "Aw will be taken care of."

"Taken care of? Like Kirkpatrick, ye mean? That lad's fair mad, he is. Belongs in Woodilee, if ye ask me."

Jessie and Gus listened grimly, and I wanted to ask if they knew the voices, but I daren't miss any of the conversation.

"I'm sorry I let ye talk me intae this," the man said. "Come noo, Mur, let's gae on ootae 'ere, while we still can. It's nae too late."

"I've put too much wark intae this. I'm nae givin' oop!"

"An' who d'ye think ye be, Lady Macbeth? He's gaun mak a queen o' ye, aye, wi' aw his grand claims? Grow up, Mur, an' see what's full gaun on! Yer *drenched* in bluid, an' ye'll nivver come clean o' it."

"I'd nae talk. Yer haunds bint clean neither. I've seen what ye keep in tha' boat o' yers, yer special deliveries, aye?"

"Well, I've nae signed on fir murther. I brought what ye asked fir, but count me oot whativver ye twa're planning next." A chair scraped—whereupon Jessie seized Gus and me each by the shoulder and hauled us toward the window.

It yielded readily now that we had thumbs to undo

{ 281

the latch, and Jessie wasted no time lifting Gus down before I scrambled over the sill, into the waiting paws of Minna, Peony, and Calpurrnia. Minna wriggled with relief, slashing the air with her frantic tail. I grabbed Peony, but Calpurrnia vanished into the trees.

"Bonnie, bonnie lass," Jessie cooed. After snuffling every inch of her mistress, Minna bounded into the trees, returning triumphantly with a somewhat battered and slobbery leather bag.

My satchel! "Guid hund!" Her tail flew with pride, even as she snuffled ravenously at the flap, hoping I had herring stashed within.

"Hame, lass," said Jessie. Minna knew this command too, and took off across the broad lawn. A huge moon shone, nearly full, and anyone spying out a Kirkpatrick Lodge window would instantly spot us scrambling for escape. I cast one last backward glance. The stately brick building sat respectably in a grove of trees. A horse stood tethered to a hitching post, a red jacket draped beside it. But Jessie shepherded us along too fast for me to see if it was a red hunting coat—or a soldier's uniform.

We plunged into the fringe of trees, and right now I would take the Carnivorous Deer (and/or carnivorous flowers), or Jacobite ghosts or ghost Jacobites, or any other dangers besides the killers whose clutches we'd just escaped. Minna tried to pull us back to the broad, open lawn, but Jessie kept to the cover of the wood, speeding onward as twigs and branches thwacked past our faces, and clouds of midges swarmed in our path.

"How far are we from Rockfforde?" I spat, sure I'd swallowed a midge. Or sixty. Wildly, I wondered what the Proper Etiquette for removing a midge from your mouth would be. Mrs. Craig probably knew.

Gus was doing his best to keep up. "Close." His voice was faint. "Jess has a shortcut."

"Watch out for traps," I muttered.

Although fleeing for our lives was the top priority at the moment, I managed to pepper them with questions. "That *was* Muriel," I said. "Was that Balfour with her?"

"Nay," Jessie said, with finality.

"Maybe it was that gillie, Donal."

Gus said, "Nay, he left wi'—"

"Wi' Kirkpatrick?" Jessie finished. "Probably has a sgian dubh stuck in *his* back noo, too, then."

I hadn't gotten a good enough look at the body to tell how Mr. Kirkpatrick had been dispatched, but apparently Jessie had seen plenty. That did seem the fate of all who interfered with the buzzards' plans.

"Why lure us into a kidnapping?" I said. "Muriel sounded like we weren't part of her plan. And how could they have known we'd be *right there*, anyway?"

"I wat we juist stumbled on somethin' we weren't meant tae see," Jessie said.

"The buzzards' nest," I said.

She stopped short, and I nearly thunked into her. "Why dae ye keep sayin' that?"

"It's what Uncle Augustus said—well, wrote—about feeling his enemies moving in. Why?" I asked. "Does it mean something to you?"

"Nay, it's naething." A moment later she decided to tell me. "The buzzard in the stables, wi' th' injured wing? She was shot. Wi' an arrow."

I shuddered. "That's awful."

"Aye, an' there's nae reason for it, either, except plain cruelty."

"Myrtle!" Gus cried suddenly, making me spin round in alarm. "The ghost detector—where is it?"

I gaped at him, ridiculously patting myself down, as if I'd somehow shoved the entire bulky device, along with its probe and batteries and miles of wiring, into my dress and not realized it. My first thought was how disappointed Cook would be that I'd lost it.

My second thought was *slightly* more productive.

"Red herrings," I said, heart banging with excitement. And exertion. "That's exactly it. We've been led astray this whole time!"

"I dinnae understand," Gus said.

We'd made it back to familiar territory. I could make out the shadow of Rockfforde Hall's great felled tree stump. Minna, spirits renewed, lifted her tail and trotted gratefully into her own yard. Peony squirmed away from me, and Calpurrnia lay asleep on the stump as if she'd been waiting there for hours.

Predictably, everyone at Rockfforde Hall had turned out for our inauspicious return, and Miss Judson and Mrs. Craig waited in the lamplit doorway, arm in arm and wearing identical dangerous expressions.

"And just where," Miss Judson Inquired, "have you three been all this time?"

21

LATE BUT IN EARNEST

> The animals in your care—be they pets, livestock,
> game, or wildlife—are as vital a part of your house-
> hold as its people.
>
> *A Country Gentlewoman's Guide to Estate*
> *Management*

There was no sense trying to tell Miss Judson that the
Expedition to the ruins had been Jessie's idea. She had
far too much experience to believe such a tale. Even
when we shared the news of Mr. Kirkpatrick's untimely
demise, she wasn't reassured. (Upon reflection, yet
another murder in the span of the few days we'd been
on Dunfyne Island might *not* put one's mind at ease.)
We were back in the Small Dining Room, which was
even spookier and more cavernous by night. A single
eerie candle flickered from the bronze flanks of the
stag statuettes, and I could have done with a fluorspar
lamp just then.

"We'll send a party over to Investigate as soon as

it's convenient," Miss Judson said. We all knew that by "convenient," she meant *safe*. "Do you care to proffer a defense for disobeying the prime directive laid down for everyone at Rockfforde Hall?"

Since the prime directive was Do Not Go Anywhere Alone, and we hadn't, I didn't bother. "Well," I said instead, "the good news is that we haven't been *murdered*."

Miss Judson tapped her fingers on her elbow. "So far," she Observed ominously. "Dare I ask what the bad news is?"

I turned my toe against the rug, looking to Gus and Jessie for support. But evidently the siblings had decided to sacrifice me to the jury. "We might have got a bit . . . kidnapped."

"Kidnapped! Oh, *mon dieu!*" A rapid string of French words unsuitable for publication followed.

"But look—we got free. And I think I've figured everything out!"

"You didnae tell me that!" Gus looked wounded.

"Well, not *everything*," I admitted. "But once we find The Ghosts, we'll know even more."

"This afternoon's inconclusive experiments notwithstanding." Miss Judson was unmoved. "I see you have returned without the so-called Ghost Detector. How, may I ask, do you propose accomplishing this discovery without your equipment?"

"Because they're not *real* ghosts," I said, adding—as

if there were any doubt—"obviously. And its real value was as a metal detector all along. I don't think they meant to kidnap us—they just wanted the device."

Jessie, rubbing her wrists, looked skeptical.

But Gus was keen. "For the treasure?"

Minna, during all of this, had returned her attentions to my bag, until I grew impatient and shucked it off my shoulder. "I don't have any herring." But she refused to believe me, pawing at the leather and giving us all beseeching looks.

"The metal detector?" Cook prompted.

"Er," put in Mr. Blakeney, "I know I'm new here, but isn't this latest murder rather the priority?"

"It's nae the latest murrderr," said Jessie. "It's the first murder."

"Second," I corrected. Well, we didn't actually know whether Mr. Macewan or Mr. Kirkpatrick had been killed first, come to think of it. "Oh—I mean third."

"Third!" Mrs. Craig wailed. "Wha' was the *fairst*?"

"Uncle Augustus," I said.

"*What?*" cried Mrs. Craig.

Jessie turned white, sinking onto a chair. "The Laird? Nay, he wasn't—was he? How?"

Her reaction surprised me—wasn't she the one who'd implied his death was related to the attacks on Rockfforde Hall? Thinking back, though, I might have misinterpreted her remarks. But, to be fair, she was keeping her own secrets.

Indeed, they were *all* giving me looks of wide-eyed disbelief, shaking their heads. "Nay, lassie," Mac said gently. "It were juist his heart. Saw a surgeon in Glasgow, an' there was naething they could do."

Mrs. Craig nodded grimly, confirming this report. "That were aboot the time the odd things started happening," she recalled. "An' the Laird began—I dinnae ken, prepairring, ye might say."

Miss Judson stepped in. "Like making a new will? And selling off part of the estate?" When Mac and Mrs. Craig nodded, she too sank heavily into a seat (she had to move Calpurrnia, who'd fallen asleep again). "It seems we jumped to conclusions."

Some of Jessie's color returned, flaming her cheeks. "*Tha's* why ye came, then? Becaws ye thocht the Laird was murrderred? Why didnae ye juist *ask* one of us?"

"Well, no one was particularly forthcoming," Miss Judson said.

Jessie sighed. "Ach, aye, that's true enew."

Relieved as I was to learn that the beloved Laird had died just as peacefully as Mr. Macewan had claimed (and not electrocuted by a metal detector—yet another yarn spun by Muriel to throw us off the scent), it only deepened the other mysteries.

"Someone *did* murder Mr. Macewan and Mr. Kirkpatrick, though," I said. "But in what order? And was it the same culprit?"

"Or culprits," Miss Judson said. "One or more

suspects united in a single criminal enterprise seems more likely."

Gus, Jessie, and I related our Observations of the crime scene, including the documents Gus found in Mr. Kirkpatrick's desk.

"Somebody was very keen to make everyone think Rockfforde Hall was haunted," I said. "Or to make Uncle Augustus believe it." And who had appeared in his notes about nearly every incident? Muriel, the superstitious housemaid.

"Buzzards," Jessie said thoughtfully. "But naebody wi' any sense believed those tales. If what ye say is true, even the Laird was skeptical."

"Which is why they had to raise the stakes—that's when the vandalism began. If they couldn't scare you off the island with superstition, then they'd do it with real threats."

"But *why*?" said Mac. "Why gae tae all the trouble, then? Just fir an auld bauble wi' a tale o' its ain attached? Right daft, that."

"Not everybody thought it was daft," I said. "Mr. Macewan believed it—and he convinced somebody else too. They had his book at Kirkpatrick's, and it looked like they'd been studying it. And not just for the treasure, but for all the history. *Minna!*" I wailed, as the silly hound had *still* not abandoned her plaintive attack on my satchel.

In frustration, I plopped it onto the table and

started digging through it. "There's nothing in here—" And then my fingers closed on Something. I yanked it out, nearly as excited as Minna, who let out a very lady-like bark and dived into my lap to retrieve her prize.

Everyone watched this unfold. Jessie rose slowly, fishing in her jacket pocket until she retrieved the bird-call. "Min—" She whistled to get the dog's attention. Minna, nose buried in the battered tweed cap of Donal Airlie, Mr. Kirkpatrick's gillie, glanced up, sniffed once at the birdcall, then thumped her tail happily in confirmation. Jessie just stared.

"What's this mean?" Mrs. Craig spoke up quietly. "Whose hat is that, lass?"

It wasn't clear if she was asking me or Jessie—or even Minna—but I let someone else answer. "Gus?" My friend had been sitting quietly all this time, hunched into his jacket and looking pensive. I wanted to tell him I was sorry I'd thought Uncle Augustus had been murdered.

He started out of his thoughts. "I told Myrtle it belonged to Donal."

"Donal—Airlie?" Mac shifted in his seat by the fireplace, his expression unreadable.

"We need a chart," Mr. Blakeney broke in cheerfully. "It's like a football scrummage—new players keep being added."

"Don't we ever," said Cook.

I turned to Jessie. "Could Donal have been the man

with Muriel? The one who—planted the herring?" I managed to change course before saying, "who kidnapped us," and reminding Miss Judson that we were in trouble. "Did it sound like his voice?"

"I cannae say," Jessie admitted. "What wuid they be doin' mixed up in such a scheme anyway?"

"Aye was a dreamer, that lad," Mac put in. "Ye remember, Catriona, when Donal were a bairn, and Bess filled up his head wi' tales o' the auld clans?"

She was nodding. "Aye, and if that rogue Macewan gave 'im an earful, he'd've latched on for sure."

That sounded plausible. We all knew how eager Mr. Macewan was to share his interest in clan history with anyone who would listen. And it seemed that Mr. Kirkpatrick's gillie was keener than most.

Gus broke in. "Donal used to tell me that he was really descended from a clan chief, and someday he'd get his rightful inheritance."

"The *MacJudd* clan chief?" Miss Judson looked alarmed. "Could there be any truth to that?"

"Ach, nay." Mrs. Craig was instantly dismissive. "His faither was a nae-guid poacher wha' ran off when he were a bairn, leavin' him and his mam tae starve, 'til they were took in by the Laird. Bess juist didnae want him tae ken the truth."

Gus disagreed. "His nan told him his father was *really* the son of a great Laird, but he'd had to marry in secret because his mam was lowly. It *could* be true," he insisted. "I asked the Laird once, and he said such things happened."

Miss Judson, Mrs. Craig, and I shared an uneasy Look. Was it possible—?

"Catriona." Miss Judson's voice was soft but firm, and Mrs. Craig took a long breath, looking at nobody. Then she reached out her hands and drew her grandchildren to her. Candlelight flickered across their pale faces, their worried grey MacJudd eyes.

"It's nae true, Gus," Mrs. Craig said softly. "Or—it's nae true aboot Donal, believe me. I kent Jamie Airlie, and he were no laird's son. But aye, sich things do happen. And the Laird kent it better than aebody—because it happened tae his ain sister." She tilted Jessie's head up. "*Isla.* Your real Gran."

If she'd expected Jessie and Gus to be pleased with this news—that they were really MacJudds in true—she was sorely disappointed. Then again, Jessie had had rather a trying few days.

"How could he nae tell me?" she cried, voice raw. "How could *ye*?"

"It wuid've made nae difference," Mrs. Craig said, but Jessie pulled away.

"It wuid've made *all* the difference! *Everything* wuid be different now! Ach!" She looked like she wanted to hit everything.

For his part, Gus merely looked stunned, drawing more than ever into himself. His wide eyes flicked to mine, and I reached out to take his hand. Fortunately, Peony intervened before I could embarrass myself (or him), bunting him solidly in the head and snuggling into his lap. "*No*," she scolded, adding, "brrrb."

"That's about the only thing anyone's said in the last ten minutes that I understood," said Mr. Blakeney.

Miss Judson made a tentative overture to Jessie. "I'm glad to know it," she said softly. "You're my only family in Britain. I would enjoy having cousins to share Rockfforde with."

Jessie only blinked at her. "Ye dinnae *understand*. Oh, how cuid ye? *That's* what he was on aboot, those last days. *That's* why he—" She took a choking breath. "Alan!"

We stared at her. "What's Mr. Balfour got tae do with aething?" Gus asked, face twisted with confusion.

Jessie flailed. "Dinnae ye see? If I'd only kent! I cuid've stopped him—none o' this wuid've happened!"

I could practically hear the gears clicking in Miss Judson's brain—but this time I beat her there. The love token in Mr. Balfour's desk had never been intended for Muriel. It was meant for someone potentially in a position to sport such fine jewelry one day. And it explained why Mr. Balfour needed money from Fyne Fisheries—£100 would go a fair way toward establishing his ability to support a family. "Were—were you and Mr. Balfour—erm—sweet on each other?"

Jessie managed a hoarse laugh at my awkward

phrasing. "He begged me tae leave wi' him, and the Laird, he—" Her eyes grew wide at the memory. "The Laird accused Alan of stealing Dunfyne's treasure."

She put a hand over her face, realizing at last what Uncle Augustus had meant. What he'd called her. What she'd called *him*. And this time, when Miss Judson put her arms around her, Jessie didn't pull away.

Something still wasn't adding up. With everything Jessie had just confirmed, it was harder than ever to imagine Mr. Balfour behind all the threatening incidents, the hauntings and the vandalism—let alone the murders. Jessie Craig falling in love with someone so villainous was unthinkable. But if Alan Balfour hadn't killed Uncle Augustus, then why had he fled so suddenly, without his belongings?

I picked up the birdcall from where Jessie had dropped it on the table. I couldn't help myself, and gave the little whistle a sniff, wondering what Minna had detected. The birdcall led Minna to Donal's hat, but not before we'd been turned around and led a merry and unproductive chase that brought us straight into the arms of metal-detector-snatching kidnappers.

"Red herring," I muttered, trying to clear my head of the muddle of false scents.

"What's that, Stephen?" Mr. Blakeney scooted closer to me, perhaps relieved to have something to focus on besides distraught Scottish relatives.

"It's Mr. Balfour's birdcall, but it's Donal's hat. We

got the hat in Tighnabruaich—no." My heart gave a thud. "We got it on Lt. Smoot's boat."

Mr. Blakeney nodded agreeably, although he couldn't possibly have followed any of that. It gave me a surge of warmth, and I pressed on, forcing my thoughts to make sense. "Mr. Balfour left all his tools behind. Why would he do that? They belong to him, don't they, not the estate?"

Only Cook and Mr. Blakeney were paying me any mind. The others were enmeshed in the Tearful Reunion of MacJudds. "Aye, lass, so they do," Cook said. "He'd nae leave them if he were off tae a new hoose." Mr. Blakeney and I both stared at her, but did not comment on her adoption of the local *patois*.

"So it's strange he'd leave his birdcall too." I spun it on the table. "Maybe somebody else has been using it." Somebody who had shown a marked dislike for Mr. Macewan—and who, more to the point, had been in the vicinity of *both* birdcall incidents: when Jessie was lured to the ruins *and* when the kennels were smoked—no, *smeeked*—out.

Minna chomped thoughtfully—and noisily—on Donal Airlie's cap. The cap that had last been in the possession of Somebody Else, and which no doubt had *his* scent all over it, too.

Somebody Else whom we had not seen all day, but who claimed to spend his time on the island "patrolling for danger." Had he patrolled right into *us* earlier this afternoon?

"Who're you thinking, then?" Mr. Blakeney said.

"Lt. Smoot," I replied. "He's a soldier who always seems to be in the wrong place at the right time."

"Smoot?" Mr. Blakeney's brow creased. "Fitz-something? I know that name. It was in Mr. Macewan's files."

I pounced on this. "Why? Does he have a criminal record?"

"No." Mr. Blakeney gave me a quizzical look. "Nothing like that—he has a share in Fyne Fisheries—along with your dead Mr. Kirkpatrick. Conceivably, with Kirkpatrick gone, Mr. Smoot could inherit substantial control of their interests."

I sat back, stunned. That was even more than I'd expected to hear. "Smoot has everything," I breathed. "Motive—getting control of the whole island! Means—he's the only person who has a boat, he admitted to knowing how to build the smoke trap in the kennels, and he probably keeps a drawer full of sgian dubhs on that yacht of his! *And* opportunity—he's been right in the vicinity of every single crime: the bag-snatching, the attack on Jessie, the attack on us—he must be the one who grabbed us!" He'd probably been aided and abetted by that horse outside the Kirkpatrick lodge, the one with the *red jacket*. I was half out of my seat with this theory, coming fully formed at last. "He's also the one who told us that Mr. Balfour was gone. They're obviously—*Oh*."

And with that, I thudded back into my seat once more. "Poor Jessie." As the threads spun out, the picture they wove was even darker than I'd first realized. Jessie heard her name and spoke up sharply.

"What aboot Alan an' Fitz? Why 'poor Jessie'?"

Now I looked from her to Miss Judson, unsure which was worse—for her to keep believing Mr. Balfour was the villain who'd attacked her, or for her to learn the truth? I took an uncertain breath. "I—I don't think Mr. Balfour is responsible for all the attacks."

"But ye juist said—"

Miss Judson grabbed Jessie's hand and held fast. Jessie hung on, knuckles turning white.

"What'rre ye saying?" Her voice had gone very soft.

"I don't know anything for sure," I hedged. "But he disappeared so suddenly, and he left all his things behind. He's not sent for them, nor even sent word of where he's ended up. He didn't come back for Uncle Augustus's funeral—and he would have, if just to see you. I don't think he *left*."

My unspoken words sunk in. Jessie shook her head, backing into the wall. "Nay. *Nay*. It cannae be—he cannae be—nay." She took a sobbing breath and covered her face.

Her tears lasted only a moment, however. "I want them," she said, voice low and dark, hands balling into fists. She turned her deadly gaze on me. "Ye better ken where they're hidin'."

I shoved my chair back from the table, the legs stuttering against the carpet. Everyone turned toward me with expectation.

"As a matter of fact," I said, "I do."

22
PETIT ALTA

Old houses make noise.

> *–A Country Gentlewoman's Guide to Estate*
> *Management*

We resumed our Ghost Hunt of Rockfforde Hall as we'd left off the other afternoon. Except now we had two advantages, even without the Ghost Detector. First, it was dark, and we would see the Glowing Specters if they made their appearance. Second, I finally knew what I was really looking for.

While Cook, Mac, and Nelly were taking up defensive posts to watch for escaping buzzards, Gus had gone to the library to fetch the plans for Rockfforde Hall. We spread the page across the enormous Small Dining Table, and Miss Judson held a lamp aloft so we could read it.

"This is what I figured out, back at Mr. Kirkpatrick's." I pointed to the rooms where we—and

Uncle Augustus—had heard the Ghostly Disturbances. "Muriel used these old hidden back corridors to come and go throughout the castle as she pleased—including places nobody's been in years." I drew my finger down the map, stopping at a nook labeled *Garderobe*. I could not help a brief accusatory glance at Mrs. Craig. "This whole wing was blocked off after the last renovation.* It makes a perfect hideout."

"I ken that place," Jessie said. "But ye cannae get tae it anymore, nae since the Grreat Storrm."

Gus agreed. "The Laird always said it was too dangerous—structurally unsound."

"Muriel must have found a way, probably while she was spying on everyone from her service corridors."

"She was rather keen that we stay away from this area," Miss Judson Observed. "It seems she's been orchestrating the entire haunting from inside our very own castle walls."

"They assumed everyone would leave once Uncle Augustus died," I said. "They'd have the whole island to themselves to look for the brooch."

"They?" said Miss Judson.

"Muriel and Lt. Smoot," I replied impatiently. "And maybe Mr. Macewan. He was probably in on the scheme, too. He didn't count on your uncle changing his will—or that you would actually *come* here, and

---

* If you asked me, Improvements should have included more indoor bathrooms, not blocked them off.

bring the rest of us too. They had to try even harder if they wanted to scare *us* off."

But Mr. Macewan must have had second thoughts—that's why he'd sent his map to Miss Judson, far away from the buzzards' clutches. And when his co-conspirators realized he'd backed out of the plan, they'd killed him.

"Just how valuable is this brooch?" asked Mr. Blakeney. "*Really* enough to commit murder? It would practically have to be the Crown Jewels. Or a tiara."*

"It's not enough for one of *us* to kill somebody for," I said. "But those artifacts, that history means a lot to people here. Especially if it would help get their hands on Rockfforde Hall."

Jessie scoffed at this. "Naebody wuid kill for this ol' heap o' stones!"

I met her gaze. "Wouldn't you do almost anything to protect Rockfforde Hall?"

Her return gaze was just as steady. "*Almost* aething." She pushed her bedraggled hair from her eyes. "Enew. Shew us where ye've tracked our quarry to ground."

"Not ground." I traced my finger up the plans—all the way up, up, and up, past the cavernous Great Hall, above the Gallery, and far beyond the reach of

* Mr. Blakeney referred to one of our previous Investigations.

the twining staircase. "Attic. More precisely, the attic of the closed-off wing."

A keen look dawned in Miss Judson's cool eye, and she offered an arm to Mr. Blakeney. "Shall we?" she said, and we set off in search of ghosts.

I led everyone to the dead-end stairs near the Trophy Room. It was a long and eerie walk from the Small Dining Room, through the deserted Great Hall with its monstrous Bird Stump, up the grand staircase hung with weapons, and down the convoluted corridors in the suffocating darkness, illuminated by one lamp and one candle—neither of which offered much in the way of light *or* comfort. I recalled Mrs. Craig's warning upon our arrival: *I dinnae recommend wanderrring aboot efter derk* . . . and found myself pulling closer to Mr. Blakeney.

Everyone clung together, hushed with tense expectation. What if I was wrong about this? I was relying on a lot of supposition and very little hard evidence. But I pushed on. Somewhere in these derk passages were the answers to all of Rockfforde Hall's mysteries. The ghosts were eerily silent, tonight of all nights—because Muriel and Smoot were off hunting for the brooch.

I hoped.

A low moan sighed through the walls, making everyone jump. Fingers clutched my sleeve, and I made no move to shake them off.

"What was that?" somebody whispered.

"Wind," Miss Judson said firmly, though nobody believed her. I glanced about, worried we'd see a flash of fluorspar green. Worried that we *wouldn't*. What was I hoping for, again?

Finally we came to the passage outside the Trophy Room. Moonlight trickled through panes of colored glass, and outside a restless owl called a raspy, lonesome cry to its mate. "Over—" My voice was a creak. I cleared my throat. "Over here."

"This is where the Grey Lady's seen," Gus whispered. His pale hair made him look rather ghostly himself, eyes huge and haunted.

"We're naewhere near the locked wing," Jessie objected.

I glanced to Gus. "Ye cannae get there from here." He giggled—high and nervous. "But you *can*. Look."

The stunted staircase that had baffled me the other day now drew me forward. I ascended the cramped passage, up as many steps as I could before my head was bent down by the low ceiling. Three more steps continued before stopping dead against the blank wall. Only not *exactly* blank: behind the tapestry was a decorative panel of inlaid wood, depicting a roosting bird of prey. A buzzard's nest.* I held the candle to it, as the others milled about for a look.

---

* Jessie, unromantically, later informed me that it's actually a raven.

Gus said, "Oh," just as Mr. Blakeney said, "Ah," and Miss Judson said, "*Et voilà.*" (Peony said "*No,*" but she was outvoted.)

I hoped my next move would not result in an embarrassing anticlimax. Miss Judson held the candle as close as possible while I probed yet another of Rockfforde Hall's secrets. I tapped the edges of the short, narrow wall, pressed into the corners, even tried prying at the almost imperceptible gaps between planks. But nothing happened. Fashed, I scowled at it.

Peony wriggled through to reach two white paws up for a languid scratch, pulling her claws down the buzzard panel in long raw scars.

"Peony!" I yanked her out of the way—and then we both nearly fell backward as the wall went *click* and the panel swung outward, almost hitting us. A set of stairs unfolded themselves, like from a carriage door, revealing a cavity beyond, cramped and dark as the grave.

"Oh my," said Mr. Blakeney.

"Wuid ye luik at that!" It was so rare to hear appreciation in Mrs. Craig's voice, I almost didn't recognize her.

Someone, Mr. Blakeney perhaps, gave a whistle of admiration—and someone else gave a soft but distinct thunk from *inside* the hollow space.

"What was *that*?" Jessie sounded strangled, breathless.

I craned my ears, throat tight. Had Muriel come back?

"The plot thickens," said Mr. Blakeney. "Rap once for yes and twice for no." He knocked sharply on the wall, to an answering knock from deep within—and an answering sharp knock from my heart.

Swiftly, painfully, several things thunked into place. "The ghosts wouldn't be trying to talk to us!" I banged hard on the staircase wall, shouting up the passageway. "Hello? Are you there?"

"Myrtle—"

But Miss Judson's warning was forestalled. *Clunk, clunk, clunk* came the sound of the ghost, followed by an eerie moan. (Actually a rather uncomfortable moan, like someone waking with several dogs on his head.) A streak of black slipped past me, alongside a tottering fluff of mottled brown, as Peony and Calpurrnia vanished together into the hidden passage.

Jessie made a whispered sound, almost a word, hand to her lips. "I cannae bear it . . ." She turned into her grandmother's arms.

"Quick!" I cried. Since everyone else was immobilized with surprise, and since Peony *would* find something in there and eat it, I pushed forward.

Clunk! Clunk! "Maaaooompph!" That, Dear Reader, was the ghost.

"Myrtle—" Miss Judson thought better of it. "Go ahead."

Before she could reconsider, I grabbed Gus by the hand. "Let's get the ghost," I said—and Observed that he was grinning. Jessie made to follow, but Mrs. Craig held her fast. She'd had too many shocks this week already. If we were wrong . . .

"Dinnae be wrong," she said, eyes blazing.

Dear Reader, I had not believed that Rockfforde Hall could possibly get any darker, but it surprised me. All traces of illumination vanished within moments of stepping foot on the first rickety step. "We need a light," I said.

"I've got one." Gus had found something in the darkness. Miss Judson handed up the candle, and I made out the shape in his hands—a familiar contraption (though more securely constructed) of a hunk of fluorspar lashed to the body of an oil lamp. He lit it, letting its eldritch glow fill the stairwell with haunting green light. At his feet, folded neatly, lay a length of finely woven ivory cotton. Mrs. Craig's missing muslin.

The thunking and moaning were growing more urgent, and I heard another much less ghostly sound from the darkness up ahead—a violent metallic clatter, followed by a loud, affronted "Brrrb!"

"That way." I grabbed Gus and urged him after Peony. We squeezed through the snug stairwell into a set of former living quarters, now hopelessly derelict. Faded darkness filtered through boarded-up windows, giving dimension to the space. Once-yellow walls with delicate wainscoting were stained with generations of rain—and other substances—leaking through the collapsed roof, and the surface underfoot went unpleasantly *squish*, a damp carpet of moldered rug, rotting leaves, and rodent droppings.

And in the corner, a heap of old, discarded weapons, and one very put-out cat. She glared at me with green eyes that plainly said, *Why are there so many SWORDS in this place?*

"Look," Gus whispered, holding his green light to the walls. "The Jacobite rose!" The wainscoting had been molded into curlicues surrounding a six-petaled rose, secret symbol of the uprising. "This must be from Angus MacJudd's time—some kind of hidden parlor for them to meet."

"He didn't hide his brooch here, though," I said. "Or Muriel would have found it by now." Indeed, the buzzards had been hard at work combing through the wreckage. Old furniture had been systematically dismantled, plaster walls torn open to search their hollow interiors, carpets pulled away from corners to uncover potential cavities in the floorboards.

And all of it scraping, rattling, and clunking through the walls to the rest of Rockffforde Hall. "She used the existing ghost stories to cover their work in here!" I continued. "And to make it more believable, they built that lamp, to mak sikkar Uncle Augustus actually *saw* a ghost."

"He didnae really believe, though." Gus—in the role of ghost, eerie green lamp flickering off his pale hair and slight form—looked around, expression unreadable.

"No. And he died before he could figure out what was really going on."

As if to punctuate our conclusions, a voice groaned out, *"Moooophh!"*

Gus clutched my arm, and I let out a brief hysterical laugh.

"No," Peony scolded.

"Ahem. Quite." I smoothed down my skirts, waiting for my heart to stop clattering. "Hello?" I called out. "Where are you? Say something if you can hear me."

"Mmmmupph!" *Clunkclunk.*

"Brrrb!"

Gus, face set, held up the lamp. "That way."

We crossed the Jacobite parlor, through an arched doorway (the door itself having long since vanished), and into a smaller sitting room. Well, whatever it had once been, it was a sitting room *now*. Waiting politely in a dark corner, well away from exterior walls where a cry for help might be heard, knees drawn to his chest and ropes about his ankles, was a gentleman in a dusty brown suit—with a burlap bag over his head that a cat was chewing on.

"Oh. Hello." Gus stopped short and I nearly ran into him. I eased my way past to shoo Peony aside and whisk the bag from the poor man's head. Lucky him—*his* bag was clean. More or less.

A pale face, round and sparsely bearded with a shaggy moustache, blinked back at me.

"Mr. Balfour!" Gus cried, rushing forward. I'd expected it, but still felt a shock of surprise and—well, not exactly recognition. It was really him. *Not* dead, *not* a ghost, but a prisoner. Right here in Rockfforde Hall, all this time. I scarcely believed it.

"Mmmmph," the face said, brown eyes blinking gratefully. There was a rag stuffed in his mouth, and I gently tugged it out. "Thank—thank ye, lass. Gus, lad! Are ye a sight for sorrre eyes."

"We thought you were dead! Well, Myrtle *said* you were dead." Accusation tinged Gus's voice.

"I promised you a ghost, didn't I?" I knelt to untie Mr. Balfour's bound hands. I was making giant deductive leaps that I was not inadvertently setting free a murderer, but given the state of his clothes and the room, I didn't think he was guilty of anything besides accidentally breaking Jessie's heart. "Stop that, that's Not Food. Shoo. Go find Calpurrnia."

Calpurrnia had, predictably, curled up beside her good friend and fallen asleep, and the satisfied little roar of her eponym filled the hollow room—a much nicer sound than ghosts. Although this ghost was quite a welcome discovery!

Mr. Balfour rubbed life back into his stiff wrists and ankles. "Ye—" He coughed, and I wished we'd brought water. "Ye'll be the lass with the Laird's niece, aye? The clever one?"

How did he know all that? "With Miss Judson, yes. I'm Myrtle."

"Weel met." Mr. Balfour offered me a weak smile, and I gave him my hand to help him up. In ordinary circumstances he surely would have tugged me right off my feet, but he must have lost condition, here in the dark for days on end, with only Muriel for company. We were lucky we found him before he starved.

"Erm—may I ask—" I looked around, but no tactful way to put this was to be found. "Why didn't they just kill you? They've killed three—oh, wait, just two—other people." (Mr. Blakeney was right. We did need a chart.)

"Myrtle!"

"Nay, she's right." Mr. Balfour wavered slightly on his feet. "Ah have somethin' they want. Or they think Ah do."

Gus and I both stopped short. "The brooch!" we cried together, and Mr. Balfour gave a surprised little chuckle.

"Well, the answer tae one of the Laird's riddles, at least."

This was Mr. Balfour's story to tell, but he was weak with privation and we were in something of a rush, so I took over. "You found the Laird's bod—the day he—er. He *was* looking for the treasure. With the metal detector!"

"Aye." I heard sadness in his voice, recalling that the last time they'd met, he and Augustus had quarreled.

"He must have found something," I posited.

"Atwixt stump and stane!" Gus said.

Still rubbing his wrists, Mr. Balfour sighed. "I called him an auld fool, puttin' his stake in th' legend, when there's anither way t' save Rockfforde. But I jalouse he was richt, aw alang."

"*Right all along*," Gus translated softly.

"What was it?" I cried, scarcely containing my impatience.

"Ah dinnae ken." Mr. Balfour scratched his scruffy chin sadly. "Ah wish Ah did. He was gaun afore Ah got therre. But he'd ta'en apairt his ain device, like he kent he didnae need it anymerr."

It made sense now. That's why they'd held Mr. Balfour hostage—they were trying to get him to give up the clue. "If you'd told them—or admitted you didn't know—they'd just have killed you."

Mr. Balfour gave me the odd look people get when I say things like that, but he nodded.

"Um." Gus shifted from foot to foot. "They still

might. We should—" He jerked his head back the way we'd come.

"Yes sir," I said. "Let's get you out of here. There are some people who will be very happy to see you."

A broad smile brightened Mr. Balfour's face, making him unexpectedly handsome, despite the eerie green lighting and his overall dishevelment.

As we passed back out of the small chamber, shapes in the opposite corner caught my eye. "What's that?"

"*No*," Peony warned, but I drew closer anyway.

"Were you sleeping over here, sir?" An abandoned candle stub lay beside a pile of old blankets, not unlike Gus's own nest in the library.

"My guard, Ah wat. Nae that Ah was gaun aewhere, aw tied up wi' nae way oot." Mr. Balfour gazed around, recognizing the space. "Tha's where Ah've been? The Jacobite Wing? Cannae believe ye fund me."

"Myrtle found you," Gus said proudly. "She figured out everything."

Not everything. I was still staring at the makeshift campsite. The guard—whoever it was—seemed to have brought along all his belongings, tied up in tartan bundles. "It looks like someone's been *living* here." That notion was even more disturbing than the discovery that our ghost was a kidnapping victim stashed away in the rafters—the murderer, sleeping under our very roof, unseen.

Peony, entirely *un*disturbed, trotted over to see if Someone had left anything edible behind, as Calpurrnia gave a sleepy stretch and poured herself onto the dirty blankets, purring madly.

"Who?" Gus said. "*Why?* Muriel has a room. Nicer than this, anyway."

"Tae keep an eye on their prisoner," Mr. Balfour said, just as I said, "To hide out."

He gave me a grave look, and I shivered, hugging my arms about me. "But who is it?" I could not, somehow, imagine Lt. Smoot crawling about up here, no matter what the buzzards had offered him.

Mr. Balfour shook his head. "Nivver saw the man's face," he reminded us. "An' Muriel did all the talkin'."

But looking at the primitive living quarters, an ugly idea unrolled in my mind. I crept closer and gently shifted aside a corner of blanket. Lovingly wrapped in a fine tartan scarf embroidered with the MacJudd crest was something hard and squarish. I unwound the wool, revealing a book bound in green leather. A novel Uncle Augustus had once given to a faithful servant.

And, like that, the final piece thunked into place, and I knew who our last buzzard was. I'd been wrong: it was no outsider. It was someone raised on Dunfyne Island, who knew every inch of the castle, who was an experienced outdoorsman, used to sleeping rough, skilled in all manner of weapons, comfortable in any terrain, able to remain still and move soundlessly while setting his traps, so as not to alert his prey. Someone who'd sneaked up behind Mr. Macewan and plunged a sgian dubh into the back of his neat blue suit.

I breathed out a single word—the distinctive Scots one I'd committed to memory. "Gillie."

23

HAUD AT HUNDS

A thorough survey of your grounds will identify
hazards in the landscape. Neglect this most critical of tasks at your peril.

–A Country Gentlewoman's Guide to Estate
Management

"Donal Airlie!" Gus gazed around the buzzard's roost,
the truth sinking in. "I thought he was our friend."

Mr. Balfour shook his head. "That lad. Ah told
Kirkpatrick he was more trouble than he was worth—
settin' traps all over the island, poachin'. Shootin' birds
juist for the cruel fun o' it."

"Would he murder Mr. Macewan?" I asked softly.

Mr. Balfour looked surprised. But not for long.
"Mebbe. Aebody who'd hurt a poor cratur athoot
compunction . . . The Laird hoped sendin' him tae
school wuid turn him roond. But draggin' a lass like
Muriel intae his schemes? And murther? Ah cannae
figure it."

Maybe Muriel had dragged him into *her* schemes.

Gus had a pressing question. "Where's he gone now?"

We'd found our ghost and rescued Mr. Balfour, but there *were* still two (or three) murderers at large, which meant everyone on the island was still in danger. As long as Muriel and Donal were distracted searching for the brooch, we might be safe, but when they couldn't find it—assuming they couldn't find it—they'd come back for Mr. Balfour.

And us.

"Quick, we maun gae." In my anxiety, a bit of Scots slipped in, and Gus grinned at me.

Before we decamped, I made a quick search of Airlie's quarters. There wasn't much, just the tattered blankets, the candle, and a crust of brown bread, gone stale, which did not prevent Peony from sampling it. Tucked in the corner was a pair of men's dress shoes, entirely out of place. (Admittedly, *everything* here was out of place.) I retrieved them, carefully lifting from the inside. "These are Mr. Macewan's!"

"How can you tell?" Gus asked.

I turned them over, studying their seams and soles, the fine craftsmanship and quality leather. "Mr. Macewan was wearing dirty boots when we found him. Dirty boots that *disappeared* from the body. Muriel claimed she burned them. What if she lied—and she gave them right back to Donal instead?"

"Why take a dead man's shoon, though?" Mr. Balfour crouched beside me.

"The ghosts maun walk silently," Gus said slowly, "an' leave nae trace. Boots work outside, but he'd need shoes like *that* for inside the castle, so as not tae leave footprints on Gran's floor."

Mr. Balfour gave a small chuckle. That was it exactly! Mrs. Craig had just polished every floor in the castle—as she'd taken pains to point out—and Muriel wouldn't dare risk her wrath by letting Donal Airlie tromp all about Rockfforde Hall in muddy boots. We'd seen her scold Jessie often enough.

I regarded the shoes with some disappointment. I'd been rather hoping for a fascinating tidbit of physical proof, perhaps even something worthy of a Scholarly Treatise on trace evidence unique to this part of Scotland. Now I had to content myself with a culprit who simply didn't want to get the floors dirty. Dear Reader, occasionally Investigation is not as thrilling as one might wish.

I prodded Calpurrnia gently from the blanket so I could wrap the shoes up. They made a bulky parcel of evidence—but I wasn't letting *this* pair out of my sight!

After that we made haste to rejoin our party. Mr. Balfour, recalling the route his captors had taken, led us to the corridor behind the Thistle Room, where an access hatch was set into the service passage, like a small cupboard door. I couldn't believe it—we'd been so close to the entrance this whole time! I shuddered again, realizing how close the ghosts and buzzards had been to *us*. To Miss Judson. It explained all the "pranks," and it was more unsettling than ever to think of Muriel (I *hoped* it was Muriel) in our room, moving our things and writing on our mirror.

"How did they—er, snatch you?" I Inquired, as we eased into the Thistle Room, which still smelled of bonfire. The constables, if any ever showed up, would want the full details of Mr. Balfour's ordeal.

"At the quay," he said. "Ah helped Kirkpatrick wi' his hounds." He held the passageway door open for Gus. "Ah wat it were a trap, then."

"Everyone thought you'd quit," Gus said quietly. "I thought so."

"Leave Dunfyne? Nivver." He gave Gus's shoulder a fatherly squeeze that sent warmth through me. I could imagine how Gus felt.

"*No*," Peony agreed—and I sincerely hoped that was a simple meow, not an expression of her own future plans.

I still wasn't totally satisfied. "Why did Fyne Fisheries pay you a hundred pounds?"

Mr. Balfour pushed a hand through his dusty hair. "Ach—that. They wanted tae send a survey team tae th' island, thocht I cuid talk the Laird intae it. He refuised, of courrse, but Ah gave them permission anyway. We needed that information as much as they did!" he said. "The land rrrecords are a hundred years oot o' date. I was sure I'd get the Laird to come roond. In the end." He shook his head sadly—the end had come before the Laird could reconsider.

"Now *Ah've* a question, if ye dinnae mind." Mr. Balfour gazed at us sternly. "Why is aebody still on Dunfyne with sich things afoot? An' why did it take twa bairns tae rescue me?"

"There's nae boat," I replied. "Donal scuttled it."

"And we're small," added Gus.

◦◦◦

The reunion with the rest of Rockfforde was brief but touching. As soon as we stepped out the Thistle Room door, Jessie flung her arms around Mr. Balfour like she'd never let him go again. Mrs. Craig fussed over him, Mac couldn't stop grinning, Cleveland leaned against his leg with a blissful sigh, and Minna did a Highland fling of pure joy.

Miss Judson stepped forward to introduce herself. "Mr. Balfour, I am terribly sorry it took so long to free you. The culprits will be apprehended and dealt with, I assure you."

He smiled and squeezed her hands like she was *his* long-lost niece. "Aye, you're the new Laird, for sure. Your faither was right aboot ye."

"My—my father? What do you mean?"

"The Laird were troubled these last months," he said. "Wi' naebody to leave Rockfforde tae."

I interrupted. "But what about—" I nodded pointedly to Jessie, who put her hands on her hips.

"Aye, what aboot it?"

Mr. Balfour held her hand. "He didnae want tae burthen ye, lass. Said ye shuid be free tae choose whativver life ye wanted." His fingers twined in hers, it was easy to see what choice she'd make.

He returned to Miss Judson. "The Laird kent yer parents wouldnae leave Deil's Island, but I told him tae ask anyway. Yer faither suggested he pick ye. Said if aebody cuid help bring order tae Dunfyne, it was his bonnie lass."

Miss Judson's brow creased as she tried to work this out. "But—" She didn't have a chance to ask the question, whatever it would have been, as Jessie was growing impatient.

"What'rre we to do aboot Donal an' Muriel, then? They maun pay fir what's happened."

"I expect they've fled by now," Mr. Blakeney said, but we all shot that idea down.

"Not without the brooch," I said.

"Aye." Mrs. Craig was grim. "If that lad promised Muriel a treasure, she'll nae leave athoot it."

I turned a pleading gaze to Mr. Balfour. "Are you

sure you don't know what the Laird found? Donal and Muriel already have the map."

He looked quizzical. "Map? Oh, aye—Hector Macewan was on aboot that. The Laird put *his* stock in the riddle."

"I knew it!" Gus was eager.

"Wait, wait." Miss Judson interjected a breath of practicality into the debate. "Muriel and this gillie are searching for the brooch. But *we* want to find *them*."

"They cuid be aewhere on th' island by now," Jessie said.

"Not anywhere," I said. "Just between stump and stane."

"Or aneath X! It's aw nonsense!"

Minna's elation at the rediscovery of her beloved Mr. Balfour had cooled slightly, and I could see her sniffing the air, clever nose at work. She gave a snuffly little bark, alerting Cleveland, who looked up from having his ears stroked to add his own "Wuff!" to the mix.

Observing this, I flipped open the flap of my satchel. "I have an idea." I pulled out Mr. Macewan's shoes, unrolled them from Donal's blanket, and handed them off to Miss Judson.

"Thank you?" she said.

I shook the blanket at Minna and Cleveland. "You know this scent. Can you find him?" We still had Donal's hat, but the blanket was fresher.

"Oh, ye clever lassie." Jessie rewarded me with a

rare grin. "We kin do better'n tha'." Taking the blanket, she whistled for the hounds, then headed off down the stairs, to the front door of Rockfforde Hall, and out into the courtyard.

It had taken longer to free Mr. Balfour from the buzzards' clutches than I'd expected, and night was lifting, a hazy mist over the moss and heather of the lawn.

The Wild Hunt cry in the kennels had only intensified over the hours—the hounds were hungry and eager to hunt. Jessie was just giving them an unexpected quarry.

"Alan, can ye ride?"

"Aye, Jess—Ah'll get Garnet saddled, too."

"Ah'll help ye, lad." Mac clapped a friendly hand on Mr. Balfour's shoulder and accompanied him to the stables.

Jessie strode straight to the kennel gates and flung them open. First the females, who poured out in a sea of white, then the males, bounding with wound-up energy. Exhausted though she was, I knew Jessie would see this through. She held the blanket to the snuffling, greedy noses of her pack, letting everyone get a good long taste of the scent. By the time Mr. Balfour made it back with their horses, Jessie and her dogs were ready. With the help of a knife, she ripped the blanket in two and handed half to Mr. Balfour, then flung her section over Garnet's saddle and swung herself into place.

A grin spread across her face as she met Mr. Balfour's eyes. "Tallyho."

~

Dear Reader, I must share the disappointing news that my first foxhunt was that short. We horseless humans remained at Rockfforde Hall as the hounds poured away, Jessie on Garnet and Mr. Balfour on a tall bay mare* beside them. In the distance, color was touching the sky, and Peony decided it was time for breakfast.

But the New Laird didn't give anyone a reprieve. "They have a head start," she said, pacing before her household like a military commander. "They have the map. They have the metal detector. But we shall not let this deter us. The brooch belongs to Clan MacJudd and Dunfyne Island, and no interlopers shall take it from its rightful home."

The rest of us weren't quite sure what to do with this new version of Miss Judson, but Gus ran up and flung his arms around her waist. "*Audere*," he said—motto of Clan Judd of Dunfyne.

She squeezed back. "Thank you, Gus. Now. Assembled here are the finest deductive minds in Britain. We shall make swift work of this so-called riddle. Gus, report."

He shuffled his feet, studying our part of the map. I hadn't been able to make heads or tails of it, but I

---

* Gus tells me, anyway. To me the horse just looked brown.

hoped Gus had had better luck. "Well, the first line is *Atwixt stump and stane*, and it leads to 'the Means,' whatever that is. That's the clue the Laird was looking for with his metal detector. I always thought it must be here, in the courtyard"—he gestured to the old tree stump—"but the Laird was at the castle ruins, and if I'm reading the map right . . ." He trailed off, and then his eyes grew huge, and a little laugh escaped him. "Oh! That's it! It's nae atwixt stump and stane—" He gave a dismissive wave to Rockfforde Hall. "It's atwixt stump and *stane*! The old stone ruins!"

I was impressed. That was a wholly logical deduction. "I agree with Gus," I said to Miss Judson.

She was smiling. "Lead the way, Master Craig. Everyone, bring treasure-hunting supplies." No one knew exactly what this meant, so we each offered our own interpretation. Gus brought the map. Mac brought a pick and an old iron shovel (his "scube dubh," he called it). I brought Mr. Blakeney. And Peony brought a leaf she'd found in a corner of the pond. Calpurrnia stayed behind with Cook for a nap.

The path to the ruins was just as silent and deserted as before, but in the distance we could hear the wild baying of the hounds as they harried their quarry—an unearthly, blood-chilling sound. I missed Minna.

"*No*," Peony said, somehow not dropping her leaf.

Mr. Blakeney fell in beside me. "I figured the clue must have something to do with that bird stump thing in the hall," he said companionably. "I must say, I'm relieved."

I had a dozen irrelevant questions I wanted to ask—mostly about Father and Miss Judson and whether things would ever be like they were before this trip—but he wouldn't have had any of the answers I needed. Instead I stuck my hands deep into my jacket pockets and said, "Do you think they'll find him?"

"Your missing gillie? No doubt." He said that with his typical blithe confidence—which meant he wasn't sure at all. But I still nodded and marched onward.

We reached the ruins just as sunlight rimmed the stones with gold, leaving their feet deep in boggy shadow. I was weary and hungry, dust covered, and wearing an absolute *ruin* of a pair of stockings, and beholding the impossible scene before us, I felt a wave of desolation. Without the metal detector, and only half the map, how would we ever find whatever Uncle Augustus had discovered that day? We hadn't even managed to find it *with* the metal detector. I sank down upon a rock—not part of the ruins—and picked at the run in my stocking. It unraveled even more, exactly how I felt this morning.

The others spread out happily, bolstered by the excitement of the treasure hunt. But what if Muriel and Donal had been here already, and they'd taken the clue? Or worse, found the brooch and left the island?

And what if we *found* the treasure? What then? Would it somehow save Dunfyne Island and Rockfforde Hall? Would Miss Judson want to stay and make good on all the repairs she'd planned? Would she fix up the Thistle Room and turn the Trophy Room into an art studio? I kicked rather petulantly at the rock.

Something shifted. I gave a squeak and hopped off. My boot heel had caught on something—a sharp edge concealed by centuries of lichen and moss, and half buried in the grass. Except *not*. I knelt beside the rock, suddenly eager. Mr. Blakeney bent down beside me.

"What have you got there, Stephen?"

"A stane," I breathed.

Mr. Blakeney fished a case of vestas from his pocket, lighting one for a hint of illumination. The sharp edge I'd kicked was a broken bit of bronze—like a nameplate. Or a marker. Heart hammering, I braced myself for disappointment. "What if Donal and Muriel got here first?"

"You won't know until you know. See what it is."

I reached for the nameplate, vaguely realizing that Gus, Mac, and Miss Judson had joined us. Peony leaped onto the rock, in exactly the spot I'd just been sulking. She reached down a white paw and batted at the brass.

"I think Gus should look." He'd been working on this much longer than I had, after all. I scooted aside.

Gus was even more nervous than I. With trembling

hands, he pried off the old bronze marker. We studied it briefly, then both of us broke into a laugh.

"What is it?" Miss Judson asked, and I passed her the metal plate, watching as she rolled her eyes. "Naturally," she said. "A stump." Embossed on the marker was the badge of Clan MacEwen: a tree stump sprouting anew, and the word *Reviresco*.

"Between stump and stone," said Mr. Blakeney.

"Should I look now?" Gus's voice was very soft, a bit shaky. He reached inside a small cavity within the stone and withdrew— "Oh. That can't be right."

It was a tin of herring. A *new* tin of herring. Well, not new-new; it had been opened, rinsed out, and re-used— but it certainly had not been residing within this rock since 1745. Gus gave it a little shake, and it rattled.

"That's promising," Mr. Blakeney said.

As we all watched eagerly, he prized the lid free, and a little iron key fell out, along with a note in familiar handwriting. Gus unrolled it and read: "*Atween lock and key: the Might.*" He groaned. "We know that already!" He shook the key in frustration.

The sound of the hounds was coming closer. Gus flung the scrap of paper onto the ground and gave the stone a furious kick. "I hate him!" he cried, in a raw, angry voice. "Why did he have to go and leave this stupid note behind! I hate you!"

I stood back, biting my finger, as Gus flailed out his

grief and anger. Peony, atop the stone, gave a burble of concern. Finally, Miss Judson put a gentle hand on Gus's shoulder, saying nothing. But she cast me a look that said volumes. Carefully, I retrieved the herring tin and the note and tucked them into my bag.

It felt like this day would never end.

24
I Open Locked Hearts

Even the most familiar of houses can possess surprising secrets.

-A Country Gentlewoman's Guide to Estate
Management

As we packed up our equipment to begin the weary
trudge back to Rockfforde Hall, the commotion in
the distance abruptly became a *nearby* commotion.
The high skirling of the hounds pealed through the
morning, mad and gleeful. Miss Judson gathered us up
like a hen collecting her chicks, just in time to see a
bedraggled man lunge out of the woods, wild-eyed and
panting.

"Donal!" Gus gasped.

With a thump, I backed into Mr. Blakeney, who
seized me by the shoulders like a Jacobite gripping

his shield. Miss Judson took a cautious step toward us. Donal cast about the scene, mouth slowly shaping into a grin.

"Weel, noo," he said, words coming in ragged gasps. "Isnae this a bonnie sight?" In the next moment, he held a knife—not a sgian dubh, but a great angry hunting knife, huge steel blade glinting in the sun. He circled us warily. His tattered tweed coat hung off one shoulder, and he'd lost a boot somewhere in his flight from the hounds. And he'd lost his hat, days ago in Tighnabruaich.

Gus stood like a frozen hare, staring at Donal Airlie.

And before any of us could react, Donal grabbed him.

"Aye, what're ye gaun dae noo?" He sneered, holding Gus round the chest in one arm, the knife in the other hand. I could almost see it dripping blood: *I mak sikkar.* Donal would make sure none of us left this island alive.

"It's too late, Mr. Airlie. You're cornered. There's nowhere to run. Give yourself up now, and we'll be merciful." Miss Judson's lofty words would have made me laugh, if the moment hadn't been so deadly serious.

"Merciful?" he spat. "What mercy did the MacJudds ever show me?"

"They gave ye a home, Donal," Mac said, warm and low.

Donal spun, taking Gus with him. "My home!" he

cried. "Mine! Rockfforde Hall is my birthright, and all of ye conspired to steal it frae me!"

"As a matter of fact, it's not." If Miss Judson had happened to have a handy genealogical chart, she'd have unfurled it right there as a visual aid. "The story your grandmother told you? It was about Gus and Jessie's father—not yours."

"Lies! It's all lies! It's—"

We never found out what he meant to say next. In the shocked cold tension of the moment, I'd failed to track the approaching storm, until a surge of white poured like a maelstrom into the ruins: dozens upon dozens of foxhounds, soaring through the morning. The sound was *deafening*: a piercing cacophony of joy and triumph. With a shriek of terror, Donal flung Gus away from him—straight into me—and stumbled out of the ruins, limbs flailing as he tried to gain his footing.

He never made it. Jessie and Garnet flew out of the trees, leaping with elegant precision over a stone wall in a beautiful silvery red arc and skidding in front of him. It was a miracle Garnet didn't land *on* him—proof of Jessie's skilled equestrianship. And something else, as she could easily have killed him where he stood.

Donal screamed again, whimpering—but it was too late. The Rockfforde Hunt was upon him, and a streak of gold had him pinned to the mossy earth, tail flipping frantically, too fast to see. Minna was next, then Nelly, and Jenny with the black ears, and little Rusty who reminded me of Gus . . . and too many to count, let alone name. Well trained, they did not tear their quarry apart—but too friendly, they could not help themselves from nearly smothering him to death in their sheer delight at having run him down: the reward for a good morning's fun.

Gus gripped me hard as Mr. Balfour rounded through a moment later, reins in one hand and a pistol in the other. He dropped to the earth just as Mac was wading into the sea of canine frolic to pluck Donal to safety. Holding Donal by the collar, Mac looked like he'd pulled a struggling mackerel from the waters of Loch Fyne—and wanted to throw him back.

Miss Judson strode forward, the dogs all settling down as their mistress passed among them. She stopped before Mac, somehow looking far more regal than an erstwhile governess in a brown work dress and paint-splattered apron ought to manage.

"Now, Mr. Airlie," she said—and it was *like* her Schoolroom Voice, but not quite. There was an extra layer to it that sent a sort of shiver through me and made me stand straighter. "You have exactly one chance to come clean before I let these dogs—who have not had dinner *or* breakfast, mind you—have their way with you."

Donal tried to be defiant, but the panic in his eyes as they flicked to the hounds gave him away. Minna licked her chops, and he gave a little moan.

"Where is Muriel?"

"Gaun," he spat. "Off th' island, halfway to Inveraray by noo. Yer sodger boy took 'er."

I groaned—we'd never see either of them again, then.

"Lt. Smoot? What's his role in this?" Miss Judson's voice was hard and icy.

Donal knew when he was caught—enough to lie his way out of it. "Ran the whole thing—him an' Kirkpatrick. *He* killed Macewan, nae me!"

"And I suppose he took his shoes and replaced them with the ones—one—you're wearing now?" I recognized that boot from its cracked heel and mud-caked leather. "And he tried to steal Miss Judson's bag? *And* smoked—smeeked—us out of our room?" My voice grew shrill. Evidently I'd lost a bit of Professional Objectivity on this case.

"I suggest you try again," Mr. Blakeney said to Donal. "And I'll advise you, Scottish law still permits the Laird to mete out justice on his—her—own land." I had no idea if this was true or not—and strongly suspected Mr. Blakeney did not either—but it did the trick. Donal's wild blue eyes went from his face to Miss Judson's, and he paled visibly.

"I want a lawyer," he snapped.

"That," Miss Judson said, "is the first smart thing you've said." She turned to her loyal retainers. "Mac, Mr. Balfour, do we have anywhere suitable to restrain this man until the constables can arrive?"

A dark glint lit Mr. Balfour's brown eyes. "Ah wat we kin mak room in th' dungeon."

"It might still be flooded," Jessie added, arms crossed over her chest. The ragged blanket still hung from her gloved hand. "Hope ye dinnae droon afore aebody finds ye."

Miss Judson's eyes went round the circle and she nodded. "That sounds just about right."

ం

The mood at Rockfforde Hall that afternoon was subdued. It was a relief to finally have the culprit safely locked up in what Mrs. Craig assured me was a secure cell. (Mr. Balfour had been exaggerating about the dungeon; Rockfforde Hall wasn't *that* old, after all. It was really just a dank storage room in the cellar, full of old dog blankets and even older turnips.) But the long exhausting days had taken their toll. Even Mr. Blakeney seemed discouraged. The instant we arrived back at Rockfforde Hall, Gus had fled up the stairs and vanished into the castle's labyrinth of passageways and rooms. As much as I wanted to go to him, I let him be. I knew too well how he felt.

Donal had offered a partial confession (I think it was the hungry looks Minna and Cleveland gave him from outside his cell door), full of half-truths and accusations, but we were able to sort out a few details of the crimes. Mr. Macewan had got his money for the map from Mr. Kirkpatrick, who then pressured Macewan into his schemes against Uncle Augustus. The solicitor agreed to accompany Kirkpatrick to Dunfyne Island that fateful morning, under the guise of convincing Miss Judson to sell. When they realized Mr. Macewan meant to back out of their plans, Donal killed him in a fit of rage.

"But it didnae sit right wi' Kirkpatrick." Mac had listened patiently to Donal's explanation of events, relating them to us now. "An' he made the mistak of threatening Donal wi' the police."

Mrs. Craig received this tale with resignation. "We didnae ken he was sae—"

"Troubled," Miss Judson offered—though to my mind, Donal Airlie was much more than *troubled*.

"What about Lt. Smoot and Muriel?" I demanded. Mac explained that Macewan had hired the lieutenant to keep an eye on Donal, in exchange for a share of the profits from the sale of the island.

"I cannae think o' Fitz involved in murder," Mac said, but he looked unsettled. "Small-time smugglin', aye, but nae killing aebody."

That explained the things Lt. Smoot had sold to

Uncle Augustus for extra cash. The maid's disappearance was especially worrisome. I suspected she was more involved than Donal was saying, and I wanted *everyone* responsible for the deaths on Dunfyne Island to be held accountable.

That wasn't the only mystery, though. Although we had solved another clue from Angus MacJudd's riddle, our expedition still felt like a failure, as it had not uncovered the object at the heart of all the Strange Occurrences on Dunfyne Island. And until that was found, things at Rockfforde Hall never really would be settled.

"Well, I'm not giving up," I said, glaring at the key, the herring tin, and the note. Gus had accused Uncle Augustus of leaving behind another cryptic clue. The tin probably wasn't part of the puzzle, just a safe receptacle for the key, yet I couldn't seem to put it down. It wasn't like a pilchard tin, with the top that peeled back, but a proper little box of scarlet metal, a leaping fish on the lid with the words *Torquay Fisheries: Packed with Pride in Cornwall.* It had come a long way to be hidden in a rock on a loch in Scotland.

With a jolt, I dropped the box, and the key.

"What is it, Stephen?"

"Between lock and key," I said, then: "between *loch* and *quay.*"

"You said that."

"No, I didn't." I couldn't sit still. Miss Judson came

over. She'd just put the finishing touch on a portrait of the heroic Minna and Cleveland seizing their quarry at Castle Dunfyne this morning, and charcoal still dusted her fingertips.

I shook the herring tin, laughter bubbling out. "Red herrings! Misdirection! Oh, Uncle Augustus!" I hadn't known the man, but I cast my gaze to the ceiling to talk with his ghost. "Very clever. Lock and key!"

"What's funny?" Jessie had slipped inside, refreshed after a bath and a nap and a long talk with Mr. Balfour. Rose tinted her cheeks, her eyes shone with a new kind of fire, and she held fast to a pendant round her neck—intertwining hearts holding a green crystal in their embrace. I had given Mr. Balfour back the love token, and it, too, had found its way home at last.

"Lock and key!" I cried again. "Loch and quay!"

"Please stop saying *lock and key*," Miss Judson requested.

"I'm not! I'm saying *loch* and *quay*!" The word was spelled oddly, having immigrated from France, but it was pronounced *key*. "*Locchh*," I said, giving the word a Scottish growl. Then I pointed at the word on the tin. "And *kway*. Q-U-A-Y—*key*!"

Mr. Blakeney gave the tin a little spin, grin growing. "Well, now. How about that?"

"We need Gus," I said. "We have to go down to the boat landing!"

Twenty minutes later we'd assembled once more

where our journey had begun: at the stone landing—the *quay*—where boats rarely docked at Dunfyne Island. Gus was nearly hopping with excitement.

"I can't stand it," he said. "You do this one, Myrtle."

"Not me," I said. "It's not my Whole Estate. In Scotland." I gave a pointed look at Miss Judson.

"Ah," she said. "I knew the reason you made me bring these would become apparent eventually." She held up a pair of tall black Wellies, which she swiftly pulled on over her own smart boots. The tide was low, and she only had to hitch her skirts to a perfectly modest knee-length to wade into the water.

Sunlight sparkled the gentle waves, and a stout fresh breeze blew off the loch. Miss Judson's hat and skirts were buffeted, but she stayed upright, like a ship's mast.

"Can you see anything?" I called from my dry position well inland.

Miss Judson splashed down the stone landing and stepped into the depths—well, the shallows—of Loch Fyne, blue, blue water lapping her boots. An elegant black shadow swooped overhead in a long, graceful arc. A buzzard, come to monitor our progress. I waved, as if Uncle Augustus had sent it.

"So, were I to look *between* the loch and the quay . . ." Miss Judson bent low, peering at the edge of the stone where it met the water, running her fingers along every inch of the ancient structure. Finally a little smile quirked her lip. "There's something here—a sort of shelf."

"What is it?" Gus clutched me—and I clutched right back. I could hardly bear the suspense.

"It's jammed in here. Just . . . a . . . moment . . . aha!" With triumph, she lifted a small metal chest out of the water and held it high for all to see.

"Open it!" we cried.

"May I get out of the water first?"

"No!"

Gamely, Miss Judson set the box on the bank, well out of reach of the greedy waves that would yank it back at the first opportunity. "The key?"

Gus passed it to her. A moment of excruciating tension passed while she inserted it. "It fits," she announced, and we all sighed. She paused, pushing a stray curl from her forehead with her wet hand. "I certainly hope there's something worthwhile in here, for all the trauma it's causing you two. You three," she amended, including Mr. Blakeney, who appeared to be gnawing on his fingertips.

"Mrrow!" agonized Peony.

"Just open it!" I begged, and Miss Judson turned the key.

She lifted the lid with great ceremony, pausing only momentarily to peer inside before holding the chest up once more for us to behold its contents—a small water-logged leather bag, just large enough for a piece of important jewelry. (Far too large for *certain* Important Jewelry, however—although if Father had *any* romance in his soul, he might have engineered this entire trip and the treasure hunt as a rather elaborate proposal. Although probably not the murders.)

Miss Judson withdrew the pouch and tugged on its drawstring. Turning it over, she spilled out the prize: a circle of silver, the size of a small bannock, glittered in her palm. It looked like a miniature shield, embossed and engraved in swirling knotwork, a sort of tower at its heart holding up a misty green stone.

For a moment—or an hour, or a day—we were all silent. Then Gus put out a pale, trembling finger. "Is it real?"

"It feels real." Miss Judson passed it to him, and he cradled it in his hands. But she cast me a look, pride mixed with pragmatism. I understood: We'd found it, the Treasure of Dunfyne Island, lost for generations and now recovered. We had followed the hidden path and restored what was lost. But it was not immediately clear how this piece of medieval jewelry would restore Rockfforde Hall's fortunes. Even I could tell it wasn't gold, and its stone was merely a pretty specimen of fluorspar.

I didn't say any of that to Gus. He was passing the brooch around, glowing with pride. I wondered when he'd realize what this had all really been about.

"That box hasn't been there for a hundred years."

Mr. Blakeney spoke quietly, out of Gus's earshot. "The metal would be tarnished."

"More like weeks," agreed Miss Judson.

"The old man knew he was dying," Mr. Blakeney deduced. "And he wanted to leave his nieces and nephew something to remember him by."

"But *he* had to find the brooch first," I pointed out. "Before he could leave the herring tin in the stane. He never did figure out *Aneath W,* but he got the rest, thanks to his metal detector. Gus just wasn't here when he did. This way they could still find it together. It still counts."

Mr. Blakeney put a hand on my shoulder. "Aye, Stephen, that it does."

❧

The excitement of recovering the brooch—and the relief at catching Mr. Macewan's killer—did not dissipate overnight. The whole castle was abuzz the next morning when the dawn chorus of hungry hounds woke me. All things considered, I prefer the dawn solo of a hungry cat, even when accompanied by teeth. But Minna and Cleveland *were* awfully nice. I liked the odd, salty smell of Cleveland's huge rough paws.

I went out into the yard to help Jessie with the dogs that had saved the day. She seemed a new person, not a bit the angry horsewoman who'd greeted us just last week. Mr. Balfour was nowhere to be seen—although Miss Judson had urged him to rest and see a doctor, he'd insisted on going straight back to work. "Ah wat a fair bit needs mendin' hereaboots," he said. "No tellin' what Airlie's left us to deal with." He'd ridden out early to check fences and dens . . . and get a look at the grim scene at the neighboring lodge.

Cook had finally finished her repairs to the fireplace, and she and Mrs. Craig celebrated by cooking a massive breakfast over a massive fire. Welcoming smoke puffed cheerfully from a sturdy chimney, entirely free from birds' nests. Mac arrived in a freshly pressed kilt and a green suit coat cropped short, furry leather pouch at his waist (that nonetheless did not hide his bare knees) and small knife tucked in his plaid stocking. A narrow wool cap crowned his bushy red hair, which he'd done his utmost to tame, and he carried a cluster of bluebells and bog myrtle.

In response, Cook had donned her own best trousers and a pair of Wellies she'd appropriated from the Rockfforde Hall collection. And the frilly little hat she'd worn on the ferry. Arm in arm, they set off together, Nelly trotting ahead, discussing plans for the water pump or perhaps Improvements to the old stone boathouse.

Gus sat on the wall overlooking the courtyard, looking thoughtful. He hadn't let go of the brooch all night, even though it technically belonged to Miss Judson, and the fluorspar at its center glowed faintly. I climbed up beside him, snagging my last good pair of stockings, and Calpurrnia unfurled herself from her sunbeam long enough to take two steps, stretch, and lie right back down again. Peony walked up to her, swatted her in the chin, and then set about washing her face, as the muscovy cat's deep throaty purr rocked the wall we sat upon.

I held out my hand, and Gus passed me the brooch. It really *was* old, and I could feel the weight of its age and its connection to this island. Mr. Macewan had given his life for it. It was worth far more than money.

"I have a weak heart, too," Gus said abruptly. I looked up in surprise, to see his slight hand resting on his narrow chest. "From the rheumatic fever. That's why I don't do sport, why Jessie's so protective. The Laird understood what it was like. When I had to be inside, resting, he showed me his books and collections, taught me history." He sighed. "I miss him."

I said the only thing I could think of. "After my mum died, Miss Judson was there. It's not the same . . . but . . ." I stopped, because I had no idea how to say what I meant. How Miss Judson had walked into our lives and changed *everything*. I couldn't promise she would do that for Gus, because in a way, I didn't want her to. She was mine, and I wanted her back in Swinburne.

But Gus reached for my hand. "I know," he said. Calpurrnia stretched out her cozy marbled paw into my lap, until they were both holding me fast in the Rockffforde Hall circle.

The moment didn't last long. Jessie turned the hounds loose to frolic in the courtyard, watching them with pride. They might only chase the foxes of Dunfyne Island, but yesterday they had more than proven themselves among Scotland's great hunts. Miss Judson appeared, holding what I first assumed was a sketchbook. She strode across the courtyard, heels tapping like the telegraph Dunfyne didn't have, and looking every inch the Laird.

"Jessie."

Jessie spun round, happy expression cooling to suspicion. "Aye?"

Miss Judson did not let this deter her. "I have a proposition. I believe I've found a way to make Rockffforde Hall and Dunfyne Island profitable. As you know, the island has few valuable natural resources."

I could see Jessie curling in on herself, her hedgehog spines rising. But Miss Judson went on as if she hadn't noticed.

"This will capitalize on something the island does have in abundance, however. But there's a hitch."

"Oh, aye. An' *coorse* there's a hitch."

Miss Judson regarded her coolly. "As I was trying to say, this will require local management. Someone with—shall we say—boots on the ground?"

"Oot wi' it, already! If yer sellin' the Hall, juist sell it. Dinnae tease us wi' your plans an' schemes."

"Actually," Miss Judson said, withdrawing a sheaf of

papers from her book, "I believe they're *your* schemes. Mr. Blakeney found your proposal to turn Rockfforde Hall and Dunfyne Island into a holiday resort, and I think it's a fine idea."

Jessie stepped back apace. "Ye—ye do?"

"Aye, Ah dae. And I think you're just the person to run it."

"*Me?* Why?"

"Why not? I won't be here all the time, and you've already done all the legwork. Your figures and analyses are very impressive. Now, we don't have the capital to get it up and running straight away, and I for one am not eager to take on much more debt, so I think a limited lease of the water power from Rockfforde Falls might bring enough income to get things off the ground. Of course, we'll need a new lawyer, given what happened to our last one."

"Oh, and I wat ye ken a solicitor we kin afford, do ye?" Jessie, color high, entered into a new debate with passion. But she caught Gus's eye and gave him a great mischievous grin. "Well, I dinnae cotton to your English lawyer, mind. I want a proper Scotsman, from Argyll, wha' kens the law an' the land. An' ye'll be wantin' all sorts o' fancy repairs, noo, too, I wat—a roof an' walls."

"And plumbing."

"Plumbing! Oh, luik who's too guid fir the land her ancestors bled fir . . ."

The cheerful argument continued, but was drowned out by a new sound. A sharp eager bark from Minna and a "Wuff!" from Cleveland alerted us to voices and footsteps coming up the path. I nudged Gus and we slid off the wall, trotting across the courtyard.

The first thing I saw was a flash of red uniform. "Lt. Smoot!" I cried.

"What's he want?" Gus scowled—but only slightly. With Mr. Balfour back, the sleekit soldier was no longer such a threat.

Marching behind the lieutenant were three black-clad constables. The police! He'd brought the police at last! He must have taken Muriel straight to the authorities—*not* fled with her as we'd all believed. I almost couldn't believe it. Then I halted, uncertain. Maybe the constables had brought *him*.

Trailing somewhat warily behind this group was a roadworn (lochworn) man with a ginger beard, squinting against the very bright Argyll sun despite a smart straw hat. "Father!" I breathed.

Miss Judson, who was far across the yard with Jessie, discussing their plans to turn Rockfforde Hall into a Haunted Hotel with Optional Treasure Hunt Excursion, somehow caught a telepathic hint from me and whirled about. Color drained from her face as she beheld the form of her employer materializing from the woods.

I ran to greet him, and he grabbed me up in a

jolly—and thoroughly embarrassing—embrace. It was all I could do to brush myself smooth after he let me down. "Hello," he said, sounding abruptly shy.

"Hello." I kicked at a clump of moss, equally bashful. Father wore a summer suit of white flannel, with a jaunty straw boater, and looked exceptionally dashing. He carried a valise but no brief-bag; and I Observed with some trepidation the outline of a small, box-shaped Item in his breast pocket. I didn't dare ask about it. "How was your trip?" I said politely instead.

"Long," he growled, but tousled my hair absently. "And rather informative. If you'll excuse me, I need to have a word with your governess."

My governess was currently having A Word with the Argyll Constabulary, but Father wasn't going to let that stop him. He dropped his valise and marched forward, brushing past the constables and Lt. Smoot.

"Miss Judson," he said, in his absolute sternest Prosecutorial Voice, the one that makes defendants quake with terror in the dock. It even startled the constables.

She turned slowly, as if it were no more than usual to see Father striding out of the Scottish woods dressed for a yachting holiday. Before Father could say another word, she forestalled him.

"Mr. Hardcastle, we need to discuss the terms of my employment."

He stopped and regarded her dispassionately. It was impossible to tell what he—what they were thinking, but both of them looked Exceptionally Cross.

"Yes, we do," he finally replied. "You're fired."

I clapped my hands over my mouth, stifling a howl to do Nelly proud, and *Glared* at him.

Miss Judson was caught off guard as well—which as you know is quite the achievement, Dear Reader. She stood, mouth agape, in her brown housedress and painting apron, utterly speechless.

And in that state, Father took Miss Ada Judson, Laird of Dunfyne Island and Rockfforde Hall, Twenty-sixth MacJudd, in his arms and kissed her.

A roar of approval rose up from the assembled company—Rockffordians, constables, hounds, and all. When Father finally let her go, her color had returned, deeper than ever. A moment later, she grabbed *him* and repeated the gesture, to even more rousing applause.

I felt someone behind me. "Saw that coming, didn't you, Stephen?"

Mr. Blakeney had the strangest look on his face—half silly grin, half oddly . . . wistful.

"I am a skilled detective, you know," I reminded him.

"I would never forget it."

When I glanced back, Father had bent to one knee,

getting grass stains on his white trousers, and Miss Judson was the very picture of statuesque composure, although one springy curl refused to behave and kept bouncing into her eye.

I started to join them, but Mr. Blakeney interrupted me. "I say," he said. "Wasn't that stump . . . dead a day or so ago?"

I turned and beheld something Scientifically Impossible—almost less likely than Father finally proposing to Miss Judson. Shoots of green had broken through the surface of the old felled tree stump, reaching for the spring sunshine.

Reviresco.

I blinked, shaking my head at the improbability. A shadow in the distance drew my gaze, and I bit my lip in disbelief. Clearly visible in the courtyard window of Rockfforde Hall, where I'd first seen Gus, was a face. Against all reason I lifted a hand in a tentative farewell—and a moment later, the vision faded.

"We didn't see that," Mr. Blakeney said, and I shook my head in dumbstruck agreement.

Back at the center attraction, Father had risen, and he and Miss Judson stood hand in hand, grinning like silly schoolchildren.

"Here." Mr. Blakeney handed me something. "My sister liked this one. Before she got kicked out, that is." It was a brochure for Boswell Academy for Young Ladies of Quality, a boarding school in Leicestershire.

"What's this for?"

"Well," he said. "I don't think you'll have a governess anymore after this, do you?"

Peony sat on my foot, watching the Romantic Tableau with considerable skepticism. I followed her gaze, feeling everything at once. It was strange. It was terrifying. It was perfect.

"*No*," Peony said cheerfully, and stalked off, tail high, to give Father and Miss Judson her own opinion on the matter.

Finis

(Then again . . .)

APPENDIX: HARDCASTLE & CRAIG'S BRIEF SCOTS LEXICON

Compiled by H. M. Hardcastle & E. A. Craig
Dunfyne Island, Argyllshire, Scotland, 1894

aebody (anybody)

aheid (ahead)

ain (own)

athoot (without)

auld (old)

aw (all)

awa' (away)

aye (yes, always)

bahootie (backside [of a person])

bairn (baby, child)

baudron (cat)

blather (foolish talk, nonsense)

bluid (blood)

braw (fine, excellent)

burthen (burden)

cannae (can't)

craig (rock)

cuid (could)

cursit (cursed)

dae (do)

deil (devil)

dinnae/didnae (don't, didn't)

disnae (doesn't)

dreich (cold and rainy)

dun (done)

elachie (alarm)

enew (enough)

forrit (forward)

fower (four)

frae (from)

gae (go)

gangin (moving, in working order)

gaun (going, gone)

gillie (a hunting and fishing guide on a Scottish estate)

glaikit (flighty, foolish)

gowk (a foolish person)

graith (gear, equipment)

guid (good)

hame (home)

hant (haunt)

haugh (hall)

hoose (house)

jalouse (suspect)

jist, juist (just)

ken, kent (know, known)

laird (lord)

lang (long)

loch (lake)

lossit (lost)

luik, luikit (look, looked)

mak (make)

maun (must)

muscovy (with *cat*, tortoiseshell)

nae (not, not any)

naebody (nobody)

nane (none)

nay (no)

noo (now)

ontil (until)

oor (our)

oot (out)

ootbye (in the vicinity of [some distant place])

ower, owre (over)

peerie (small, used fondly)

saxty (sixty)

Scube Dubh (a mystery-solving Great Dane)

scutch (scratch, scuff)

sgian dubh (Gaelic "black knife," a small knife carried in the stocking)

shoon (shoes)

sikkar (sure)

skirl (the sound made by bagpipes)

sleekit (sneaky, crafty)

smeek (smoke, fumes)

sodger (soldier)

swither (hesitate)

therty (thirty)

thocht (thought)

thrawn (stubborn)

twa (two)

wat (know, presume)

wha (what)

wha' (who)

whigmaleerie (thingamajig)

wuid (would)

A NOTE FROM THE AUTHOR

Clan MacJudd, Dunfyne Island, Rockfforde Hall, and the lost clan brooch are entirely fictional, but Clan Ewen of Otter and the MacEwen families (however the various branches spell it) really exist, boasting descendants all over the world. As of the writing of this book, Clan MacEwen has undertaken the lengthy process of naming a new clan chief for the first time in 530 years—since Sween MacEwen died without heirs in 1493. Information on the progress of Sir John R. H. McEwen's claim can be found at the Clan MacEwen Society website, clanmacewen.com/chiefship. *Reviresco*.

The lost brooch was inspired by other legendary clan artifacts, such as the Ugdale Brooch (said to be from the plaid of Robert the Bruce himself) and Clan MacLeod's Fairy Flag of Dunvegan Castle. The setting of this story, Loch Fyne in Argyll, is likewise real, and although ferries no longer run from Tighnabruaich to Otter Ferry (it's a twenty-minute drive by car), they were once the most efficient mode of travel in the area.

Scotland is home to three native languages: English, Scottish Gaelic, and Scots. Scottish Gaelic gives us beautiful words like *Tighnabruaich* and *sgian dubh*. Scots—a close cousin of English—sounds tantalizingly familiar to English speakers, and Scots speakers often blend it freely with English, choosing whichever language best expresses an idea. I must express my gratitude to everyone who helped tune my ear—and my pen*— for Scots: the Scots Language Centre (scotslanguage .com), a tremendous resource for anyone interested in the rich linguistic heritage of the Scottish people; Billy Kay's *Scots: The Mither Tongue*; and especially author Anne Reilly, who read the manuscript tae mak sikkar I didnae imbarace mesel'. Anie mistaks are me ain.

For giving us the *Scots Thesaurus* and a book of clan mottos way back when, knowing they'd come in handy someday, thanks to big brother Scott McKuen. *Think more!*

The nineteenth century was a period of vigorous scientific innovation. Scientists investigated every aspect of the natural world—and the supernatural world. With the aid of new technologies like electricity and electromagnets, telegraphy and radio, and sound recording, researchers were inspired to take a scientific approach

---

* There's no pen; it's a laptop.

to the study of paranormal phenomena like ghosts. Groups such as the Society for Psychical Research (spr.ac.uk), of which Arthur Conan Doyle was indeed a member, brought together scholars from all disciplines to investigate hauntings, spirit mediums, and psychic encounters. Some claims were readily debunked. Others remained unexplained. Although the organization, and others like it, continues its work to this day, it's safe to say that no universally satisfactory conclusion regarding the existence or nature of ghosts has yet been reached. *Post funera fœnus.*

For assistance with manufacturing my own nineteenth-century Scottish haunting, thanks to geologist Elizabeth J. Catlos from Jackson School of Geosciences at the University of Texas for answering my questions about luminescent minerals, and to the marvelous staff at Crescent Springs crystal shop in Overland Park, Kansas, for walking me through them in real life. *Lux in tenebris.*

As always, my thanks and admiration go out to my amazing team at Algonquin Young Readers, all the folks who have contributed to bringing you five Myrtle Hardcastle Mysteries (so far): the editorial guidance of Krestyna Lypen and Ashley Mason; the artistic vision of Laura Williams, Brett Helquist, Leah Palmer Preiss, and Carla Weise; the eagle eyes (or is that buzzard eyes?) of Sue Wilkins and Dan Janeck; the marketing and publicity prowess of Shae McDaniel (how did

I miss naming a character after you?) and Meghan O'Shaughnessy; and the organizational efficiency of Adah Li. *Huc tendimus omnes.*

And to Myrtle's first and forever editor, the incomparable Elise Howard, who retired right before I turned in the first draft of this book—but who, like the stalwart Myrtle fan she is, took the manuscript home to work on even afterward. Myrtle and I could not have had a better champion, guide, or friend. (Rather like a beloved governess of our mutual acquaintance.) *Et custos et pugnax.*

To the legions of loyal Myrtle fans whose passion for my irrepressible heroine and her sidekicks has helped this series grow, you are the absolute best readers any author could dream of. Keep Investigating, keep Making, and never stop asking questions. *Constant and faithful.*

First, last, and always, for being the most supportive partner imaginable, my love and thanks to my very own MacEwen, my occasionally kilt-wearing legal consultant, C. J. Bunce. *Fortis ceu leo fidus.*